If I Fall

Merilyn Davies is a former Crime Analyst for the Metropolitan Police and she is married to a serving officer with the Met. She was co-founder of the Chipping Norton Literary Festival and now works for Oxford City Council. She lives in Oxfordshire with her family.

Also by Merilyn Davies

When I Lost You

If I Fall

MERILYN DAVIES

arrow books

1 3 5 7 9 10 8 6 4 2

Arrow Books
20 Vauxhall Bridge Road
London SW1V 2SA

Arrow Books is part of the Penguin Random House group of companies
whose addresses can be found at global.penguinrandomhouse.com.

Penguin
Random House
UK

First published in Great Britain by Arrow Books in 2021

www.penguin.co.uk

A CIP catalogue record for this book is available from the British Library

ISBN 9781787461567

Typeset in 11.04/16.21 pt Times New Roman by Jouve (UK), Milton Keynes
Printed and bound in Great Britain by Clays Ltd, Elcograf S.p.A.

The authorised representative in the EEA is Penguin Random House Ireland,
Morrison Chambers, 32 Nassau Street, Dublin D02 YH68

For Eva and Polly. You are both superheroes x

*Just as Sodom and Gomorrah and the surrounding cities,
which likewise indulged in sexual immorality and pursued
unnatural desire, serve as an example by undergoing
a punishment of eternal fire.*

Jude 1:7

Prologue

Event: THE REUNION
Date: 12 NOVEMBER
Venue: Rooftop, The Varsity Club, Oxford
Time: 20:00
Group status: This is a private Facebook group. Only invitees may attend The Reunion.
Description:
Secrets have a way of finding their way out into the world . . .
This is a chance to meet and share old stories. When people come back together, they bring with them echoes of the past. Some of you have nothing to fear. Others do. The Reunion will prove which one of those is you.

Invited: Simon Morris, Hannah Barclay, Ash Desai, Alice Baxter

Comments:
Simon Morris: 'Seen this?'
Hannah Barclay: 'Who sent it?'
Ash Desai: 'Anonymous account.'
Hannah Barclay: 'What do we do?'
Simon Morris: 'We go.'
Ash Desai: 'Are you mad?'
Simon Morris: 'No.'
Hannah Barclay: 'Have you seen who else is invited, Simon?'
Simon Morris: 'Yes.'
Hannah Barclay: 'What does it mean?'
Simon Morris: 'Well, it means *Alice is back*.'

One

Despite cold night air, the rooftop bar at Oxford's The Varsity Club was busy. Groups huddled under blankets, heated seats working with gas burners overhead to warm the space around them.

Carla Brown pushed her way through the crowd, coat done up to her chin, wine held high. As she reached Baz, already halfway through his pint, she put down the glass, hopped onto the high bar stool and threw her bag by her feet.

'It's freezing,' she said. 'Whoever thought an open-air bar in England was a good idea needs to have a word with themselves.'

Baz took a mouthful of beer before replying, 'You're always cold. Want to go inside?' He was dressed in work clothes – paint-splattered trousers, a battered sweatshirt, pair of off-white trainers – and Carla briefly wondered when he'd stopped dressing up for her.

'No, it's OK, here's good.' Truth was, inside was virtually empty, meaning they would be alone with all the long pauses and loaded silences that implied. Plus, work was slow, CID were hogging all the good cases to get their stats up and she felt like people-watching – she liked to watch people's interactions, trying to piece together the sort of person they were and the lives they led; probably should have been a psychologist rather than a crime analyst, but then she did love her job, mostly.

Pulling a blanket over her legs, Carla took a sip of wine, enjoying the quick hit of it, and let Baz's talk of his day wash over her. She looked around the rooftop, a mixture of people in workwear, the odd group of women gearing up for a long night with their lipstick and heels, before spotting a woman standing by the wall to Carla's left. She was shrouded in shadow but – even so – Carla could tell she looked out of place. About twenty-eight, she was dressed in a black bomber jacket, hair tucked under a scruffy hat, face obscured by a thick wool scarf, and she seemed to be looking for someone, as her eyes darted around the room, briefly alighting on Carla before looking quickly away.

'And then the damn woman wanted different tiles in the bathroom, as if she hadn't made enough changes,' Baz was saying, beer almost finished. Carla turned back to him.

'Do you see that woman?' She gave a light nod to the woman by the wall. 'Don't you think she looks, well, odd?'

Baz followed her stare before shrugging and downing the last of his pint. 'She's obviously homeless and has come in for a bit of warm. It's not a crime, Carla, even though the police would probably like to make it one.'

She ignored the dig. Ever since she'd hidden from Baz that she was still using contraceptives, which she'd fully admitted was a terrible thing to do, he had increasingly made negative comments about the police in general and her colleagues in particular. She weathered it, figuring it was a price worth paying for him to trust her again, but every time a jibe came it was just a reminder he didn't.

Baz stood. 'I'm getting another pint, want another?'

The mood he was in made her want a whole bottle, but she said, 'No thanks, I'm good.'

She watched him walk off and felt a pang of love – but whether it was for what they had now or a memory of what had been, she couldn't tell.

Taking a sip of wine, she looked back at the woman by the wall. She hadn't moved. Carla thought how small she looked, as if she was trying to make herself invisible. Maybe Baz was right – she was homeless and hiding from bar staff, but there was something about the way she kept scanning the crowd which made Carla think she was waiting for something.

Suddenly, the woman took a step out of the shadows – her face pale, her thin lips and nose overshadowed by wide, dark eyes, giving her a lost look. She appeared to have found what she was looking for, eyes fixated on a spot to the right of Carla, but the strength of the crowd made it impossible for Carla to see what it was.

Then everything happened at once; or in a sequence Carla was unable to untangle, even days, weeks later. Baz was coming towards her with a pint of beer; the woman was taking a step back, then another; Baz was near to their table and no one seemed to be concerned with the frightened woman by the wall; no one seemed to care about the look on her face – fear, panic; no one was looking to see what she'd seen so they could help and no one seemed to know what Carla knew: the woman was about to jump.

Carla stood, shouted to Baz, the sound muffled in her head. He looked to where she was pointing. Shoving his beer on the nearest table, she watched as he pushed his way through the crowd; as the woman slowly climbed the wall; as Baz was two feet away when the woman opened her arms; the woman looked up to the sky and, just moments from Baz reaching her, the woman leant back, someone shouted, 'Alice,' and then she fell.

There were screams, staff scrambled to see what had happened, pushing through to get to the spot where she'd fallen. People leant over the wall, peering at the road below before turning back, hands clutched to face. Baz, a few feet in front of Carla, wasn't moving. She knew she needed to go to him, to check he was OK, but she couldn't seem to make herself walk forward. She felt suddenly cold but a flash of heat to her face made her stomach lurch. Oh God, she was going to throw up; she couldn't, not in front of everyone – not when a woman had died. She reached to her left and grabbed the table. Sort it out, Carla. The police would be there soon and the last thing she needed was for them to see her, a civilian, that way; it was bad enough fighting to get their respect, without finding her passed out on the roof terrace.

The crowd was subdued, after the initial panic, groups reformed and hushed conversations followed; staff by the door fending off those who wanted to leave before the police got there. Baz walked back to the table, took one look at her and said, 'Jesus, are you OK, you look grey.' When she didn't reply, he took her elbow, and slowly helped her onto the tall stool.

'Is she dead?' Carla didn't want to picture the woman on the road below, and yet it was the only image she had – a body crumpled, limbs at wrong angles, blood slowly pooling around her head.

Baz pulled up a stool next to her and took her hand. 'I think so.'

Carla nodded, gave his familiar hand a squeeze, suddenly full of gratitude he was there. They sat like that, watching staff fence off the area where she fell with chairs, trying to keep the chill of shock at bay. A group behind them were talking quietly, huddled close, they stood beneath a printed sign pinned to the wall, bold black letters – THE REUNION – indicating the space they occupied was prearranged, and it struck her as odd there were only three of them; surely a reunion of three didn't need to be planned? Distracted, it took Carla a few seconds to realise that the group were talking about the woman who fell from the roof, as if they knew her.

'Are you sure it was her?' The woman speaking was tall, long brown hair tucked under a hat, and her expression matched the concern in her tone. 'Are we sure it was Alice?'

'I knew we shouldn't have come,' the man's voice was posh, deep, agitated. He kept running his hand through his blonde hair, glancing over at the spot where the woman had fallen. 'It was a set-up,' he went on. 'Alice got us here and this is the ultimate payback.'

'For God's sake, Simon,' the woman snapped. 'Are you seriously telling me Alice organised this whole thing, just so she could kill herself in front of us for something stupid that happened years ago?' She sounded more frustrated now, than upset – but whether by the comments made or the woman's death, Carla couldn't tell.

'I agree with Hannah,' the second male said; softly spoken, the slight wobble in his voice made Carla think he was frightened.

'I can't imagine anyone doing that,' he went on, 'not even Alice.' He was shorter than the rest, slight, and Carla got the impression he was the outsider in the group from the way the man snapped back.

'Then what were we invited for, Ash?' Simon replied. 'The Facebook event made it clear that this was all about Alice – that she would be here too. We came to see what she wanted, and clearly this was it.'

They fell silent for a few seconds and Carla glanced briefly behind her; Simon – white, he was dressed in chinos and a pink shirt, which seemed to match the accent. The second man, Ash, was a good foot shorter: thin, Asian, he wore glasses behind which darted worried eyes. And Hannah, taller than the men, long dark hair and skinny jeans, was staring crossly at the spot where Alice had fallen. Carla sensed they were very familiar with each other, their bodies turned inwards, not away from the group, and it made her feel they were close – certainly closer than needing a reunion as an excuse to meet up. So what was it about Alice that had brought them here?

'Do you think it was Alice who invited us?' Hannah asked, her voice certain, as though it wasn't a question at all but a fact.

'Of course,' Simon snapped. 'Who else would? No one but us and Alice was involved.'

There was a pause before Hannah said, 'Rachel did.'

Even with her back to them, Carla could sense the shift in mood, as if Simon's anger seemed to radiate.

'This is nothing to do with Rachel,' he said. 'Leave my wife out of it. She's the one innocent in all this.'

'If you say so,' Hannah replied, and Carla could almost see the shrug that accompanied her words.

'The police are here,' the second male said, and Carla turned to the door where three uniforms were speaking to staff.

'What are we going to tell them?' he asked, the fear back in his voice. 'What do we say? Do we tell them about the invitation, that we knew Alice?'

The scorn in Simon's voice was obvious. 'For a university lecturer, you can be really stupid sometimes, Ash. We're not going to tell them anything. We're going to say we were meeting up for a drink after work, that's all. They've sent three plod to confirm a homeless woman has killed herself and, when they have, that will be it, case closed. There are dozens of witnesses to say she jumped, even the police couldn't mess that up.'

The three officers began to marshal customers, keen to gather statements as quickly as they could, and Carla had to agree with Simon: usually they'd go through the motions, check the facts but do no more than that, and file it away as another sad case of the homeless in Oxford. But Simon didn't reckon on her. Something wasn't right: the invitations; the secret about Alice they all shared. No, tomorrow morning she was going to get that case from CID and then she'd damn well give Alice the decent investigation she deserved.

Two

DS Nell Jackson rolled over, propped herself up by her arm, and took in the figure next to her. The woman's hair – blonde – was strewn across her face, which was pink from sleep. Nell tried to remember the colour of the woman's eyes, brown? No, green. Or possibly blue. Shit, did she even remember her name? Matilda. That was it. Relieved she lay back down and stared at the ceiling. Man, she needed a can of Coke and a shed-load of carbs if she was to stand any chance of getting her arse into work.

The woman – Matilda – stirred and smiled across at Nell, her eyes . . . brown. Damn it.

'Hey you.'

'Hey.' Nell turned over and returned the smile, resisting the urge to bolt. She wondered if the woman remembered she was Welsh or if her accent came as a surprise, but if it did, she gave no sign.

'What you up to today?'

Nell couldn't remember if she'd told her she was a cop or trotted out the usual line, 'I'm in finance,' so she just said, 'Just the usual, you?'

'Well, as I'm mid-thesis I imagine I'll be in the Bodleian Library attempting to write, but instead, I'll probably be staring onto the quad thinking of you.'

Nell had to admit she delivered it well; the light tone suggested a joke, but the eyes said it could be serious if Nell wanted it to be. Which she didn't. Nell rolled over and picked up her phone.

'You fancy meeting up after work?' The light tone came now with a tinge of hope. Nell screwed her face up and checked her messages. One from DCI Bremer. *Got a new case. Dead body. No rush.*

Nell frowned. How could a dead body not be urgent? She threw off the covers and grabbed her bra and jeans.

'I've got to go, sorry.' She picked up her biker boots and tried to ignore the look of disappointment on Matilda's face. 'Help yourself to anything in the kitchen.' She hesitated, then leant over and kissed the woman on the cheek. 'Leave your number, OK? And I'll call.'

Matilda smiled up at her and relaxed back onto the bed, pulling the duvet down just a little, to show Nell what she was missing. 'You sure you can't stay for longer?'

'Don't tempt me.' She grinned, and kissed her again, even though the truth was she wasn't tempted at all.

*

Nell put her phone on speaker, pulled the car onto Jericho's high street, then dialled Bremer.

'DCI Bremer speaking.'

'It's Nell. How the hell can a dead body not be urgent?'

'And good morning to you too, Sergeant. Looks like a cut-and-dried suicide, but still needs a look.'

Nell felt nauseous. She needed that Coke. 'OK, well I'm twenty minutes away. Carla there yet?'

'She is, which is why we have the case.' He sounded irritated, annoyed even, and Nell didn't feel up to asking why.

'OK, give me fifteen and I'll be there.' Ending the call, she pulled into a petrol station, grabbed a box of paracetamol along with two cans of Coke and a black coffee. Squeezing two tablets from their packaging, then a third, she downed them with the Coke before putting the car into drive. Why was Carla making a fuss about a suicide and, more importantly, why the hell did Bremer agree? She knew he was still relatively new to the team, arriving from the Met with a strange obsession for including civilian crime analysts in every minutiae of a case, but this was extreme even for him. Pulling the car into a bay and swiping in through the back gate, she had a sinking feeling this was going to be a long day, chasing nothing and getting nowhere, a feeling only strengthened when she opened the office door to see Carla in Bremer's office, gesturing wildly.

'What's going on?' She threw her bag down on her desk and looked down at an amused Paul. The DC had his feet on a chair, phone in hand, half-drunk coffee on the disorganised desk next to him. His tattoos poked out from under a faded grey T-shirt, covering arms that had obviously spent copious hours in the gym.

'There was a suicide at The Varsity Club in town last night. A homeless woman, we think.'

Nell was watching Bremer hold up his hands as Carla continued to speak. 'So why have we got it?'

Paul took his feet from the chair and swivelled round to face her. 'Carla was there. Saw it all. And seems like she's got some theory it wasn't a suicide at all.'

Nell frowned. 'Well, it either is or it isn't.'

'Exactly. But try telling her that, because Bremer has and she's having none of it.' He took a swig of coffee and winced. 'Cold. CID are furious that Bremer has pulled rank and he's told Carla she has it for twenty-four hours. After that he's bouncing it back.'

Nell assumed that was the argument currently under way in Bremer's office. 'She's lucky to have it for that long. And I suppose we're going to get roped in?'

'You assume correctly.'

The door to Bremer's office flew open and Carla strode out, took a seat at her desk and wheeled her chair to face them. Her cheeks were pink, her expression serious, but she looked tired – as if she hadn't slept, and it occurred to Nell this might have been the first death Carla had been a witness to; she told herself to go easy on her.

'What's up?' she asked.

'There was this death at The Varsity Club last night and I want some time to work on it but Bremer's being pig-headed about it.'

Nell glanced at Paul who held up his hands. Turning back to Carla, she said, 'Paul said it was a suicide?'

Carla threw him a look. 'On the face of it, he's right. The woman was on the wall, she held open her arms, and fell back.' Carla paled as she spoke and Nell chose her next words carefully.

'Were people standing near her?'

Carla shook her head.

'What was the nearest someone was to her, roughly?'

Carla thought for a second. 'Maybe four to five feet?'

Nell extended her arm. 'Bit longer than an arm's reach then.'

Carla suddenly deflated, head bowing, hands falling to her side. 'I know, I know. But there's something about it that wasn't right.' She looked up at Nell, brown eyes wide. 'And I just want the chance to find out what that something is.'

Nell glanced at Bremer's office. 'Well, he's given you twenty-four hours. So, we'll work hard to see if we can find anything.' She ignored the look from Paul. 'Can you put your finger on what it is you think is off? Somewhere to start?'

Carla became animated again. Walking over to her desk she picked up a pile of statements and held them up. 'There was this group, three people, who'd been invited there and they knew the victim – Alice Baxter – they knew her and seemed worried she was going to be there, something to do with their past.' She was speaking quickly, clearly desperate for them to understand. 'And when the woman – Alice – climbed on the wall, one of them

13

shouted her name right before she fell.' She stopped and looked at Nell. 'Tell me that's a coincidence. They turn up for a reunion, the only other person invited is Alice, and she dies that night.'

Nell got why Carla would read something into that – hell, she probably would too, and it was definitely worth a look. But facts were facts, and attending a reunion where someone you know kills themselves wasn't a crime.

'It doesn't look like a coincidence, no,' she said carefully, 'but we have to keep an open mind, Carla. Just because they knew her doesn't mean they were involved on any level.'

Paul tapped his phone on the desk. 'Exactly. She still jumped, right? So coincidence or not, it's still suicide.'

Bremer appeared at his door. 'Has she told you about the thirty people who all state she jumped?' He walked towards them. 'Or the witnesses who put this "group of three"' – adding air quotes with his fingers – 'at least ten feet from Alice when she jumped?' He turned to look at Carla, who had flushed. 'In fact, they were standing behind you, were they not?'

Carla remained silent, so Bremer went on. 'And did any of the witness statements you've so far only skimmed indicate whether the group interacted with her in any way prior to her jumping?'

Nell almost winced. She'd not seen Bremer like this, and certainly not to Carla, and she wasn't keen on his bullying tone.

'I assume we haven't got a scene layout yet, so how can we tell where the witnesses were standing or what they could see? We need to be able to place them on the rooftop to be sure what Carla says is correct.'

Bremer glared at her, but she went on. 'Surely that's worth a look?'

'You want to go and look at the scene?' Bremer asked.

'Why not? You've given us a day to look into it, and it seems as good a place to start as any.'

Bremer looked between her and Carla. 'Fine. But I want this closed, Nell. CID want to close this because their stats are scraping the floor, and they only agreed to give it to me because their analyst is off sick, so they see it as a way for us to do their work for them.'

Nell wasn't sure why he'd even bothered if he was so convinced Carla was barking up a dead end, but she just said, 'Of course, sir.'

'You go too, Carla. Check out all the angles you need to in order to get this off my desk. I want Paul to stay behind in case anything comes in in the meantime, and Nell' – he stood – 'if it does, I want you back here pronto.'

Nell gave a mock salute. 'Received and understood.'

Picking up her Marlboro Lights she winked at Carla. 'Come on, one for the road.' But as she followed the analyst down the corridor – all trademark pencil skirt and white-blonde hair – Nell hoped this wasn't Carla's way of creating work for them so she could take her mind off her home situation. Because, as sympathetic as Nell was to that, and as much as she trusted Carla's intuition, her hangover had its limits.

Three

I don't believe it's possible to wake up knowing someone is dead, but if I did, I'd be convinced I knew Alice was gone. I'm lying in my narrow childhood bed, sheets too thin for the cold room, mattress too hard for adult bones, and all I can feel is a sense of absolute hopelessness and loss. I try to tell myself it's nerves at the reunion last night, at not being able to find Alice to warn her not to go, and I want to get back home to Simon to be reassured all is still as it was.

Downstairs, my parents are seated at the dining table, places set for breakfast just as they were every morning of my child-hood. The feeling in the room is austere; despite the expensive ornaments and vases, silverware on decorated plates, and I take my seat in silence just as I always did.

'Good morning, Rachel.' My mum is pouring me tea into a

china cup; she doesn't make eye contact. I smooth down my dress – suitable length, high enough collar – and smile at my dad.

'Yes, thank you. It was nice to be back in my old bed,' I lied.

My dad nodded, pulled the napkin from its brass ring and lay it on his lap. 'Rather small for you now, I imagine. It's good Simon doesn't go out often.' There is a hardness to his tone which takes me by surprise – my parents adore Simon; he is, after all, my protector, the way they once were. Taking the cup in both hands I decide I must have misread the tone. I'm unsettled, paranoid; I just need to get through breakfast, call a taxi and get home.

'Your father and I will drive you home,' my mum says, stirring her cup with an antique spoon. I try to look relaxed.

'Oh, please don't worry, I'm fine taking a taxi.'

My mum looks up at me – eyes blue in their deep-set sockets – and holds my stare before I look down.

'Nonsense,' she says. 'It's been decided. And we'd love to see Simon. We haven't seen our son-in-law for weeks.'

There it is, that tone again. What's happened? What's been said behind my back, am I in trouble? I feel suddenly cold – do they know I went to find Alice? Do they blame Simon for not being there to stop me? But no, that's impossible, I was careful, so so careful.

I put the cup down and dig my nails into my wrists, pushing down hard to ease the pressure I'm feeling, willing myself to draw blood so I can get some escape from it. My mum puts a sausage on my plate along with a slice of fried bread. The smell turns my stomach, as it has done for the last twenty-eight years, the smell of grease making me feel faint.

'Eat up,' she says with a bright smile. 'And then we can go.'

Simon opens the door to us and, as he hugs me, I can smell sourness on his breath and cigarettes in his hair. As he greets my parents, who stare disapprovingly at the stubble on his chin, I sense the same tension I felt in their tone. Simon leads them to the front room, with its grand fireplace and sweeping views of the garden, as I go to make tea, but as I set the cups on the tray, I see I am shaking.

I start to hear voices, raised, angry, coming from the front room. I walk quietly to the door, straining to hear what is being said, but the door has been shut and all I can gather is it's my parents who are angry. Hearing footsteps, I hurry back to the kettle; I am expecting Mum to appear by the door, but it's Simon.

'Are you going to be long?' He looks cross. His cheeks are flushed and the space between his eyebrows is furrowed in the way it always is when he is angry or concerned, and I think how funny it is you can sometimes know someone so well, yet also not at all.

I turn to put the milk on the tray. 'Two minutes.' I keep my tone light, uninterested. 'Is there something wrong?'

'Why do you ask that?'

I have my back to him, but I can still see the tense shoulders, the brief clench of his jaw. I am a constant source of annoyance to him, so I know those mannerisms well. 'I just thought I heard raised voices.'

He lets out a practised sigh. 'It's nothing to concern yourself with. Not everything is about you, you know, Rachel.'

And I almost laugh, because we both know it is.

I turn with the tray and hold it out to him. He hesitates and I wonder if he's going to make a point of not helping me, but we both know that would only confirm I am the source of disagreement and so he steps forward to take it from me.

'How was last night?' I say, as he turns to leave. He stops, silent; I begin to feel a tightness in my chest, a weakness in my legs, and it's unbearable to not ask, so I do. 'Did Alice go?'

He slowly turns towards me. Instead of the anger I expected, his face is pale, slack, all tension gone. I try to work out if this is a good thing, that she didn't turn up, and is still out there somewhere, safe.

'She did,' he finally says. I wait for more and when it doesn't come, I ask, 'How was she?'

He looks in pain, his face contorted in a way I've never seen before, mouth open to speak but unable to form the words he has to say. I grab the table; I can't feel my legs, the room has become too hot, I pull at my collar desperately – tugging and tugging until the material bites into my skin. Simon puts the tray down, takes my wrists, pulling them down beside my hips and bends his head down to catch my eye. 'She died, Rachel.'

I stare at him, no thought of how or why, just thoughts of the gulf that's opened up inside me and which I'm about to fall into.

And for the first time in his life, Simon says, 'I'm sorry.'

Four

The entrance to The Varsity Club was in Oxford's covered market – a small warren of indoor market shops above which ran painted ornate iron castings. Carla and Nell walked down the fake grass runner to the dark narrow entrance, climbing the flight of stairs which opened up into a large bar, hundreds of glass bottles lining the blackened wall behind a well-polished bar top.

Nell opened her warrant card and held it up to the bartender. They were the only ones there, but at such an early hour she'd have been worried if they weren't.

'DS Jackson. I'm here about the woman who died last night. We'd like to take a look around if that's OK?'

'Sure. If you head up to the roof, Adrian is there cleaning up. I think he was on the late shift yesterday so he may be of some help.'

Thanking him, they headed to the stairs.

Nell looked over her shoulder to Carla. The analyst looked pale, hesitant to climb the stairs. Nell got it. 'You drink here often?' she asked, keen to distract.

Carla gave a short smile. 'Is that what you say to all the ladies?'

Nell laughed. 'It's fail-safe, I tell you.' They turned the corridor and began the next flight.

Nell glanced over her shoulder. 'How's it going? With Baz, I mean.' She'd been reluctant to ask, now Carla was back with her fiancé, but she'd been there to pick up the pieces when he'd found out she'd been taking the pill behind his back, when he'd thought they'd been trying for a baby, and you didn't just bounce back from that.

'He's trying to show he trusts me,' Carla said, following. 'But we both know he doesn't, so instead putting on a brave face and pretending we're the same couple we were before.'

They emerged onto the roof terrace; overhead heaters trying to battle the damp fog obscuring Oxford's skyline; a mishmash of heights, spires and lead-laced windows. Nell stood for a second, scanning the long table down one side, scattered with cushions, glass table-tops slightly frosted, lights along the wooden floor. 'Posh,' she said, grinning over at Carla who had pulled out a map she'd scribbled before they'd left the office.

'Baz must really be trying to get in your good books if he brought you here.'

Carla grimaced and looked down at her map. Walking over to Nell she pointed at the page.

'I've plotted where the witnesses were, as best I can remember, given the time.' She looked up, took a breath, and pointed to the wall at the far end to their left. 'That's where Alice jumped, so it will have been visible from everyone standing here' – she extended her arms – 'to here,' she said, walking a little the right.

'Where were you and Baz?'

Carla walked to a small round table, high up in the centre of the terrace. 'Here.' She pointed behind her, a little to the right. 'And the group of three were just there.'

Nell walked to where Carla had pointed. 'Here?' she asked, stopping. Carla nodded. Nell looked to the wall where Alice had jumped. Definitely no way they could have reached her from here, and a clear view when it was empty.

'Do any of the witness statements suggest people were standing in front of here?' Nell gestured to the space before her.

Carla looked at her map. 'Possibly, these and these' – she indicated a handful of numbers on the paper – 'but I won't know if that's significant until I get back and go through their corresponding statements.'

Nell could tell Carla wanted to get back to the office, her comfort zone, where she could plot out the statements on a timeline to check who agreed with whom, trying to spot the inconsistency which would lead her forward. Nell spotted a man in the far corner, clearing a table near where Alice had jumped. 'Give me a couple of minutes and we'll head off, OK?' Then, without waiting for Carla's reply, Nell went over to him, holding up her warrant card.

'Hi, DS Jackson. Are you Adrian?'

The man looked immediately concerned, a standard response. Nell smiled in what she hoped was a reassuring way. 'The guy downstairs said you were working last night. I wondered if you saw anything around the time a woman jumped from here?' She indicated a little to her left. Adrian relaxed back onto the wall, obviously relieved.

'I spoke to the woman a few minutes before she did it.' He looked off to the left, recalling the conversation, before looking back to Nell. 'It was pretty obvious she was homeless, but we don't have a policy of chucking them out, not like other places. We just like to have a quiet word, we want no problems, that kind of thing.'

Nell nodded and took out her notebook. 'And how did she seem when you spoke with her?'

Adrian frowned. 'Confused.'

'Confused?'

'Yeah, like she didn't know where she was.'

'So on drugs then?'

Adrian hesitated. 'I've seen lots of people off their faces in my time.' He gave Nell an apologetic smile. 'But I didn't get that sense from her. Sure, she was confused, a little agitated, but it didn't seem to be because of something she'd taken, it just felt like something was distracting her, like she was worried.' He gave a slight shrug. 'Sorry, I can't explain it. It's just a gut feeling I had that she wasn't high or drunk, just disassociated somehow. As if something real was bothering her.'

Nell got it, sometimes you had a feeling about a situation, even if you couldn't describe why. Hell, it had got her out of enough scraps when she'd sensed things were about to kick off, or made her chase a lead when there was no evidence to say she should. 'Did she give you any indication of what she was worried about? Any idea of why she might have come to the bar last night in particular?' Nell didn't want to lead him to say something he couldn't naturally recall, but a little nudge in the right direction wouldn't hurt.

'She kept asking me if they were here yet.' He gave another apologetic smile. 'But that was it. She just kept repeating it, getting more and more agitated when I said I didn't know what she meant.' He sighed. 'She was so small, tiny really. And even though she was dressed in old clothes, you could tell her old life was still there, like she hadn't quite been able to let it go like the others do.'

Nell frowned. 'Do you think she was newly homeless then?'

Adrian shook his head. 'No, she didn't have the same sense of shock; didn't seem as lost as they look when they first arrive in Oxford. You know?'

She did. When she'd worked the city centre as a uniform, the thing she hated most was befriending a newly arrived homeless person – fresh with tales of family breakdown, redundancy and divorce – to come across them one month later, barely able to recognise her through the drink and drugs.

'And she didn't mention anything else; not a name, anything?' Nell asked. Adrian's eyes narrowed, thinking.

24

'She said a name, a man's, I think, but I can't remember it.'

'It was definitely a man's name?'

Adrian shook his head. 'I can't be sure, but yes, I think so.'

Nell walked back over to Carla, who was sitting on one of the long benches, staring out at the skyline. She took a seat. 'Beautiful, isn't it?'

Carla nodded.

'When I first arrived in Oxford, from a little farm in Wales, I would spend my whole time looking upwards, amazed by how beautiful it all was.' She smiled at Carla. 'Even now I don't think there's a week goes by when something doesn't make me stop and stare.'

'I grew up in an estate by Blackbird Leys. All this' – she waved across the view – 'was just another kick in the teeth for us; another example of how posh Oxford didn't care about poor Oxford. We were just invisible at best, a blight at worst.'

Nell felt surprise then guilt she didn't know this. But then she'd spent the first six months of their working relationship trying to exclude Carla from the team, so she hadn't bothered to know.

Nell pulled her Marlboro Lights out of her jeans, lit two, and handed one to Carla. 'Seems Alice was agitated last night. Mentioned a man's name?'

Carla became instantly animated. 'There were two men in the group – Simon and Ash – standing behind me, talking about Alice.'

Nell checked her watch. 'Come on, twenty-one hours and

counting before Bremer kicks this case back to CID. Let's get you back to the office, see what you can dig up on Simon and Ash.'

Carla was out of the seat before she'd finished the sentence. But as Nell watched her scoop up her bag and stamp her cigarette out, she couldn't help worrying this case wasn't about Alice at all, it was all about Carla. She just had to figure out how and why before their twenty-one hours was up.

Five

Back in the office, Carla flicked through the witness statements. She knew the first names of the group of three, so she just had to hope there weren't many Simons, Hannahs or Ashes to eliminate before she found them. It took longer than she'd hoped, but after comparing statements – noting positions they were standing in, similarities in statement content – she finally narrowed it down to the three she'd heard speaking behind her.

Simon Morris: twenty-nine years old, white, lived in Summertown, Oxford

Hannah Barclay: twenty-eight years old, white, lived in Botley, Oxford

Ash Desai: twenty-eight years old, Asian, lived on Cowley Road, Oxford

If all three lived in and around Oxford, maybe they'd all

studied at either Oxford University or Oxford Brookes University? It would make sense for a reunion held in Oxford. Carla made a note to follow that up, and to check if Alice had studied at either university, before re-reading each statement.

All three had told the police merely that they'd met for a drink after work, and all stated they'd never seen Alice before that night. The statements were short, all denying they'd even seen Alice on the wall, let alone called out to her, but each statement did list their dates of birth, addresses, and contact numbers. Carla ran each through the criminal records database. No hits, no police record, not altogether surprising – most people didn't. Opening up the intel database, she inputted the same details – again no hits, but she hadn't expected any, given their clean record. At this stage it was all a process of crossing off the list of potential sources of information, moving through it until you found a source which took you further.

Opening Google she began with Simon. A couple of hits came back about his work as a financial consultant in London, a hit on LinkedIn which she made a note to check later, and a picture of him running the Oxford half marathon two years back. Hannah's Google results centred on her work as a vet in Botley – a piece in the *Oxford Mail* about her work with a homeless charity Dogs on the Street, a puff piece about a cat she'd taken in after it had been left on the doorstep of her vet's practice where she appealed to people to treat their pets with kindness, and a hit on LinkedIn. Ash's results focused on his work at Oxford University as a professor of Ancient History; if the papers he'd published were anything to go by, he seemed to specialise in the early history of Greece and Rome, followed by a now predictable hit on LinkedIn.

LinkedIn was a site Carla didn't really understand. She assumed it was like Facebook for businesspeople, or Twitter for sensible people, but either way she'd never really had cause to use it as an intelligence source, until now. Opening up a new browser window she created a fake account and searched for Hannah, Simon and Ash – they were all there, faces smiling in their profile pictures: Hannah on her own, Ash with his arm around a man Carla assumed to be his husband given the wedding scene in the background, and Simon staring intensely into the camera, his blonde hair perfect, teeth bright white, blue eyes vivid. And there it was, the link between them all – Oxford Brookes University.

Carla leant back, took out her leather tobacco pouch and began to roll a cigarette. If she could link Alice to Oxford Brookes, she could prove they were all connected, maybe that they even knew each other. She wasn't sure that would be enough to convince Bremer to let her keep the case – probably nothing short of a DNA link would do that – but it was a start and it may buy her more time. Now all she had to do was find a way to see if Alice had studied there too, but a quick search of LinkedIn and Google brought back nothing. Frustrated and desperate for a nicotine hit, she googled the contact number for O'Hanlan House. If Alice had been homeless, she'd almost certainly visited the homeless shelter in central Oxford, so maybe they'd have some information on her.

She picked up the phone. 'Hi, Thames Valley Police here, I just want to check on one of your residents.' She heard someone sigh on the other end of the line and, when she spoke, the woman's tone was resigned.

'Who do you want to hound now?'

Carla tapped her pen on the table and tried not to bite. 'I'm interested in Alice Baxter. I believe she was staying with you?'

'We can't give out personal information, you should be well aware of that.'

'I know, but I'm afraid Alice died last night so she is no longer covered by data protection.' It sounded clinical and, when the woman replied, voice shaking, Carla regretted her abruptness.

'How? It's not that cold, was she attacked? But who would hurt Alice? She always made so sure she kept herself to herself.'

Carla shut her eyes, tried not to apologise; once you did that you were on the back foot, so she had to keep going. 'I'm afraid Alice died after falling from a building.'

Silence.

'Hello?'

'You mean she killed herself?' The woman's shock was palpable.

'We won't know that until cause of death has been established,' Carla explained.

'Christ.'

Carla waited a couple of seconds, gripping the pen in an attempt not to speak, a deep sense of dread telling her she was going to say the wrong thing. Again.

'What did you want to know about Alice?' the woman finally asked.

Carla placed the pen carefully on the table. 'It would be really helpful if you could confirm Alice stayed with you and, if so, we'd like to speak to staff and residents about her movements over the last few days.'

'I'll confirm that. She's been staying here, on and off, for the past three months. Staff will be happy to speak to you, but I wouldn't hold out much hope about our residents – most aren't your biggest fans.'

'Yeah, understood.'

'I suppose you'll want her belongings?' the woman asked.

'Sorry?'

'Her stuff, it's all in our lockup. Some of our residents pay a couple of quid to keep their belongings safe during the day. The council encourages it,' she added.

'That would be really useful, thank you. Can you make sure no one touches them until we get there, please?'

'Sure, everything is in solo lockers so no one will have access except staff, and they'd have no reason to go into it, but I'll leave a note to everyone just in case.'

'Thank you. One more question. I'm having a hard time tracking down family for Alice and we'd really like to notify them. Do you know where she was from or where she had previously worked? Anything that could help us?'

'I don't know where she was originally from, I'm afraid, but she once mentioned working for Oxford Brookes University, does that help? She didn't say when or doing what, but I got the impression she left under a bit of a cloud.'

Bingo. A link between Alice and the group of three. Making a note on her pad, Carla asked, 'A cloud?'

'I might have got it totally wrong, it was just a feeling I got, like she was ashamed whenever people mentioned it.'

'And you believe she worked there rather than studied there?' Carla asked, underlining 'Oxford Brookes University' and 'work'.

'Oh yes. I sensed some form of "issue" with her employment which eventually resulted in her being with us.'

'So, she became homeless after her employment with Brookes ended?' Carla asked. 'Do you know how long ago that was?'

'I don't, I'm afraid. She's been homeless for a while, definitely over two years. It's not an uncommon story; people lose their jobs and things just start to crumble.'

Thanking the woman, Carla ended the call, then dialled Oxford Brookes University and asked to be put through to their HR department. It was a long shot, they were unlikely to give her anything, but she wanted to at least give it a go.

'Hello, yes, Carla Brown here from Thames Valley Police. I was hoping you could help me with a case we're working on. I think the victim may have previously been a member of staff?'

'We don't give out information on employees, past or present,' a bored-sounding woman replied.

'Yes, I thought that would be the case. It's just this is a murder inquiry and any help you could offer would be really helpful.'

'Sorry, no can do.'

Carla reiterated the point about data protection, but the woman wasn't playing ball. She glanced at Bremer's office. 'How about if my DCI pops in for a chat while we gather the relevant documents for you to release the information? Would that work?' She couldn't tell if the resulting silence was one of consideration, or irritation, so decided to give it one last push. 'I mean, it would save us all time as we both know I'll get the permission, so . . .'

'Fine,' the woman snapped. 'If you can get here before four this afternoon, ask for me, Sammy, at reception. If not, you'll have to ring again tomorrow.'

Carla checked the clock plenty of time to send Bremer over there before her twenty-four hours was up. 'That's perfect, thank you.'

The woman had hung up before she had finished speaking.

Carla picked up her notepad and went to Bremer's office. Peering round the door, she asked, 'Good time?'

Bremer was sitting, sleeves rolled up, behind his big wooden desk; a picture frame sitting empty behind him on the sparsely filled bookshelf, a coffee cup, glowing laptop and a mobile phone the only signs of recent activity on his desk. Anyone looking at it would think he'd moved in last week rather than a year ago.

'Sit.' He gestured to the chair Carla was already heading for.

'What you got?'

'OK, so, Alice was staying at O'Hanlan House where her belongings remain. They've secured them.'

'Good work. Nell can go and pick them up.'

'That's not all.'

Bremer gave a brief smile. 'Somehow I didn't think it would be.'

'The woman at the shelter said she thought Alice worked at Oxford Brookes before she was made homeless, so I gave them a call and they've agreed to see you if you can make it before four.'

He leant forward, hands on the desk. 'Without a warrant?'

'Well, it's for a "chat", so you might not get much, but worth a reconnaissance mission maybe, before we apply for the order? Because the thing is, Simon, Hannah and Ash all studied at Oxford Brookes, and it would be good to see if their dates overlap.'

Bremer was studying her face as she spoke. 'Right, I'll let Nell know about the belongings over at O'Hanlan House and then . . .'

Carla knew what was coming.

'We'll head over to Oxford Brookes.' Clocking the look on her face, he said, 'We've been over this, Carla. I want you out and about just like any other member of the team, not stuck behind a desk all day seeing only one side of the investigation.'

She knew better than to argue. It was old ground, and she'd come to accept Bremer's ways; not that she was sure she could say the same for Nell, who viewed a civilian trailing along as akin to a health hazard. And Carla had to agree – what if she said the wrong thing, ruining the CPS case with the wrong question? She'd already almost messed up the O'Hanlan House call, so what's to say she wouldn't do the same now?

Bremer was waiting. Carla stood. 'I'll get my coat.'

'Isn't that my line?' He gave her the Bremer smile, one you couldn't help but return, then picked up his mobile. 'I'll meet you in the yard after I call Nell, then let's see if we can get anything out of the university about why Alice left.'

Six

I've been put to bed. For the first time in my life, my mother stroked my hair as she whispered psalms to me, and I let the words of God carry me to sleep. In my dreams I walk barefoot in a wood, His gaze lighting the narrow path covered in moss, broken branches, until into sunlight I walk to find Alice waiting for me.

I wake. It's dark and I can hear the hum of the heating as water heats the pipes. I stare at the ceiling, arms folded across my stomach, feeling the rise and fall of my chest as I breathe. Alice has gone. I start to panic, feeling like I'm falling, so I sit up and clutch the covers to convince myself I'm not, that I'm still in this room, safe.

Sounds filter up from downstairs: more raised voices, the slam of a door. I look at the bedside table and see my phone light up. They left me my phone. As I stare at it I feel the smallest triumph amongst the heart-crushing grief. Picking it up I see a message from Ash.

'Are you OK? Call me if you can. But only if safe.'

My mouth goes dry. I look to the door then back to the phone. Do I dare?

I pad softly to the door, leaning against the wood, trying to hear footsteps but there is nothing. Silence. I look back at the table, digging my nails into my wrist as hard as I can. Then, before I can change my mind, I run over, grab the phone, and sit cross legged on the bed. Ash answers almost before it's had time to connect.

'Rachel?' His voice is low and I know it's because he's mirroring how mine will sound; he doesn't have to speak quietly, but I do.

'Are you OK?' he asks.

I realise I'm crying, tears fall onto my lap, because it's so good to hear his voice.

'Alice has gone,' I say, before putting my hand over my mouth, letting out the sound which feels like it's being forced out of me by the pain. Ash is silent, leaving me time to cry; he's always been good at helping me manage pain – both physical and mental – after the summer we spent together when we were nineteen. He'd been Simon's friend at university, but the moment we met we knew we recognised something in one another – a sense our secrets were the same and our struggles familiar – so we'd gravitated towards each other during the weekends I'd visit, able to relax, to feel safe and uninhibited in a world where we always felt wrong. That summer had been both painful and wonderful – the hours sitting in the garden, taking in the watery sun, glad to be out of our rooms and feeling new air on our skin.

'I'm so sorry,' he said.

And I know he is, not just for Alice's death, but for all the things that went before it. Just as I know that from the moment he found his husband, Eric, Ash has felt guilt that I never got my Alice. 'What happened?' I ask.

'Simon didn't tell you?'

I rest my head on my hand. 'No.'

'Christ. OK . . .' He lets out his breath and I listen with mounting disbelief to what he tells me.

'But she would never do that.'

Ash is silent for a moment. 'We don't know her any more. She was homeless, destitute, probably high on drugs. Hannah said she was in a bad way when she saw her.'

I don't trust a word Hannah says, but then how would I know, I never did find Alice the day I'd gone to warn her, because I let myself be scared off by a woman and her dog. 'My parents are here,' I tell Ash now. 'I think they are arguing with Simon about something.'

Ash is briefly silent again. 'I see.'

'Do you think it's because of Alice?'

'Do you?' he asks.

I think. Do I? 'Possibly,' I say. 'Hannah saw her, so I assume she told Simon, and if she told him, it's likely he'd tell my parents.' I paused. 'Do you think they had something to do with her death?'

'But how could they? I saw her, Rachel. I saw Alice climb onto that wall and disappear with no one anywhere near her. It was suicide, it couldn't have been anything else.'

I know what he says is true, but I can't help but remain unconvinced. Maybe I just want them to be to blame, to block out the feeling I have that actually the one to blame is me. 'Who do you think invited you all? Who arranged the reunion?' Could my parents have done that? I don't think they have a Facebook account and I know they certainly wouldn't approve if I did. 'It's the Devil's work, Rachel, stay away, stay safe, stay loved.'

'I think it was Alice,' Ash said. 'I think she got us all together to punish us for getting her fired. She wanted us to see what it had done to her, and to leave us with guilt for her death.' He spoke quickly, as if ideas were forming as he spoke and he was trying to keep up. 'Because who else would have done it? Hannah, me and Simon were invited, so it couldn't have been one of us, it wasn't you, so who else knew what we did and how far we went?'

My parents, I think, they knew.

I wipe my face. I need to go downstairs, face them, be bright – the perfect daughter, the perfect wife. 'Ash?' I ask.

'Yes?'

'Did Simon tell you what he did to her, before he filed the complaint?'

I can hear him breathing down the phone and I know the answer.

'Yes, he told me.'

I nod. 'It was a terrible, terrible thing to do.'

Ash's voice is quiet. 'It was.'

'God punishes those who commit acts like that.'

I hear him sigh and I understand. He no longer believes in God's word, not after our summer. He doesn't believe that the love of Jesus saves us from sin, so neither does he believe the wrath of God against those who dishonour His word. But I do.

'I've got to go, Rachel; will you be OK?' He sounds worried and I want to reassure him but I have one more question first.

'Did you tell Eric about our summer together?'

He's silent.

'Ash? Does Eric know what happened?'

He sighs again, voice low, he says, 'Yes. He's my husband, of course I told him.'

I nod, biting my lip. 'Does he hate me?'

Ash gives a short laugh. 'No, Rachel. He doesn't hate you. It makes him sad but he understands.'

I'm instantly relieved. I'd hate to lose Ash because of one summer, especially now Alice has gone. 'Maybe we can have dinner one evening? You and Eric could come over and we could get a takeout or something.'

Ash hesitates. 'Yes, maybe. That would be lovely.'

But I know from his tone he won't come.

'Take care, Rachel,' he says.

'Take care,' I reply. 'Love you.'

'Love you too.' And with that, he's gone, and I'm all on my own again.

Seven

The homeless hostel was tucked away on a side road in the centre of Oxford, close to the magistrates' court, on a street named 'Luther'.

'Apt.' Nell nodded to the street sign as they passed, before pulling up outside O'Hanlon House, looking as grey and unwelcoming as the sky above it.

A group of men and one woman were seated outside, stereo on, drink in plastic bottles; they eyed the car with suspicion.

'Anyone would think we had police tattooed on our foreheads,' Nell muttered, grabbing her notebook from the glove box.

Paul eyed the group. 'Probably not the first time they've met police.'

Walking into reception, a woman – dip-dye blonde dreadlocks tied up in a ponytail – was trying to placate a harassed-looking man.

41

'I just want her stuff, that's all. It's not yours to keep, she was Luci's girlfriend and she wants it.'

'That's not how it works, and you know that, Guy.' Her tone was friendly but firm and Nell could tell the woman was having none of it. 'And anyway, Luci can come and ask me herself, if she wants it. But then, I haven't seen her around today . . .'

Her words hung pointedly between them, the man – around six foot three tall, dark lank hair and a pin-thin frame – shuffled, unable to remain still.

'Luci asked me to get it for her. Seriously, Sarah, I need to get Alice's stuff, she's got things of Luci's in there, things she needs.' His tone had become pleading, but Sarah looked unfazed. Paul threw Nell a look, but she shook her head, keen to hear what the man had to say before he knew who they were and inevitably clammed up.

'What sort of stuff?' the woman asked.

'Just stuff . . .'

'You know we have a no-drug policy here, Guy.'

'You seriously think Alice had drugs on her?'

Sarah smiled and shrugged before clocking Nell and Paul.

'Look, Guy, I'll do my best, OK? I'll come and find you and let you know.' Turning to Nell she beckoned them over. 'How can I help?'

Guy remained where he was, blocking their approach to the desk. The smell of alcohol emanated from him, along with stale and fresh cigarette smoke, but Nell could see he cared about getting access to Alice's belongings. The question was, why?

Nell waited, holding Guy's stare until he muttered, 'For fuck's sake,' and disappeared through the double door leading into the hostel. Definitely one to follow up on.

'Sorry about that,' Sarah said, 'things are a little emotional here at the moment. We've had a death and it's rocked everyone a bit.'

Nell nodded, holding up her warrant card. 'Alice Baxter?'

Sarah looked surprised, then, 'You're here for her things, aren't you?'

Nell shoved her warrant card in her back pocket. 'If that's OK, yes.'

Sarah glanced after Guy.

'Problem?' Nell asked.

Sarah looked apologetic. 'It's just that Guy says Luci wanted the opportunity to go through Alice's belongings. Luci was Alice's girlfriend,' she added.

Paul was writing notes, 'Surname?' he asked, looking up. 'Of Luci.'

'Sorry, I don't know off the top of my head. I can look it up?'

'Great, thanks,' Nell replied, glancing over at Guy. 'And I'm afraid it's not possible for Luci to look through Alice's belongings. Of course, we can return them to her when we have finished with them, unless a relative comes forward,' Nell added.

'But it was a suicide, wasn't it? Surely she could just have a quick peek? Take anything of sentimental value?'

Nell felt a stab of irritation. What planet were these people on? 'Cause of death has yet to be established, so we really will have to take her belongings.' Lucky they'd got there when they did; a couple of hours later, and it was clear Sarah would have buckled and had Luci rifling through Alice's stuff as if it were her own.

'Do you know what Luci is looking for?' Paul asked. 'You mentioned drugs – is that probable?'

Sarah gave a sad smile. 'You'd have thought so, wouldn't you, but I highly doubt it. Alice abused alcohol at times, but I never saw her do drugs. She was quite unusual, as it happens; didn't really fit in with the rest of them. I often wondered what she was really doing on the streets, and whether it was her attachment to Luci that kept her here.'

'They were happy then?' Paul asked.

Sarah smiled, revealing rotten teeth, making Nell wonder if she'd been homeless once too.

'Yeah, they were,' Sarah said. 'I think that's why it's hit everyone so hard. There was no suggestion she was depressed and, in fact, quite the opposite. She and Luci had a really strong relationship which was really helping her – Luci I mean – get off the drugs. Alcohol is still an issue, but you have to celebrate the small steps when you can.'

'How long had she and Luci been together?' Nell asked.

'I've known them for six months, and they've been together for the whole of that time. I think it's been almost a year in total.' She looked earnest. 'And that's no mean feat when they are in a situation such as theirs. Maintaining a stable relationship in such a chaotic lifestyle. I mean, Jesus, most of us don't manage that when we've got everything going for us.'

Nell wasn't in a position to dispute that and, frankly, she thought, neither was Paul.

'Any chance Luci will have a chat with us now we're here?'

Sarah shook her head. 'I haven't seen her today, sorry. She doesn't often come in because of Billy.' Then, clocking Nell's blank look, added, 'Her dog. A little pit-bull called Billy; he doesn't leave her side.'

'How about Guy?' Nell pointed to the door. 'He might know where we can find her?'

Sarah looked doubtful. 'He's not in the best of places at the moment.' She gave a short laugh. 'Figuratively as well as literally. But I can ask him.'

'Thank you, I'd appreciate that.'

As Sarah left, Nell looked around the well-worn reception room.

'They say we're all two steps away from homelessness,' Paul said, following her gaze.

'Do you believe that?'

'Yeah, I think I do.'

Nell thought about what would happen if she lost her job and home: she could go back to Wales, stay with her parents, but what if they were dead? What would step one be for her then? 'Maybe,' she said. 'Not sure I'd stay here, mind.' She waved her hand around the room. 'Think I might prefer to take my chances on the street.' But then she supposed that's what Alice had done, and that hadn't worked out so well.

An angry-looking man stumbled in through the doors, yelled

for Sarah and, when it was clear she wasn't there, he looked at Nell. 'Where the hell is she now?'

'She'll be back in a minute.' Nell took in the blackened fingers, the matted hair and too-big jacket, the slight sway as he tried to stay focused on her.

He pulled out a half-full bottle of wine and offered it over to her.

'No thanks, I'm good.'

He eyed her suspiciously. 'Got a fag?'

She handed a couple over and the man relaxed. 'Cheers.'

'No worries.' She looked at Paul who was shaking his head. 'What?'

'You know what. You're supporting him being on the street.'

'By giving him a couple of Marlboros? Don't be a dick.'

Paul shrugged. 'Got to be tough to be kind, Jackson.'

Nell spotted Sarah hovering behind the doors, speaking to a reluctant-looking Guy.

'Well, I'll take my chances, thanks.' She nodded towards the doors. 'Looks like we might be in luck.'

Paul looked over his shoulder. 'Want to take him down the station?'

'For what?'

'Just might loosen his tongue a bit.'

'Jesus, why have you suddenly gone all hard right on me? Can't help them out with a fag or two, drag them down the station for absolutely nothing. I thought we were only two steps away from being just like him? Let's see what he gives us first, yeah?'

Paul shrugged. 'Sure, but I bet it's nothing.'

Nell ignored him, kept the cigarettes in one hand, flicking her lighter with the other. Maybe Paul was right; it wasn't as if she wasn't prone to sweeping generalisations, after all, but it didn't hurt to give it a go with some humanity first. And as Guy walked hesitantly towards them, she fought the headache starting in her left eye, and held out her hand.

Eight

The journey to Oxford Brookes University was twenty minutes from the office, taking them from the green fields of West Oxfordshire to the built-up suburban enclave of Headington, where cafés and charity shops littered a main road dotted with bustling market stalls.

A little way down the hill, Bremer pulled into the car park of a modern-looking building, a far cry from the dusty halls of Oxford University just down the road, and ten minutes later finally found the HR manager's office through a maze of corridors and workspaces.

'Thank you for seeing us at such short notice,' Bremer said, shaking the HR manager's hand and taking the seat across from her.

'No problem at all, I'm Miranda.' She gave a brief smile. 'I've fond memories of Alice so it's been very sad to hear of her passing.'

Bremer nodded. 'So, she didn't leave on bad terms then?'

Carla had to admire him, he certainly got straight to the point. Miranda looked taken aback.

'Well, there was an unfortunate misunderstanding, and Alice felt it best she leave.'

'Misunderstanding?'

Miranda gave an apologetic smile. 'I'm afraid I really can't release confidential information about the case, There were others involved and their rights have to be protected too.'

Bremer smiled. 'Of course. So there was more than one complainant?'

Miranda looked a little flustered. 'Well, no, just others were asked for their version of events.'

'Did they corroborate the complaint?'

'In part, yes.'

'I see.'

Carla waited for Bremer to say more and, when he didn't, she asked, 'Miranda, was a man called Simon Morris involved in the complaint? Either as the accuser or a witness?'

Miranda looked surprised, opened her mouth to speak then shut it again. Carla went out on a limb. 'After Simon made the complaint, did he stay at the university?'

'Oh yes, Simon was never going to leave, he was always going to achieve big things.' Then, realising what she'd said, she put a hand to her neck and fell silent. Too late, it was obvious the complainant was Simon, but complaint about what?

Miranda looked between them both, as if deciding whether she should say more, before leaning back in her chair and clasping her hands together. 'Alice worked in the lab and she was really good at what she did. It isn't fair when students come in and look down on the staff who help them.'

'What did she do in the lab?' Bremer asked.

'Set out equipment for the students, assisted their experiments, tidied everything away when they'd gone. She was always cheerful, went out of her way to help them if they had a problem; nothing was too small or big an ask for Alice. Her knowledge far outweighed her role here. By rights, she could have been a lecturer.'

'Do students often look down on them? These assistants?' Carla asked.

Miranda shook her head emphatically. 'No, it's very rare. We aren't like Oxford Uni where it's all about the elite. We are real people here with real students, creating great jobs for themselves by working hard. But you always get one student who found daddy's money couldn't buy them into the posh uni and resents slumming it here at the new one.'

'And Simon was one of those?' Bremer asked.

'No, actually. From what I can remember, Simon didn't come from money. I think that's what made him so angry.' She looked out of the window. 'Simon was the type of student who wasn't privileged, so made up for it by adopting the very worst of their traits: rudeness, arrogance, a belief that the world owed you a living.' She stopped, face flushed. 'I've really said enough, I'm so sorry I couldn't be more help.'

Carla expected Bremer to push her further but he smiled and held out his hand. 'I fully understand, and I appreciate how frank you have been.'

She smiled gratefully, walking them to the door. 'Let me know if I can help with anything else.'

'What did Alice do, to upset him?' Bremer asked. Miranda folded her arms, sighed.

'What he accused her of and what she actually did, are two very different things. But as Alice left before the complaint was processed, we were never able to prove who was telling the truth.'

And Carla thought it was pretty obvious from Miranda's tone whose version of the truth she believed.

Back in the car, Carla looked across at Bremer. 'Not the biggest fan of Simon, was she?'

He laughed. 'No. And he doesn't sound the most charming of men.' He glanced over at her. 'What impression did you get of him?'

Carla stared out at the darkening sky, glad of the warmth from the heater as it pumped out hot air, and tried not to picture Alice's face as she stood on the wall. 'He seemed the one in charge, the one the others looked to for guidance. Arrogant, dismissive of Ash's concerns that they shouldn't have gone there to meet.'

Bremer tapped his finger on the steering wheel. 'Sounds about right.'

Carla turned back to him. 'I wonder what Simon's complaint was about.'

'Aren't complaints usually about sex?'

'You think Simon accused Alice of sexually assaulting him?'

'Could be she refused his advances, and that annoyed him enough to get her in trouble?' Bremer pulled onto the ring road, smoothly moving to the outside lane to overtake a blue van.

'But then why did Alice leave? Why wouldn't she have stayed and fought it?' Carla asked.

'Well, Miranda alluded to there being witnesses, so maybe Alice felt she didn't stand a chance.'

Carla nodded. 'I bet the witnesses were Ash and Hannah. We need to look at what sort of group they were. Would they have been the sort to rally round Simon if he made a false allegation, and if so, why? What was so special about Simon that they'd ruin a young woman's career for him?' Carla itched to be back at her computer, to dig up more on Ash, Hannah and Simon. 'Someone got that group to The Varsity Club for a reason, and it has to be this, don't you think?'

'Certainly an interesting lead.' He looked over at her, an odd look on his face.

'What?' She knew him well enough now when he had something to say. 'Spit it out.'

'How are you feeling about Gerry?'

Carla turned to look back out of the window. This was not a conversation she wanted to be having. Gerry was the man who'd taken her under his wing when she'd first joined the police, been the man who she looked up to and trusted until six months previously she'd found out everything about him had been a lie.

When she didn't reply Bremer said, 'It's his sentencing this week, isn't it? How do you feel about that?'

What did he expect her to say? Great? Happy? Sad? Because she seemed to feel all of those things, and none. 'I'm OK,' she finally replied. 'Trying not to think about it, I suppose.'

'Not always a good idea, that.'

Carla could hear the smile in his voice.

'It's understandable to find this stage emotional. He was, after all, something of a father figure to you, wasn't he?'

Carla snapped round to face him. 'Yes, but he was also a DS who covered for his murdering psychotic wife, which almost got him killed. So, not much better than my own dad, it turns out.' She looked out of the window ahead. Rain being pushed to the side by the slow whoosh of the windscreen wipers. 'And I'm not using Alice as a way to distract me, if that's what you're getting at.'

His silence told her it was.

Back at her desk, Carla decided to search Facebook. LinkedIn had proved they all went to Brookes together, but Facebook was the most likely platform for them to socialise, and she was sure they'd mentioned Facebook last night. She just couldn't remember why.

Annoyed, at herself, at Bremer, she typed in Simon's name, finding his account moments later, partially open – she could see his friends as well as profile pictures. She'd take that. She opened two more pages and searched for Hannah and Ash, then with all three profiles now on her computer, she began to search for links between them, anything to suggest how close they were both past and present.

She quickly found that Hannah and Simon were friends, but while Ash also appeared on the former's profile, the two men appeared not to be Facebook friends. She sat back. Was that odd? Maybe not: Hannah could be the link between the two. Perhaps she'd got them all together for old times' sake. But that explanation didn't feel right. The way Miranda told it, Simon sounded as though he was going to be the dominant link in the group. So why was Ash not on Simon's friends' list?

Frustrated, she began to search through each of their available pictures to see if any had been captured of the three of them together, or, crucially, in the years they would have been at university. She found no answer either way.

Giving up, Carla searched for Alice. Seconds later she found a picture of a happy but slightly shy-looking young woman, her head lowered so that she peered up at the camera, arms around the neck of a beaming friend. She looked so different to the tiny worried woman she'd seen last night. Here was a woman who'd been alive, happy, but whose body was now lying on a mortuary slab. What had gone so wrong?

Carla scrolled through Alice's profile, scrutinising each picture for signs of a life before last night, trying to piece together an image of her that could combat the one of her face as she stood on the wall, images of her lying dead on the road below. Carla forgot the case, no longer searching for a link to Simon's murder, and focused instead on humanising her, on making Alice a person again, with family and friends who loved her and would miss her.

Carla peered at picture after picture of pre-homeless Alice, standing with an older man and woman she imagined to be her parents, the little dog at their feet, a much longed-for present; she scrolled through Alice being hugged by the woman in the profile picture, sitting with a man by a campfire – face again lowered, eyes looking out from under a fringe, then another of her running with a street dog through the streets of Oxford, looking back at the camera and laughing in an oversized coat, all wild hair and a grin.

'You got anything?' She heard Bremer's voice from over her shoulder.

'Not really, but I've only just started. I think this woman is pretty important to Alice.' She pointed to the woman around whom Alice's arms were wrapped. 'She's in lots of photos but isn't tagged, so I don't have a name . . .' She paused, looking back at the picture of Alice running, coat flapping either side of her, hair catching the sunlight and glowing like gold.

'You'll drive yourself insane if you try to work out why.'

She looked up at him, 'Sorry?'

Bremer perched on the edge of the desk and folded his arms. 'When I was a probationer I went to a few suicides. Most of them I was OK with, you know, in so much as you can be. But there was this one boy, eighteen years old, who'd thrown himself onto a railway track and I just couldn't get him out of my head. I went home that night and did just what you are doing now, scoured the internet just so I could make him human again. You'll never really find out why she did it, and you'll go mad if you try.'

Carla looked back to the image of Alice on the screen, then back at Bremer. 'But what if it wasn't suicide, though? What if she was murdered and we just don't know how yet?'

'I think we need to focus on the facts, Carla, OK?' He spoke gently and she suddenly felt the need to cry, but whether it was because she'd let the case get to her or because things were so absent at home and she missed a man being kind to her, she couldn't tell. 'I'm going for a cigarette, want me to bring back a coffee?'

He studied her face for a moment before nodding. 'Sure thing. But don't be long. Nell will be back soon with Alice's belongings.'

Carla nodded. 'Sure thing.' She picked up her bag and Bremer put his hand out to stop her.

'I'm going to have to make a decision soon about handing the case back to CID.'

She looked at him, feeling both sick and angry at his look of concern. 'I'll be fine with whatever decision you make.'

Bremer took his hand back. 'I know you will. I just wanted to warn you.'

Without thanking him, Carla grabbed her tobacco pouch and left.

Nine

Sarah, the homeless shelter's receptionist, guided Nell and Paul into a side room. The man who'd been so keen to get hold of Alice's belongings sat on a threadbare armchair, foot tapping nervously on the vinyl floor.

Sarah smiled down at him. 'It's nothing to worry about, Guy, OK? They just want to ask you about Alice.'

Guy eyed them suspiciously as they took a seat on the narrow sofa next to him, his glassy eyes suggestive of a heavy session the evening before.

Nell leant over, elbows on her thighs. 'We just want to ask you about Alice, and about how she may have been feeling in the days leading up to her death, OK?'

Guy shifted uncomfortably under her stare, so she leant back. 'How did Alice seem, yesterday, for example?'

Guy interlaced his fingers, then released them, repeating the movement again and again. 'She was OK, normal.' He glanced up at Paul then quickly down again. His long hair, still wet from a shower, was swept to one side, revealing a pale, drawn face.

'And what was "normal" for Alice?' she asked.

Guy frowned. 'What do you mean?'

'Well, was she a happy person, sad, angry?' Nell asked.

Guy contemplated her for a moment. 'She was sweet. She looked after me, made sure I ate, didn't drink too much. When I let her.'

Nell nodded. 'Did she drink?'

'Sometimes.' His defensive tone told her it was more than that.

'And did she do anything else?'

'Drugs, you mean?'

'Yeah, I'm not here to make trouble for you,' she said, clocking his expression. 'So it won't go any further than this room.'

His foot stopped tapping. 'No, she was clean. I never saw her take anything.'

Nell believed him. 'And had anything happened in the last few weeks to upset Alice? A row with her girlfriend maybe?'

Guy shook his head, his hands stopped moving and he looked Nell directly in the eye. 'No. Alice and Luci are tight. Were tight,' he corrected. 'It wasn't to do with Luci, none of it.'

She felt the familiar deep thud of her heartbeat as the adrenalin kicked in. 'Did something happen to Alice then? To upset her.'

Guy's foot started tapping. 'No, I didn't say that.'

'But you said none of it was to do with Luci. None of what?'

Guy eyed the door, Nell felt Paul tense beside her. She leant forward.

'What happened in the days before her death, Guy?' she pressed. 'What wasn't Luci involved in?'

Guy leant back in his chair, hands motionless. 'Luci didn't say much, just that someone from Alice's past came back and it unsettled her. Alice got all anxious, kept looking out for them.'

'Did Luci say who Alice was looking for?'

Guy shook his head. 'No. She said she'd asked, but Alice had said it was better she didn't know.'

'Did Luci have any thoughts on who this person might have been? I mean, Alice and Luci must have spoken about their lives before the streets, so did Luci have a guess at who, or why they came to find Alice?'

Guy looked pained. His fingers clawed at his wrist until Nell wanted to reach out and stop him. She pulled out her cigarettes and offered him one. He looked at them warily. 'We're not allowed to smoke in here.'

Nell smiled, pulled two from the packet and handed him one. 'I'm the police, what are they going to do?'

Guy hesitated, then accepted; lighting the cigarette, he visibly relaxed.

Nell lit her own. 'What was Luci's theory?'

'Well, she thought it was a man who had come back to punish Alice for something she did before she was homeless.'

'Did she say what Alice had done in her past that would make someone want to punish her?'

Guy shook his head and tapped ash into the palm of his hand. 'No, but she thought it'd been pretty bad if it made her homeless. So maybe this person was coming back for revenge and Alice was scared? That's what Luci thought anyway.'

'And she was certain it was a man?'

'Well.' Guy gave it a thought. 'I suppose not, but it's always a man, isn't it? Lots of girls end up here 'cos of that, you know? Men beating on them.'

Nell nodded. 'Yes, I imagine that's true.'

Guy leant forward. His teeth were blackened from drugs, the dark circles under his eyes littered with tiny blue veins. His eyes flashed, and Nell would have bet a tenner a man beating on Guy might also be the reason he was there too.

'And then they end up here and men carry on beating on them,' he said, breath quickening, eyes darting around between them. 'On and on and on. Like they're a dog getting in the way.'

Nell knew when she was losing an interview; she glanced to Paul, who nodded and took over. 'Guy, going back to the person who Alice was scared of – is there anything she told you or Luci which might help us find who they are?'

Guy shook his head, eyes scanning the room, before resting on the door. 'I want to go.'

Paul's tone was gentle. 'Why do you want to go, Guy? We're just trying to help find out what happened to Alice.'

Guy started to shake his head, hair falling over his face. 'No, Luci said I mustn't tell.' He stood, Paul followed. Nell watched Guy, judging whether it was worth pressing him a little further – what did he know that he couldn't tell them?

'I want to leave now,' he told Paul.

If they were going to carry on the interview, it would have to be back at the station, and Nell didn't think that would do anything other than make him shut down completely. She held up her hands. 'OK, Guy, of course you can go. But can I ask you one more question?'

His back was to her. 'What?'

'Do you think Alice killed herself?' she asked.

Guy didn't move. 'No,' he said quietly.

'Do you think someone hurt her?'

Silence.

'Thank you, Guy, you can go now.'

Nell watched as he bolted for the door; when he'd gone, she turned to Paul. 'Thoughts?'

'That whatever drug he's taken is working?'

'Yeah.' She pictured Guy's face, pain mixed with fear, laced with defensive anger. 'But I think he was telling us the truth,' she said. 'Someone made contact with Alice in the weeks leading up to her death, someone she was scared of.'

Her phone vibrated in her pocket. 'We need to find Luci. Find out what she knew about this person from Alice's past.' Pulling the mobile from her jacket, she checked it, before shoving it back again.

'Bremer wants us,' Nell said as she pulled open the door, a waft of cigarette smoke pushing past her. 'Let's pick up Alice's belongings. Maybe something in there will give us a clue as to who it was that she was so scared of.'

Ten

Carla watched Nell walk into Bremer's office, put Alice's belongings on his desk, and walk out again. She looked to Paul for an explanation, but he just shook his head and stared down at his phone. Nell paused by Bremer's door for a second, maybe waiting for an acknowledgement of some kind, and when one didn't come she walked over to Carla and slumped in the chair next to her.

'I'm not going to lie,' Nell said, 'I think your theory has legs, but I know he's going to pull the case. CID are going to want it back to keep their case numbers up and we've not got much Bremer can use to convince them to let us keep it.' Nell looked at Bremer's office and shook her head. 'Bloody politics.' She turned back to Carla, pointing at her. 'If I ever say I want to be anything higher than a DS, shoot me, OK?'

'Why do you think he's going to pull the case?'

Nell almost laughed. 'Because what have we got? Secrets in the past that have come back well, who the hell hasn't had their fair share of that?' Nell shook her head. 'But there's something there, something's not right about this whole thing, I know it.'

'Then tell Bremer?' Carla said. 'Tell him you think we should keep the case.'

Nell leant forward, held Carla's eye. 'There's this man, Guy, he says Alice had a girlfriend who thinks someone from Alice's past came back and messed with her head. Or more.' She leant back, clearly exasperated. 'But we've run out of time. Just when it was getting interesting, he's going to gift it back to CID who'll close it within a day.' She looked at Carla. 'Any ideas?'

Carla pictured Alice on the wall. The Alice before. 'No. If Bremer takes it off us. There's nothing we can do. It's his call.'

'Really? That's all you've got?'

Carla stared at her. 'I got us this far, Nell. No one even wanted this case until I did. Maybe it's time you did some of the heavy lifting.'

But before Nell could reply, Bremer came to his office door. 'We'll debrief in five minutes. See you at the wall.'

The briefing wall had one picture on it – Alice Baxter. No suspects, no witnesses, nothing more than a young homeless women smiling out into the room, and it occurred to Carla there was only one reason for that – Bremer had never intended to take the case from CID on a permanent basis. This had all just been about distracting her from Gerry's sentencing. Maybe he was right, and she'd been chasing answers when there weren't any; maybe this really was just a suicide. She suddenly couldn't bear to hear him say it, to see pity from Nell and Paul while Bremer gently explained why their twenty-four hours was up.

Picking up her bag she walked over to Nell. 'I'm going, tell Bremer I'm ill, OK?'

'You can't just go, Carla, it's a debrief.' Nell stood to face her. 'It's your case, fight for it.'

Carla shook her head. 'It's not and I can't. Tell him I'm sorry,' she said, before pushing open the office doors and leaving.

Two hours and three mojitos later, Carla stared out at Witney's market square, from the top of the Como Lounge. Behind her was the gentle hum of conversation mixed with music, muted lighting and dark walls creating a sense of intimacy despite the room's size.

'Hey.'

Carla jumped, and turned round to find Nell standing grinning at her, cocktail in hand. 'What the hell are you doing here?'

'Cheers to you too,' Nell said, pulling out a chair and raising her glass to Carla's.

'How did you know I was here?'

'I walked the length of the High Street checking each bar.' Nell took a gulp of her cocktail. 'So, the next round is on you, and possibly the one after that.'

Carla grinned. 'Was Bremer mad, did he drop the case?'

'No and yes.'

Carla nodded. 'OK.'

'He's worried about you because of Gerry's sentencing.'

'I know.' She looked over at Nell. 'But I really don't want to talk about it.'

Nell gave a short nod. 'Received and understood.'

They sat for a while, staring out of the window at the Cotswold stone buildings housing pubs and shops, before Nell pulled out a packet of Marlboro Lights. 'Fancy one?'

'Totally.'

Nell grinned. 'Come on then, let's brave the terrace.'

The smoking area was exposed but covered; walls adorned with Mexican designs clashing with the ice in the air. Carla rolled a cigarette, thoughts of Alice on the wall, battering her head. 'Do you think Simon put in a complaint against Alice because she was gay?'

Nell looked up, surprised. 'What makes you think that?'

'I don't know, but the complaint has been driving me insane. Bremer thinks it's because she spurned his advances, but what if it was more than that? What if he hated the fact she was a lesbian and decided to, I don't know, target her because of it.'

'Because he's a homophobic arsehole, you mean?'

Carla rolled her cigarette on the edge of the ashtray. 'Would someone do that, though?'

Nell laughed. 'Jesus, Carla, people do a lot worse than that just because of their bigoted hate.'

'Yeah. Sorry.' Like she was going to tell Nell how bad people could be to you just for being gay. And Alice had been homeless, which meant she'd probably not had family to go home to, maybe for the same bigoted reasons. 'Was it OK for you, when you came out?' It occurred to her they'd never spoken about Nell's sexuality, but then why would they, they'd never spoken about hers either.

She was about to take the question back when Nell said, 'Yeah, well, there wasn't any big reveal. It was just always sort of known.' She gave little laugh. 'My parents are basically hippies and so, if I hadn't been a lesbian, they'd probably have tried to make me be one. And they are anti-religion, so they don't have any moral reasons to object, but mostly they just think being gay is totally natural.' Nell shrugged. 'So, I always felt loved and accepted.' She downed her cocktail. 'But I know not everyone gets that lucky.'

Carla thought Alice probably hadn't been, but she was glad Nell had. She picked up Nell's glass and rested her cigarette in the ridge of the ashtray. 'Right. My round. And when I get back, no Alice, no Gerry,' and, clocking Nell's face, she added, 'and no Baz.'

Eleven

I say goodbye to my parents at the door. My mum looks worried, exasperated, her tightly curled hair a good reflection of her mood.

'Promise me you'll ring if you need us?' she says. It's a strange thing for her to say and I wonder again what's gone on between them and my husband; Simon is sulking in the garden room, whisky in hand, and my dad hasn't uttered a word for over an hour.

'God loves you, Rachel, trust in Him, always.' She squeezes my hand and I squeeze it back. 'He'll protect you,' she adds, before turning to go down the steps. My dad leans forward and gives me his awkward hug, nodding at me, like some sort of a mental pat on the head. I watch them reverse out of the drive, the gates slowly closing behind them, and consider my mum's words.

Why would I need protecting, and what would I need protecting from?

I shut the door, pour myself a large glass of wine, taking it to the garden room where I curl up on my favourite chair and pull the wool blanket over my legs. Simon is staring into the fire, which crackles and spits beside me, casting shadows across his face. I try to judge his mood, but his face is blank so I ask, 'Are you OK?'

He starts, as if he'd not realised I was there. 'Yes, why?'

'No reason.' I want to ask him about the arguing, the raised voices, but there's something I want to know first. 'Are you worried?'

He frowns. 'Worried? About what?'

I keep my tone light so as not to alarm him, but it's been on my mind since I learnt of Alice's death. 'Are you worried there's more to Alice's death than suicide? That it's linked to the reunion and whoever sent those invitations?'

I can tell he is worried by the way he's contemplating my question. 'I mean,' I carry on, 'if the person who sent them was somehow involved in Alice's death, do you think they are going to . . .' I pause.

'Come for Hannah, Ash and me?' he finishes, his tone scornful. 'No, I don't think that, Rachel. This isn't some Christie novel titled *One Down, Three to Go.*' He goes back to looking at the fire but I'm sure he looks unsettled, so I press on.

'It's just, if she didn't kill herself, then the person who arranged it might not be done yet. I mean, if they got you all together for a reason, they're going to want you to know what that reason is, aren't they?' It seems so obvious to me, because I'm convinced Alice didn't take her own life, and if Alice was killed, the others could be too, but Simon snaps his head around, glaring at me.

'Alice was the reason. And now she's dead, so what other reason could they have?'

I try to think of a reason for anyone to hurt Simon. I can't imagine one, but what if there's one I don't know about; something between him, Ash and Hannah they've not told me? It's not like Simon is averse to secrets; he doesn't know I know that my parents give him money to 'look after me', or that he sneaks off to see Hannah behind my back. But what secret could be so big that someone would kill because of it?

Simon stands, pours himself another whisky and says, 'I'm going to bed. Unless you're concerned I shouldn't in case someone offs me in my sleep?'

'Don't be silly. I'm just worried about you, that's all. I want you to be careful. Just for a while until we know for certain how Alice died.'

He looks at me as if I've gone insane, and maybe I have – I keep picturing his body, mutilated, smashed into pieces so small it would be impossible to piece him back together again and it makes me feel sick. Dizzyingly so. The idea of life without him is terrifying. He's the shield between me and my parents; without him I have no idea who I would be because he defines me. He is me; I went from them to him with no in-between because the in-between I could have had – Alice – was taken away from me.

If I Fall

At the thought of her I drain my glass, stand unsteadily, and pour myself another; spilling a little, I don't bother to clean it up because there's something niggling at the back of my head like a fly trying to get out. It's a feeling of relief. I have no idea why the image of Simon's body in a pool of blood calms me, but the realisation that it does terrifies me almost as much as the idea of him dead.

Twelve

The phone on Nell's bed-stand beeped. Groping for it, she checked the clock – 4 a.m., that wasn't good. 'DS Jackson speaking.'

'Nell, Bremer. We've got a body.'

She sat up, switched on the light and, deciding to bin the 'no smoking in the house' rule, she pulled one out. 'Where?'

'University Parks. White male. Five feet eleven inches.' He paused.

'What?'

'It's Simon Morris.'

'Jesus. Simon Morris from The Varsity Club? The one linked to the suicide?' They'd handed the case back to CID two weeks ago, much to Carla's annoyance, and hadn't heard a word about it since. 'Does Carla know?'

She heard him sigh. 'Not yet. I'm calling her next. Get down there, yes? Then report back. I need to know if it's linked to the death of Alice Baxter, ASAP.'

Nell bet he did. And if it was, she was glad it wouldn't be her giving an explanation of why they'd handed it back and now had a dead body on their hands.

The entrance to the University Parks was sealed off with police tape. One of the two uniformed officers stationed by the wrought-iron gates lifted it as Nell and Paul approached. Crunching along the gravel path, a white tent gradually came into view behind the large green trees surrounding it, and the duck pond to its left. It was a place usually filled with joggers, students, walkers, so it was strange to see it empty – the river Cherwell, running behind the pond, free from the punts usually moving slowly past – silence broken only by the quiet sound of officers slowly working the scene.

Nell walked to the edge of the tent and pulled back the flap. A man with a camera was crouched over the body, two forensics officers looking on. Noting her entrance, one held up his hand.

'It's pretty grim, so just brace yourself.'

Usually Nell would have bristled at such advice, but the look in his eyes told her this wasn't the usual patronising bullshit she got at a scene. She took a breath and stepped forward.

Simon's body was naked, lying on his back, arms down by his side. His head rested on a large stone, blood congealed in his hair, one eye closed, and it took her a second to notice the other. She pointed down. 'What's that?'

'One eye has been removed after death.'

'But not the other?'

The forensic officer shook his head. 'And so far we haven't found it.'

Paul appeared behind her. 'A trophy then?' He looked how she felt: pale, shocked, sick. Because if the killer had taken a trophy, this wasn't going to be a common-or-garden murder, and that was likely to mean a body count higher than just this one.

'That's not all,' the forensic officer pointed lower down Simon's body. 'He's got one foot missing and one hand. Both severed post-mortem.'

Nell tasted acid in her throat and swallowed hard. 'And I presume we haven't found those yet, either?'

'You'd presume right.'

Nell turned to Paul. 'Get out there and make sure all officers know what they're looking for and tell Bremer we need more manpower.' The park was huge, multiple entrances and exits, some crossing into fields. It was going to be a nightmare to find anything at all, and that was assuming they were there to be found.

The forensic officer looked up at her. 'And he has a tooth missing, again extracted after death, I'd say.'

'So, he wasn't tortured? They mutilated him after they killed him?'

'Looks that way. Cause of death is a single blow to the head from behind.'

Nell stared down at Simon. Why kill someone then mutilate

the body? Was it a message? But to who – the police, or someone else? 'Does it look ritualistic to you? Like some sacrifice or something.' It had to be a possibility – the man was laid out as if he was sleeping, yet they'd done very deliberate things to his body; neat, detailed, specific.

'Like satanic worship, that sort of thing?' the forensic officer said. Nell didn't have a clue. She'd seen programmes on things like that, though nothing in real life, but before she could answer, the second forensic officer spoke.

'Or religious punishment.'

She looked over at him. 'Explain.'

'People think the Bible just says, if you want to take revenge, it's an eye for an eye, a tooth for a tooth. But that was just the gospel of Matthew doing an abridged version of the actual version, which was in Leviticus: life for life, eye for eye, tooth for tooth, hand for hand, foot for foot.'

Nell stared at him. What was he, some sort of priest? 'And that bit in . . .' She tried to remember what he'd said.

'Leviticus,' the forensic officer offered.

'Yes, that bit in Leviticus, what's it about? Why do you get permission to cut bits off people?'

'Well, it's a misconception that it's about revenge. It's about justice. God set out ways for people to get justice for wrongs done to them. So, if someone takes your foot, then you get to take theirs; your eye for their eye. And ultimately' – he shrugged awkwardly – 'if they take a life, you get to take theirs.'

Nell looked down at Simon's body. Life for life, eye for eye, tooth for tooth, hand for hand, foot for foot. 'Like for like,' she said.

'Exactly. I mean, it's pretty metaphorical, but it's meant to give a sort of outline to a just and fair society.'

Nell wasn't sure Simon's mutilated body was fair or just, but whatever the killer thought Simon had done to justify this mess, it had to be pretty bad.

Thanking the forensics team, she walked outside, glad of the fresh morning air. Her stomach was still churning, but just being out of the stuffy tent seemed to help. Paul walked across to her, boots leaving marks in the frosted grass.

'Nothing found yet,' he told her. 'Bremer's sent in extra troops.'

Nell took another breath of air. 'We won't find the body parts.'

'You think we've got some sort of trophy-hunting serial killer here?' His tone was light, but Nell knew a serious question when she heard one.

'I think we have a killer who is different from anyone we've come across before and I don't think Simon's will be the only death.' She looked up at him. 'So, yes, I think we do.'

Thirteen

Carla hadn't thought she'd heard correctly when Bremer told her who the victim was. It was 4.30 a.m. and she was sitting on the edge of the bed, back to Baz; she made him repeat it.

'It's Simon Morris.'

Carla grabbed her tights off the floor, padded over to the door and closed it gently behind her. 'Was it suicide?'

'No. Most definitely not.' Bremer's tone was serious, heavy – and she briefly wondered what the implication would be for his career if it was found by handing Alice's case back to CID he'd indirectly caused the murder of Simon. Murder. Jesus, even she hadn't predicted that. She'd been so focused on Alice she hadn't bothered to think about the threat to the other three invited to the reunion. Maybe if she'd given him cause to think there was a threat to life he might have kept the case, and then who knows, Simon might still be alive; maybe this was her fault, not his.

In the office, Bremer handed her a coffee. He looked pale, stubble suggesting he hadn't had time to shave, and she felt a pang of sympathy for him despite the growing anger she'd felt driving in.

'I've had a call from Nell,' he said, as she shrugged off her coat and pulled out her chair.

'Simon's body has been mutilated and she thinks it may be some sort of religious sacrifice or punishment. I need you to research Leviticus and the "eye for an eye" segment.' He explained why, as she took notes, 'And then I want a full report into Simon's wife, parents, in-laws, friends, colleagues, acquaintances. And track his movements if you can, see why he was in the park, where he'd been before and where he was headed to.'

Carla stopped writing. 'And what about Alice?'

Bremer sat on the edge of her desk. 'I've left a message for the DCI in CID.'

Carla nodded. 'So, we're getting her back then? The case.'

Bremer studied her face before replying. 'Yes, we are. But I don't want you to link the two straight away. Keep an open mind. Let's get the facts straight about Simon's death first, OK? They are very different: one is a suicide, and one is a murder and mutilation.'

Unless it wasn't a suicide, Carla wanted to add, but she just nodded. 'Sure thing, I'll get to work on it now.'

She decided to focus on Simon's wife, Rachel, spouses being

the first suspects in a murder, and while Nell's description of the scene didn't seem like a spousal murder, she figured it was as good a place to start as any.

It took a while to get information on Rachel – limited internet footprint, no criminal record, no current employment and no intel reports made building a picture of her difficult – but the discovery of Rachel's maiden name through her bank details gave Carla the break she needed.

Google told her Rachel was the only daughter of a wealthy local couple, Malcom and Hilary Davidson. Living near Chipping Norton in Oxfordshire, they were known as philanthropists. Various local media articles detailed their advocacy for – and donations to – local charities, mostly religious. Rachel had, according to the *Oxford Mail* and *Liverpool Echo* articles, gone to study English at Liverpool University, where her parents had presented a large donation to a local church.

A notice in *The Times* told her that Rachel had become engaged to Simon nine years previously, while she was still studying at Liverpool University. Simon had been at Oxford Brookes, where he'd been studying economics. There was, however, no mention of Simon's parents in the announcement and, despite an hour's worth of digging, she came back with nothing. Carla leant back in her chair. Rachel's family were rich, wealthy and well connected – their numerous patronages were testament to that – so what did they think of their only child marrying a nobody?

Bremer looked out of his office. 'Anything?'

'Simon's wife comes from money. His, not so much. Not sure if that matters?'

Bremer walked across to her desk. 'Money always matters. Not enough or too much; either way, it matters.'

'Well, Rachel comes "from money", but Simon had a good job in the City' – she clicked open his LinkedIn page – 'so maybe it cancels itself out?'

Bremer considered the page. 'Not sure new money can ever outweigh old money. Even if you have more, you'll never have that same class.'

'But does that matter here?'

Bremer looked over at her. 'What do you mean?'

'Well, Rachel comes from old money, Simon doesn't, but how does that relate to his murder? I mean, Rachel wouldn't need to kill him for money. Nor would her parents, and anyway, he doesn't seem to have any money so there wouldn't be a financial gain by killing him? And, OK, her parents are religious, and his murder had religious overtones, but are we really going to go down the line they are suspects? They're coming up to seventy and hugely respected. Could they have mutilated Simon's body that way?'

Bremer contemplated her. 'But they could afford to pay someone to . . .'

Carla gave it some thought. 'But why would they? What would be the outcome? How was Simon a threat to their daughter?'

'Well, that's what I want you to find out.' Bremer stood. 'I'm under pressure here, Carla. I need your report.'

'OK, but what if my report shows a link between the deaths of Alice and Simon?'

'It won't.' He turned towards his office. 'One's a suicide, one's a murder. Just find me a suspect for the latter.'

She watched him walk away. 'You know that's not how it works?' And when he didn't reply, 'They were both invited to a reunion – a reunion we were tasked with investigating which we dismissed – and now two are dead.' Carla realised she was breathing hard, but she didn't care. 'Two other people were also invited to that reunion. What about them?'

Bremer stopped walking, back to her. 'Then find me who invited them. Find me who and tell me why.'

'And in the meantime? We don't protect the other two – Ash and Hannah?'

Bremer turned around to face her. 'Carla, policing is about budgets. You prove to me Ash and Hannah are in danger and we'll get the funds to protect them.'

'So, I have to prove it to you when you already know it?'

Bremer raised his hands in the air. 'It's seven a.m. We've been here for almost two hours. I'm sorry I dismissed Alice, OK? I'm sorry I thought you were deflecting your worries about Gerry and putting them into her case.' He stood by his door. 'But I need you to be part of the team now, Carla. I've always told you; you are – but I need you to prove it now.'

Carla watched Bremer disappear into his office. It was true, she had been deflecting her feelings about Gerry onto Alice, but it still didn't mean she hadn't been right. Turning back to her desk she wrote, 'Ash', 'Hannah', 'Simon', 'Oxford Brookes', and drew a line to connect them all, then wrote, 'Alice', drawing a line to link her to Oxford Brookes. Tapping her pencil on the notepad she thought about what Bremer had said. 'Find me who invited them. Find me who and tell me why.' Someone had to connect them all, but who?

Carla drew a question mark beside the names – indicating a person not yet known – and looked at the notes she'd made against Simon's name: his address, his car, his date of birth, the name of his wife. Rachel. Carla stared at it. And, despite having no cause to do so, Carla crossed out the question mark and wrote 'Rachel' in its place.

Fourteen

Simon and Rachel's house was a modern-style town house, contrasting sharply with the sprawling Victorian properties lining the Woodstock Road. Nell pulled the car onto the gravel drive, parking next to grey slate steps, and thought it looked like the kind of house designed by people who enjoyed teasing their less affluent neighbours with glass frontage, allowing them to see, but not touch, the wealth inside.

Paul unclicked his seatbelt. 'What do we know about the wife?'

Nell peered up at the front door, arms resting on the steering wheel. 'Carla says she's a twenty-eight-year-old housewife. Studied English at Liverpool Uni, and they've been married for around eight years, I think.'

'Kids?' Paul asked.

Nell shook her head. 'No.'

'So what does she do all day?'

Nell turned to look at him. 'And how the hell would I know that, Hare?' She looked back at the house. 'Thank God we don't have to be the one to tell her. Uniform is with her now.' She unclicked her belt. God, she hated this part of the job; grieving families, distraught and in a pain you could almost touch. 'Come on then,' she said to Paul. 'Let's get this over with.'

A uniformed officer opened the door as they climbed the steps: tall, blonde, with an athletic build, she was older than Nell, but there was a hesitancy about her which made Nell think that what she had over Nell in years wasn't matched by experience.

'Got the short straw?' Nell asked as she reached the top.

The woman grimaced. 'What else are probationers good for?'

Nell had been right then; as a probationer she'd have less than two years of policing under her belt, but when the woman rolled her eyes Nell couldn't help but smile. It took balls to let a senior officer know you were pissed off; balls, or a total lack of awareness of the way rank worked. Judging by the look of this one, Nell was putting her money on it being the former.

'Name?'

'PC Laura Sergeant.'

Nell laughed. 'Bet that's been fun.'

Laura rolled her eyes again. 'Yeah. Parade has been a blast these last few months. Never realised the police were such comedians.'

'Stick it out. They'll get bored soon enough.'

Laura gave a half-shrug and Nell suddenly hoped she hadn't given up already. Jesus, they really were crap at helping people adjust to coming into the job; just throw them in there and watch while they sank or swam.

'Were you the one to break the news to Mrs Morris?' Nell asked. They'd all been there, been the one to inform a relative of a death; you needed the experience to pass probation. Didn't make it any less grim.

Laura nodded.

'How did she seem?'

Laura looked slightly over her shoulder, considering the question. 'Hysterical, but in a measured way. Like she knew she should be hysterical but didn't really feel it?'

Nell frowned. 'As if she was play-acting?'

Laura scrunched up her face. 'I wouldn't like to say that. But she didn't seem too bothered about her husband, more about what her parents were going to say, and how would she tell them. Like he was their son, rather than their son-in-law.'

Nell couldn't tell if Laura was being overly analytical, fresh to the job and wanting to find clues when there weren't any, or if it was a valid observation. Plenty of parents loved their child's spouse; maybe they and Simon had just been particularly close.

'They seemed close though,' Laura added. 'Rachel and her husband. Place is littered with pictures of them, and about ten of them on their wedding day, although I've seen happier brides.' She threw Nell a knowing look.

'What do you mean?'

Laura shrugged. 'Just lots of them look forced. Like you know when someone wants a selfie and you don't, so the smile ends up more rabbit-in-the-headlights?'

Probably wedding-day nerves. 'OK, thanks, I'll take a look.'

Laura looked hesitant.

'Anything else?' Nell asked.

'Well, I thought I heard a scream from the house while I was waiting at the front door.' She looked embarrassed.

'A scream? From who?'

'I don't know, it sounded like a woman, but when Mrs Morris opened the door she seemed perfectly composed.'

'So someone else is, or was, in the house?'

'Maybe, I haven't been able to check.'

Nell got it. As a probationer you did the job you were told to do, and Laura had been told to babysit Rachel. Worth a look around the rest of the house, though.

'We'll check it out.' She turned to Paul. 'Right, let's go and meet Mrs Morris.'

Rachel sat in an oversized armchair, her face turned away from them, legs curled up under her. Her hair was dark brown, tied back in a ponytail; it fell far below her shoulders and her profile hinted at pale delicate features. A proper English rose was Nell's first thought.

As they walked across to the sofa, Nell took in the room – long, wide and decorated in muted colours. A large cream marble fireplace dominated the centre on which were scattered framed pictures, and a vase filled with a large bunch of white lilies. Nell glanced at Rachel, noting how the pastel shades of her clothing matched the room perfectly, giving the scene the faded feel of an old watercolour painting.

Nell stopped in front of Rachel's chair. 'Mrs Morris?'

Rachel started, pulled her cardigan close, and looked up at her. 'Rachel, please.'

Her eyes were extraordinary – deep brown, with flecks of light, they dominated her small face, itself pale, heart-shaped, and – Nell had to admit – absurdly beautiful. Glancing at Paul, Nell didn't need to be a detective to work out from his expression he was thinking the same thing.

Sitting on the large grey velvet sofa, Nell took out her notepad. 'Rachel, can you tell us what Simon was doing last night that might have led to him being in the University Parks?'

Rachel stared, unfocused, at the space between Nell and Paul. 'I have no idea why he would be there.' She looked up at Nell, painfully earnest. 'He said he was going out to meet Hannah, but she lives on the other side of Oxford, so I can't see why he went there at all. It's not even on the way home,' she added.

Nell nodded. 'You say he was going to see Hannah. Is that Hannah Barclay?'

Rachel blinked, surprised. 'Yes. They've been friends since university. They were at Oxford Brookes together, and they occasionally meet up.' She looked concerned. 'Do you think that has something to do with his death?'

'If you're asking whether we believe Hannah is involved with the murder of your husband, I'd say no, not at this stage.'

And that wasn't a lie. This was the first Nell had heard about Simon meeting Hannah the night he died. 'How did Simon usually travel to meet Hannah?' she asked, trying to keep her tone light.

Rachel thought for a moment. 'Well, he would take a bus or taxi.' She looked suddenly confused. 'I can't really remember.'

Nell smiled. 'That's OK. Why would you remember such a small thing?'

Rachel looked grateful. 'Well, yes, exactly.'

'And how often did Hannah and Simon meet, roughly?'

Rachel frowned, hugging her knees. 'Maybe once a month, maybe twice,' she looked helplessly at Nell. 'I can't remember.'

Nell gave another reassuring smile. It wasn't unusual for family and friends to go blank during questioning – hell, if she had a police officer sitting in her front room asking what she'd had for dinner the night before, she'd struggle to answer.

Nell sat back. What was she looking for from Rachel? Was she a suspect, a witness, a victim alongside Simon? For the first time in Nell's career she didn't have answers to the most basic questions, and it was beginning to unnerve her.

Frustrated, she watched as Rachel rubbed the cross that hung around her neck – simple, gold, hung from a long chain. Nell looked around the room: two crosses above the fire, a third attached to the wall by the garden doors, a fourth above the door where Laura stood. She looked at Rachel.

'Are your whole family religious, Rachel?'

'Yes, why?'

Nell pictured Simon's body – an eye for an eye, tooth for a tooth, hand for a hand. 'Was it also important to Simon?'

Rachel frowned. 'Yes, of course, I couldn't have married him otherwise. That was very important to us both, our joint commitment to God.'

Nell nodded, even though she didn't understand in the slightest, but then again, Nell and Christianity were always destined for a bumpy ride, seeing as her sexuality was pretty much outlawed by it.

Rachel was studying her. 'Why do you ask?'

'It's just an avenue we're pursuing. There may have been a religious element to Simon's murder.'

If it were possible to pale even more, Rachel did. 'What do you mean? How could someone be murdered religiously?'

'It's just something we are considering at present.' She smiled, but the woman just stared at her, brown eyes full of an emotion Nell couldn't identify – fear, maybe? But fear of what?

Rachel began to dig at her wrist. Nell noted the scars – some fresh, others not – and thought of the scars on her own body, ones she hadn't inflicted herself but which remained, nonetheless.

'My dad is a preacher at our local church, well, our family home's local church,' Rachel corrected.

'Where is that?' Nell asked, tone light.

'Near Chipping Norton, just outside Great Tew.'

Nell knew the area – the archetypal Cotswold village where you couldn't buy anything for under a million. Maybe Rachel wasn't a kept woman after all; maybe the house and the expensive clothes were because she came from money, not married into it.

'Are you close to your parents?' she asked.

Rachel smiled. 'Yes. They are very fond of Simon.'

It struck Nell as an odd thing to say: why mention her husband when she'd asked about Rachel's relationship with them, but she supposed they were speaking to her because of Simon. Still, Laura may have had a point about something feeling not quite right.

'Just one more thing, if you don't mind.'

Rachel nodded her permission for Nell to continue.

'Do you remember two weeks ago, that Simon went to The Varsity Club, with Hannah and a man called Ash?'

Rachel frowned. 'Yes, why?'

'It was for a reunion, wasn't it?'

'I think so, I can't really remember.' But there was something about the way she said it, the slight shift in the chair, a brief look away, which made Nell think she could.

'Have you noticed anything out of the ordinary between that reunion and now? Anything in the last two weeks which has seemed odd to you; something small maybe, which just struck you as strange?'

Rachel shook her head. 'No, nothing. Why? Does the reunion have something to do with Simon's death?'

'We are interested in Simon's movements leading up to his death, in his mental health, that sort of thing. Had Simon's mood changed in the last few weeks or days? Anything which gave you cause for concern?'

Rachel stared at her, mouth slightly open, fingers digging into her wrist. 'No, he was just normal. I mean.' She tucked a bit of hair behind her ear, red marks on her arm. 'He was obviously upset that he'd watched a woman die, but nothing more than you would expect.'

Nell nodded. 'Yes, of course, Alice Baxter. It's always a shock when someone you know dies.'

Rachel looked confused. 'Simon didn't know her.'

Nell feigned surprise. 'Oh, I'm sorry, I assumed because he studied at Oxford Brookes and she taught there, they might know each other.'

Rachel shook her head. 'No. I mean, maybe he came across her, but I doubt he would have remembered her. It was always just the three of them at university. Hannah, Ash and Simon.'

'Just a coincidence then.' Nell smiled and looked at Paul. 'I think that's all for now, thank you so much for your time. Laura is going to stay here for as long as you need and she'll update you with any information as and when we get it.'

Rachel looked over to Laura then back to Nell. 'Thank you.'

Nell stood outside on the bottom step and lit a cigarette.

'Is it just me or was that really weird?' Paul asked, clicking open the car.

Nell watched cigarette smoke drift upwards.

'I mean, she didn't even ask how he was killed,' Paul continued. 'Have you ever met a spouse who didn't ask that?'

'No. Can't say as I have.' She turned to Laura, who was

standing on the top step. 'Get the parents' contact details and try to listen in on any conversation she has with them, OK?'

Laura nodded.

'And guard all the electronic devices he had access to, I'm sending someone over to seize them.'

Nell's phone buzzed in her pocket. Taking it out she read it and gestured for Paul to get in the car. 'Bremer's got Alice's belongings back from CID. He wants us at the office now.' She looked back to Laura. 'Let me know if she says anything and try to get her talking about her parents. There was something odd about the way she spoke about them, like she was afraid of them. Might be something, might be nothing, but worth checking it out while you're here.'

Then, stubbing her cigarette out on the stone dog guarding the door, she jogged down the steps to join Paul.

Fifteen

Carla lay the contents of Alice's backpack on a table covered with a blue plastic sheet. Each item folded neatly by Alice prior to her death.

'Not the sort of stuff you'd normally find, is it?' Nell said, pointing to the newly laundered underwear, the well-worn but pressed hoodie and recently cleaned trainers.

Carla stared down at the remnants of Alice's past life. 'She was probably trying to keep part of her old life present,' Carla said. 'How long had she been homeless for?'

Nell perched on the edge of the table. 'We don't know yet, why?'

Carla shrugged. 'It's just, you know, when you see a newly homeless person turn up in Oxford, their clothes – the bags they carry – are all from the life they just left behind. Fast-forward a few months and all trace of that is gone, lost to drink and drugs. But it doesn't look like Alice had lost that need to keep her past life with her.' She pointed to the way the clothes were neatly folded, washed. 'She wanted to make sure she didn't lose it, and this care of her belongings made her feel she hadn't.'

Nell gave a nod. 'Yeah, maybe.'

The edge of a piece of white card poked out from beneath a pair of jeans. Carla slowly pushed them to one side, then glanced up at Nell. 'It's an invitation to the reunion at The Varsity Club.'

Nell flipped over the invitation with a pen. 'It's not addressed to anyone.' She poked around the clothes. 'No envelope.' Nell looked across at her. 'How did she get it? Was it hand-delivered or posted?'

Carla looked down at the card. 'And, either way, how did they know where she would be? She was street homeless. Hard to track someone like that down.' She watched as Nell slipped the invitation into an evidence bag.

'We'll fingerprint it and I'll get Laura to check with Rachel; see if they kept Simon's, or if she can remember anything about whether it was delivered by hand or posted. If it's the latter, maybe we'll be lucky and get a clue to where it was posted from.'

Carla could tell from Nell's tone she didn't hold out much hope, and neither did Carla, but it had to be worth a go because – right now – it was the best lead she'd got.

Bremer walked in, four coffees balanced in a cardboard drinks carrier. Calling Paul over from his desk, he looked down at the table.

'Not much to show for a whole life, is it?' He took the lid off his coffee and nodded to Nell. 'Update?'

'Simon went to meet Hannah last night. His wife, Rachel, said they met regularly.'

'As friends or something more?' he asked.

'Rachel didn't indicate anything other than friends, but then she wouldn't be likely to.'

Bremer nodded. 'We need to speak to Hannah. Carla, do you have an address for her?'

'Yes, home and work.'

'Good.'

'I'd also like to speak with Luci,' Nell said. 'Alice's girlfriend.' She gestured down at the table. 'She was very keen to get hold of this and I'd like to know why.'

'She might also be able to tell us why Alice went to the reunion,' Carla added. Bremer looked at her.

'What do you mean?'

'Well, doesn't it strike you as odd? She was the subject of a complaint by Simon, which lost her her job and must have resulted in her – ultimately – becoming homeless. So why would she want to see them again? And I know we've thought she may have wanted to punish them for that by killing herself in front of them, but that would indicate she organised the reunion herself, to make sure they were all there; but how would she have done that? Living on the street isn't exactly conducive to purchasing expensive invitations, let alone finding addresses and posting them.' She could see Bremer was considering what she'd said.

'So I'd like to know from Luci if she knew Alice was organising the reunion and, if not, if she'd been acting strangely leading up to it.' She turned to Nell. 'You said her friend, Guy, the one from the homeless shelter, had told you that Alice was scared of someone who had recently come back into her life. I think we need to find out who that person was.'

'Because that could be the person who arranged the reunion,' Nell finished.

'Exactly.'

Bremer was frowning. 'We still need the connection between Simon and Alice's death. Yes, they both were at Oxford Brookes, invited to a reunion, and both are dead, but we can't ignore the facts that those deaths are very different.' Clocking the look Carla was throwing him, he added, 'But I agree. Luci and Hannah are our priority.'

The phone rang in Bremer's office. 'Carla, find out all you can about Luci, where she's likely to be. We can't speak to her if we don't know where she is.' The phone stopped ringing then immediately started up again. 'I've got to get that. Nell, check how Rachel is doing, then go and chat to Hannah, bring her in if you have to.'

As he walked off, Nell pulled over a chair. 'Why were they all invited? What was the motive?'

Carla took a seat next to her. 'Money, revenge, love, blackmail, self-defence, sex. Pick any one and you'd be as close as I am right now to knowing.'

Nell grinned. 'It's always this way at the start. We'll get there.'

'Yes, but if we hadn't given Alice's case up, we might be at least halfway there by now.' Carla knew it was a pointless thing to say it, but it had been gnawing away at her ever since she'd heard of Simon's murder.

'Well, let's not waste any more time then,' Nell said. 'Motive for killing both Alice and Simon. It's not about sex, neither victims were assaulted.' Nell was checking each off with her finger. 'Can't be self-defence because there was no one near Alice and, from what I saw of Simon's body, he didn't stand a hell's chance of defending himself. So we've got blackmail, money and revenge.'

'I'll check Simon's accounts for signs he was having money troubles, or any indication he was being blackmailed.'

'Or was the blackmailer,' Nell added.

'Which leaves revenge. But what sort of revenge is it to throw yourself off a building?' Carla asked. 'Plus, Simon would be her main target, and she died before him.' She looked at Nell. 'Do you think there is a possibility that we are looking at two people? I mean, maybe there are two motives and two people working together.'

Nell looked as if she was considering the possibility, then said, 'I think the motive is the same for both, it has to be, because it's the reunion which connects them all. One connection, one motive.'

And there it was again, the reunion. Nell was right: so far it was the only real connection they had.

Sixteen

The policewoman, Laura, is making me a cup of tea. I need to ring my parents but every time I try to leave this chair, I can't. It's as if getting up will begin the next stage of my life, the one without Simon, and I'm not sure I'm strong enough to do that yet – I'm not sure I can bear for all this to be real.

Laura looks around the door. 'Would you like me to get you the phone so you can call your parents?'

I smile. 'Yes please, that would be very helpful,' but inside I'm just thinking 'no, no, no'. Because I know what they'll say and I don't want to hear it.

The tea is actually welcome. I sit cradling it in both hands, phone on the table beside me. After a while, I put it down and pick up the mobile, dialling my parents' number – a number more familiar to me than my own.

'Mum.'

'Darling, how are you, how's Simon?'

I don't think I can tell her, but when I finally do through the tears and the sobs, my mum is silent. 'Mum?'

'You need to come home, Rachel.' Her tone is hard and allows for no disagreement or discussion. I think of the house, of dusty, draughty rooms hidden away, secrets, wandering in corridors without light; two houses in one. I cannot go back there. I will not let Simon's death be mine as well.

'Pack your bags,' she is saying. 'Your father will come and pick you up.'

I start to panic, the familiar feeling of a tsunami coming, one I have no protection from and no ability to fight. 'I can't yet, I have a policewoman with me. She needs me to stay here.'

'Then we will come to you. You can't be left alone, Rachel, that is inconceivable.'

I think about the summer with Ash, the times I spent talking to Alice; the only times I haven't felt alone. 'I'm not alone, Mum, I have Laura the policewoman. I'll come home soon, I promise.'

She's silent and I think she's considering this, until my father comes on the phone. 'The Lord needs you at home.' It is unequivocal, definitive.

'I'll be home later when Laura can drive me,' I lie. I feel numb, weightless, as if I'm no longer part of my body.

'I'm glad that's sorted.' My mum's voice has gone back to its usual brightness but I don't feel relief. I feel nothing.

'We'll sort everything with Simon, you don't need to worry about a thing.'

It strikes me she doesn't sound upset; in fact, she doesn't even sound surprised. 'Mum, what did you and Simon argue about?'

She gives a dismissive laugh. 'We haven't argued with Simon, darling.'

'You did. The morning after I stayed the night at yours.'

'You were unwell then, dear, you must have been imagining it.' The edge is returning to her voice and I know I'm pushing my luck.

'I'm sure I did,' I press. She sighs.

'It was nothing. Just a little disagreement about money, that's all.'

I knew it had to be that, what else could it be, but what had he said to anger them? 'About money?' I repeat. 'Was Simon in trouble financially?' It didn't make sense, we had more than enough, so much so I was able to hide thousands without him even knowing. Maybe something had gone wrong, a bad business call, a stupid gambling mistake? But Simon didn't gamble. My mind is whirring with possibilities until my mum cuts them off.

'It was all sorted out, Rachel, now pack a small bag and I'll have a light supper ready for you when you arrive.'

Hanging up, I see a shadow cross the floor by the door, left ajar. Laura. I bite my bottom lip, chewing at it until it bleeds. Pressing my hand against it I allow the sharp sting to settle me. Everything will be OK. I picture the travel bags under the bed, one full of clothes, one full of money, and I look to the door again. I need to get rid of Laura. There's no way I can do everything I need to if she is still here, and I barely have enough time as it is: I need to check Simon's bank accounts for one; there's Ash, I have to find a way to see him, and then there's the woman with the dog. Because, whatever happens, I can't leave until I've spoken to Luci.

Seventeen

Carla opened up Facebook and clicked on Alice's profile. If she was going to find Luci, then this was as good a place as any, and Carla would put money on it being the woman in all the pictures she'd found of Alice in the hours after her death. Scrolling through Alice's pictures, she clicked on each one where a young blonde woman was hugging or smiling with Alice, the same pit-bull always somewhere in the frame, sometimes front and centre, other times wandering idly in the distance. But not once was the blonde woman tagged. She leant back in her chair. 'Shit.'

'Problems?' Paul put down his mobile and looked over at her.

Carla pointed at the screen. 'I just know this is Luci, but she's not tagged into any of the pictures, so I can't get a surname. I'm going to have to ring O'Hanlan House again, but I wanted to avoid that.' She looked to Paul. 'I don't want to spook her.'

'Want me to give them a call?' he asked. 'I asked them to check her surname when we visited two weeks ago. I could make out it's a routine chaser call?'

Carla wasn't sure that would be any better, and she'd rather try to avoid mentioning it was in connection with Alice's death. 'No, it's OK, I will. But thanks,' she added, as she dialled the number for O'Hanlan House. 'Hi, Carla from Thames Valley here, I'm trying to get some details about a woman called Luci? She was friends with Alice Baxter and a man called Guy?'

'Is she in trouble?' the woman asked defensively.

'No, no, not at all.'

'OK.' She sounded uncertain. 'Well, I haven't seen her for a few days now, but her surname is Mahon. Luci Mahon.'

Carla wrote it down. 'I don't suppose you have a date of birth?'

'No, sorry,' then she said, 'although actually she had a birth-day recently. The residents gave her a cake I think.'

'How recently?'

The woman paused. 'Two months ago, roughly; sorry, the days all merge into one after a while.'

Two months. That would make it September, October time. 'Do you remember how old she was?'

'God, I'm sorry, no. Late twenties, I think. Twenty-eight, maybe?'

OK, so that would make it a 1991. Carla ringed the date. It was a start. 'Thank you, that's really helpful.'

'No worries. I can confirm it with Guy, if you'd like? He might remember the exact age she was celebrating.'

'Oh no, don't worry, it's nothing urgent,' and before the woman could reply, Carla hung up.

Three hits came back on Facebook for a Luci Mahon, same age, all with no profile picture. She clicked on their photo albums but no picture matched the Luci from Alice's Facebook page.

Frustrated, she searched again, with a wider age range, squinting at each result in turn. Nothing. She pushed herself back from the desk in frustration, still staring at the screen. If Alice had a Facebook profile, she sure as hell would bet Luci had one too, so why couldn't she find it?

Pulling herself back to the desk, she took one last look at the list and was just about to shut it down when a picture of a dog caught her eye. She opened up Alice's profile again and scrolled down to the picture of her running with a dog, then switched back to the profile picture of a 'Ms M', where the same dog, looking for all the world as if it was smiling, panted back at her. The pictures definitely matched, Carla was sure of it, distinct white fur around its nose, one eye blue, one brown, which meant the owner of the dog was obviously Alice's Luci.

She flicked through the profile but Luci hadn't posted for five days. The last post was a picture of Alice smiling into the distance, a cigarette perched between her fingers, collar pulled up against the cold. She'd tagged it 'my love'.

'I've found Luci on Facebook, so at least we now have a picture,' she called to Paul, 'but she hasn't posted in days. I'm going to look for anything else I can find, but really I need a phone number. Didn't Alice have a phone?'

'Not that I've seen logged.'

'But that just doesn't make sense, how else would they communicate or post things on here? The posts are all from phones so they haven't accessed a computer but, without a phone, how would they know where to meet up?'

'Want me to double-check the evidence log?' he asked.

'Yeah, will you? If I can get her number I can try and get Luci's through the phone bill.' It was a long shot and Carla didn't hold out much hope, but Alice must have had a phone, she was sure of it, so where the hell was it?

Carla turned back to the computer and absent-mindedly scrolled through Alice's account. It had amazed her when she found out homeless people used social media just like anyone else, and she'd felt a deep sense of shame for ever having thought otherwise. That shame hung there now, a sense she was letting Alice down by not getting the answers or even knowing the questions to ask, the nagging feeling of guilt she wasn't working hard enough because Alice's life wasn't worth as much as those of others.

Just as she was about to shut down Facebook and run Luci Mahon's name through the usual police intel databases, something to the left on Alice's profile caught her eye. There, in a list of groups Alice had joined, amongst Oxford City Council and the Old Fire Station Café, was one titled 'The Reunion'. How the hell had she missed that?

Carla clicked on it. The banner across the top was a generic picture of the dreaming spires of Oxford, set against a perfectly blue sky and, even though it was a stock photo, it looked just like the view from the rooftop of The Varsity Club.

'Paul,' she called. 'Come and look at this.' When he'd joined her she pointed at the page. 'We knew there was a link to Facebook, and here it is. Four invitees: Ash, Simon, Hannah and Alice. No admin. No indication of who had set it up; the sole post, a picture of the paper invitation each had received. 'It's genius,' she said.

'Genius? How? Why send paper and e-invites?'

'Two reasons. One, to make sure they all know it's only them going. So they know it's not really a reunion, they know it's linked to their past.'

'But in that case, wouldn't you just not go?'

Carla wheeled round to face him. 'But how could they? Four people invited to a mysterious reunion via a private Facebook page, and they all just happen to share a secret? I don't buy that. There must be a fifth person who set this whole thing up. The question is who and why?'

Paul looked unconvinced.

'The challenge is for them to come and be open about their secret, just as the person inviting them has been open about inviting them.'

'And what's the second reason?' Paul asked.

'I'm not sure, but I think it's a way to document the event, and everything that happens afterwards.'

Paul squinted at the screen. 'But there is only one post.'

'For now,' Carla replied. There was something about discovering the page which had made the adrenalin kick in. Maybe it was because it hinted at a plan, a methodological approach with expected outcomes; either way it meant the murderer was going to be easier to catch – if they had a plan, that was a plan waiting to be found.

Bremer appeared at his door. 'Anything?'

'You might want to see this,' Paul said, pointing down at the screen.

Bremer walked over and took a seat. 'This is a great find. Can we trace the IP address? Find who set it up that way?'

Carla shook her head. 'Facebook never reveal IP addresses or account holders' details. Multi-million dollar lawsuits have tried and failed, so we wouldn't stand a hope in hell. And even if they did,' she went on, 'whoever is doing this is organised and methodical. This has been planned really carefully, so if I was the killer, I would have used a VPN.' Seeing Bremer's confusion, she added, 'Virtual Private Network. The internet is public so all data-sharing – including the IP address – will be public, but a VPN creates a private avenue for people to share things.'

'The dark web, you mean?' Bremer asked.

Carla shook her head. 'No, this is just a way to communicate privately in a public forum. Yes, it can be used for criminality, as can anything really, but businesses use them so it's not always sinister.'

'And you think this page is important because . . . ?' Bremer asked.

'Because if I were the murderer and I'd bothered to set this up,

I'd be planning on using it for something. Why else risk it? We are part of this game, for want of a better word, and this' – she pointed to the screen – 'is how they are going to play.' She could see Bremer's unease and she got it, there was nothing there yet for him to trust what she was saying. But Carla knew she was right; the killer wanted to tell them something and this was what they would use to do it.

Eighteen

Nell called Laura, the FLO, on her way out of the station. 'How's it going?'

'Rachel has asked me to leave.' Her voice sounded tinny from the car speakerphone. 'But I listened in on her conversation with her parents and got something that might be worth looking into.'

Nell checked her watch. 'Meet me at The Trout in ten.' Hanging up, she texted Paul to meet her at Hannah's in an hour, before heading off to the Wolvercote pub on the bank of the river Thames.

Inside, they took a seat in the far back room, navigating uneven floors dotted with mismatched tables and chairs.

Nell handed Laura a half of lager. 'How's Rachel bearing up?'

'OK, I think. Quiet. No tears and she seems to be holding it together. I'm not sure she really gets that he's dead.'

'Yeah, well, people deal with things in different ways.' Nell had once had to tell a mother her son had died playing chicken on the train tracks, and she'd been furious at him for hours before finally breaking down and sobbing her heart out for her child.

She pictured Rachel, sitting alone in that big house, not knowing why her husband was dead, or who killed him, and it occurred to her those were two questions Rachel hadn't asked.

'Did she ask any more about how he died?' Nell wondered if Rachel might have wanted more details about the religious aspects of Simon's death, but Laura shook her head.

'Nope. She didn't ask anything about him. Is that odd?'

'Truthfully? I can't tell. On the one hand it could mean she is still in shock and has no idea what's going on; on the other, we can't rule out the possibility she isn't asking the questions because she knows the answers.'

Laura frowned. 'I just can't see it. She's like an injured sparrow curled up in that massive chair like it's a nest.'

Nell thought Rachel looked more beautiful than a sparrow, but she got the point. It was going to be important to keep Laura in the house as much as possible, even if Rachel protested. Nell would have to get Bremer to agree to second Laura to the team, at least until they'd more of an idea about the level of Rachel's involvement. It would be invaluable to have someone on the inside, especially if Laura managed to gain Rachel's trust, although thinking back to Laura's attitude when they'd first met, Nell wasn't sure that was really Laura's forte.

Laura suddenly reached into her pocket and handed Nell a piece of paper. 'Simon's passwords to the laptop and his phone.'

'Great, thanks.' That would please Carla; his phone had been sitting on her desk, and Nell could see it was driving her insane not to be able to access it. She took a sip of her lime and soda. 'You mentioned something about the conversation Rachel had with her parents?'

Laura pulled out her notebook. 'OK. She called her parents about two hours ago and they spoke for no longer than fifteen minutes. It was clear they wanted her to go back to their home and equally clear Rachel didn't want to, although she agreed to in the end. Anyway, Rachel asked about an argument she'd overheard between her parents and Simon, and she asked if it was about money.'

'Money? Did she say why she thought it was about that? Had she overheard them mention it?'

'She didn't, and I didn't get the impression it was something she listened to, more that she assumed it was about that.'

Nell picked at the edges of a beer mat. 'And she didn't say any more about it, other than ask if it was about money? Nothing to indicate whether it was about Simon wanting money from them or whether they'd borrowed money off him and he wanted it back?'

'No, sorry. She just asked the question.'

Nell would get Carla to check Simon's financial records, and if that gave them something, she'd request the parents too. 'You said Rachel had agreed to go back to her parents?' That was not ideal if they wanted Laura to stay close to her.

'Yes, but there was something about the way she behaved after the call ended that made me think she wasn't going to go.'

'In what way?'

Laura gave it some thought. 'She seemed anxious, agitated, and straight away asked me to leave. She kept checking the clock on the wall and her watch, and she went upstairs for a good ten minutes, which is the first time she'd left the chair.' Laura shrugged. 'I know it isn't "facts" but it just felt . . . off. Her whole demeanour changed.'

Nell got it, sometimes you just knew there was more to a behaviour than met the eye. 'Could she have been packing?'

'Well, yes, that's what I assumed she was doing, but there was no noise, no indication she was opening drawers or wardrobes, no clinking in the bathroom, just this odd silence. And I was halfway up the stairs, listening, so I would have heard if there had been anything.'

Nell wrapped her hands round the glass and thought about Rachel's conversation with her parents. Why did she ask about the argument? Did she think it had something to do with Simon's murder? Nell tried to picture telling her parents that a loved one had died, and she couldn't imagine that would be the time to ask about something she didn't consider relevant to the news. 'Did you get the impression Rachel thought her parents had something to do with Simon's death?'

'I didn't get an impression either way, sorry,' she said.

Nell downed the rest of her drink. What was Rachel doing upstairs if she wasn't packing? Was it relevant? Two possibilities occurred to her: either she had already known her parents would want her back and she was packed already; or, and this wasn't an option Nell hoped for, she was already packed because she'd already known she would leave. 'When you got to the house to tell Rachel about Simon's murder, did she, at any time, go upstairs prior to the ten minutes you mentioned?'

Laura shook her head. 'She just sat in that chair. I even had to get the phone for her to call her parents.'

That wasn't good. If, as she said, Rachel hadn't known about Simon's murder, she wouldn't have packed ready to go to her parents. Which meant she'd already done so prior to Laura telling her the news. Whichever way Nell looked at it, that could only mean Rachel already knew about Simon's death. 'What time does your shift end?' she asked.

Laura checked her watch. 'I've got two more hours.'

Nell nodded. 'I want you to keep watch on Rachel's house. Park in the side road across from it and let me know the minute she leaves, OK?'

'Sure thing,' Laura replied, looking doubtful. 'You think Rachel is involved?'

Nell pulled her cigarettes out of her jacket. 'I don't know, but if she's going to become a flight risk, I want us to be there when she tries.'

Nineteen

After Laura leaves, I wait ten minutes to be sure she's gone, then grab my car keys and head to Oxford. The early evening crowds are starting to gather in George Street, a bustle of eateries, the odd pub, and as I walk around groups huddled on the pavement, I wonder how Alice had felt looking at all those people enjoying their lives while hers fell apart.

I decide to walk up Cornmarket, a street upstaged by the new shopping centre down the road, now just a row of boarded-up shop fronts where homeless people gather, despite the best efforts of the council to move them on.

A homeless couple are arguing in the shadows of one shop. They look drunk or high, and I am about to turn away when the man stops shouting in the woman's face and turns to stare at me.

'What you looking at?'

I freeze. The woman looks at me, half curious, half suspicious and, despite my better judgement, I grip my phone in my hand and walk over.

'I just wondered if either of you knew this woman.' I held up a picture of Luci on my phone, a screenshot from Alice's Facebook page. 'Or this one?' I scroll quickly to one of Alice laughing at a dog. It's my favourite of the ones I'd found since her death; in my hours of searching for signs of her life, putting together each piece, hoping it would give me a picture of the person I'd lost. That's how I'd found Luci. It was obvious from the moment I saw the way she looked at Alice, in the pictures on my computer screen, that they were in love; a realisation that both hurt and reassured.

'You a cop?' the man snaps, his focus on me wavering. The woman hangs back, eyeing us both with interest.

'No, no,' I say, looking down at the picture of Alice. 'She was just my friend, that's all, and I was hoping to find out about her. I hoped to speak with her girlfriend, Luci.' The woman pushes past the man and puts her hand on my arm. Rain begins to fall more heavily, hard.

'Come under here.' She tugs me towards the shop. 'I knew her and I know Luci.'

The woman smiles. 'I'd offer you a swig of wine but you don't seem the type.' Her smile turns into a grin as she flops onto the duvet on the floor, gesturing for me to join her. 'Although you do look like you could do with one, if you don't mind me saying. I could roll you a cigarette?'

I don't smoke, but the gesture feels somehow important, so

I say, 'Yes please, thank you. I'll pay you for it, obviously.' I reach for my pocket, then instantly regret it when I see how offended she looks.

'I'm sorry. It's very kind of you to offer me one. I'm Rachel.' I hold my hand out to her.

'Patsy.' She gives my hand a firm shake, before taking out her tobacco and two cigarette papers. 'How did you know Alice?' She is concentrating on lining the tobacco up. I watch, remembering Alice doing the same, her delicate fingers twirling the paper with such skill I'd been mesmerised.

'We knew each other briefly when she worked at Oxford Brookes,' I reply.

Patsy licks the paper and rolls it swiftly into a cigarette before handing it to me. 'I liked Alice. She'd always be on your side whatever, you know?' She glances at the man who was now standing smoking across the road, watching us.

'He's OK.' Patsy gives a short shrug. 'Just gets protective, that's all.'

I nod. 'Hard enough having a relationship when you have a house and money.'

Patsy grins again. 'I wouldn't know.'

I feel I've messed up again, but Patsy holds out a lighter and I lean forward, dragging on the roll-up until it takes. 'Was she OK, Alice, I mean?' I ask, trying not to cough out the smoke which fills my lungs.

Patsy studies me as she lights her cigarette. 'Well, man, she was homeless so . . .'

'I know, but I just want to know, if she was . . .' I finish, unable to say the word, so Patsy says it for me.

'Happy?'

I watch the rain bouncing off the pavement. It feels a ridiculous question; of course she wasn't happy, and I don't know what I want or expect to hear.

'She was good,' Patsy says.

The cracks in the pavement are quickly filling with water and I realise what I really wanted to ask was, 'Did she think of me?' But, of course, no one could answer that, except Alice.

My head spins from the cigarette and I feel a wave of nausea. I stub it out.

'You OK?' Patsy asks. I peer at her, trying to focus, waiting for the nicotine rush to pass.

When it does, I ask, 'How is Luci?'

'Yeah. She's not doing so good. They were real close. But she's got Billy.'

'Billy?'

Patsy laughs. 'Her dog. Won't go anywhere without him. Which is why she's not often at the hostel.'

'Do you know where she is now?'

'Probably by the back of the Westgate. There's a loading bay there which is good if you want some peace and quiet.'

That's where I'd first met her, Billy yapping at my heels, Luci's face full of anger. I look over at the Westgate shopping centre.

'Do you want me to come with you to see if she's there?' Patsy asks.

I look at her and think it would be good to have someone with me this time around. 'I would, thank you.'

We walk to the back of the old shopping centre and I scan the area for Luci or the dog, Billy. 'I can't see her,' I say to Patsy. She looks down the small side street we'd just come from, pointing to a dog.

'There, next to Billy.'

The dog looks over at us, then seeing it's Patsy, stands and wags his tail, which speeds up as we approach.

Patsy pats Billy's head. 'Hey, Luci,' she calls to the woman under a dank-looking duvet, belongings scattered to one side. 'Luci,' she repeats, and a dishevelled woman – twenty-eight, possibly twenty-nine – peers out, blonde hair, dark roots, blue eyes swimming with drink.

'What?' Her voice is hoarse as she eyes me suspiciously.

'This is one of Alice's friends, Rachel. She wanted to come and speak to you about her.'

Luci eyes narrow. 'I know who she is.' She pushes herself off the floor as Billy begins to growl. 'I bloody well know who you are, you bitch.'

I feel Patsy take a step back as I hold up my hands. 'I'm not here to cause trouble, I just wanted to meet you.'

'Well, I don't want to meet you.' She takes a step towards me. 'Not after what you did to Alice. Now fuck off.'

Patsy tugs at my arm, clearly afraid of Luci, but I can't stop staring at the woman who'd taken my place, who'd slept next to Alice on the cold, wet streets. Patsy tugs harder as a man I hadn't noticed starts to wake from the sleeping bag next to us.

'Come on,' she says, urgent, fearful. 'You need to get out of here.'

But Luci steps forward, fist raised, and before I can move back she punches me in the stomach, the face, and all I can hear is Patsy screaming at her to stop and the dog barking madly while a pain in my side makes me almost pass out.

'I'm going,' I manage to say, hands across my face, hunched over from the blows. Patsy starts dragging me back towards the road, Billy barking, strangers staring at us as we stumble forwards.

'I know what you did,' Luci yells as we turn the corner and I fall down against the wall. 'So don't ever come back.'

Twenty

Nell drew up to Hannah's house in the suburb, Barton. Paul was already waiting for her, but the lack of light from the house told her they were wasting their time. Lighting a cigarette, she walked to join him.

'No one's in,' he said. 'And I've checked her vet's practice and it's shut, no sign of her.'

Nell took a deep drag. 'Back to the office then.' She hated a wild goose chase and didn't fancy hanging around waiting for her with no intel to say when Hannah was going to be back.

'We could go and take a look around town for Luci.' He held up his mobile phone. 'Carla found her on Facbook so we've got an ID.'

'Nah, let's get back to the office. It's getting late, so even if we do find her she'll probably be off her head by now. And

Simon has to be our priority at the moment; his was a murder, after all.'

'You don't think the Alice angle has legs?'

Nell wasn't sure how Alice's death fitted into Simon's murder, but until she did she had no intention of wandering the streets of Oxford looking for a woman who probably had nothing to do with either. 'I don't know. Carla seems to think so, but . . .' She hesitated. It felt disloyal to Carla to mention Gerry's sentencing, pushed back now, just to prolong the agony for her, but she still had a sneaking feeling Carla was diverting the emotions that the case brought up onto Alice.

'It must have been hard on her, seeing Alice die. So I get why she feels she has a vested interest in the case.'

'Yeah, I do too, I just don't want it to fuck up a murder case.' She threw her cigarette down. 'Come on, let's get back, debrief then call it a night. I don't know about you but I could kill for a beer.'

Carla was seated at her desk. Nell dumped her bag on the floor and went to join her. 'Got anything for me?'

'Facebook,' Carla said, nodding towards the screen.

Nell pulled over a chair. 'Anything good?'

'Not yet. I feel like I'm just going round in circles.' She looked tired. Nell checked her watch. Man, it had been a long day.

'Can you get financials for Simon?' Nell asked, explaining about the conversation Laura had overheard about money. 'See if he was in any trouble, that kind of thing. If he doesn't have a joint account with Rachel, can you check hers too?'

Carla frowned. 'On what grounds? You know I can't check it without Rachel's permission or a court order. Or are you telling me she's a suspect now?'

'Suspect?' Bremer said from behind them. 'Who's a suspect?'

Nell wheeled around to face him, outlining Rachel's behaviour, her theory she might be a flight risk and know more than she was telling them. 'I've got Laura outside, just to see if she leaves, where she goes.'

'Good thinking.' He took a seat. 'Did you get anywhere with Hannah?'

'She wasn't there. We thought about taking a look for Luci, but I decided it would be better to do that in daylight.'

Bremer nodded. 'Good call. And Hannah has to be our priority at the moment, and Rachel,' he added, 'if your instinct is right and she's lying about her level of involvement.'

Nell could see Carla tense at the mention of priority. She was going to have to speak to Bremer about it, if Carla continued to focus on the Alice angle without giving her full attention to Simon's murder. But maybe worth a quiet word with her first. 'Do you have anything on the parents? Laura said she'd agreed to go there this evening, although she didn't get the feeling Rachel was telling the truth about it.'

'Nothing more than the preliminary research I did earlier. Want me to dig for more?'

Nell shook her head. 'Not tonight. It's getting late. I think we should clock off for the night.' She looked to Bremer for approval.

'I think you're right. It's been a long day. We'll meet back at six a.m. Hannah will be our priority, followed by a proper chat with Rachel. How long can Laura mark the house?'

'Not much longer, unless you authorise the overtime?'

'Consider it authorised.' Bremer stood. 'Get some rest and I'll see you back here in a few hours.'

With him gone, Nell looked back at Carla. The analyst had dark circles under her eyes and was paler than usual. 'Try not to let this get to you. I know it's hard, but you can't get too close or it will destroy you. And that means it will destroy my case,' she added with a slight laugh, just to reassure Carla she was joking, even though she wasn't wholly. Before Carla could reply, Nell's phone rang. She checked caller ID . . . shit. 'Go ahead, Laura.'

'It's Rachel. She's come home.'

For a second Nell didn't understand; they'd been waiting for her to leave, not return. It meant Rachel must have left soon after Laura had, but where had she been going in such a hurry? 'Which direction was she coming from?'

'Town. Using her own car. Lights are on now and gates are closed.'

Maybe Rachel wasn't going to be a flight risk after all. 'Are you OK to stay until lights out?' There seemed no point in Laura staying beyond the time Rachel went to sleep, and Bremer could thank her in the morning for keeping his overtime budget low.

'Yeah, sure. I'll let you know if there's any movement.'

Thanking her, Nell took Carla's mouse and closed down the computer. 'Need a lift home?'

Carla lifted her bag and took out her tobacco. 'No thanks,

I drove in.' She seemed distracted; Nell almost asked why but thought better of it. Sometimes you just had to let Carla work things out over time. She'd see how she was in the morning, and besides, all Nell wanted to do right then was to grab a bottle of red, sink into the sofa, and spend an hour scrolling through Netflix before falling asleep.

Twenty-one

Baz wasn't in when Carla got home. The flat was dark, just a single light in the corner, and she sat and ate the takeout curry she'd bought them on her own.

When she finished, she dragged her laptop over and opened up Facebook. Typing in Luci's name, she clicked on her profile, not expecting to see anything new, and was surprised to find a picture of her dog with a man called Guy tagged in. Hadn't that been the name of the man Nell and Paul had met that afternoon in the hostel, the one who had been so keen to collect Alice's belongings?

Feeling a beat of optimism, she clicked on Guy's profile. It was littered with pictures of Alice and Luci, but what took Carla's attention was the most recent post – added only five minutes ago – of Luci in the reception of O'Hanlan House.

She grabbed her phone and dialled Nell; when it went to answerphone she tried Paul but got the same. Shit. She couldn't risk Luci leaving the hostel. She tried Nell again and when it went to voicemail this time, she said, 'Nell. Luci is at O'Hanlan House, now. I'm going down there,' then hung up, scribbled Baz a note telling him she was working late, picked up her car keys and left.

As she drove over, she grew increasingly anxious. What was she going to do when she got there? What if Luci kicked off or Guy took exception to her approaching them? She looked down at her phone, hoping to see a missed call from Nell, but the screen was blank. Should she try Paul again? But by the time she'd decided to, she was sitting parked outside the hostel, and it seemed ridiculous to call him then. What was she going to do, sit and wait for him, like some scared little girl?

She pictured Alice, her pale face, limp hair, big brown eyes scanning the rooftop before she jumped. 'Sod this,' she said and, unclicking her seatbelt, she checked her phone one more time before heading out.

The hostel was busy; it smelt of sweat, alcohol, dogs and cigarettes. As she scanned the reception for signs of Luci, Carla focused on her heart rate, willing it to keep calm.

'Can I help you?' a woman called from reception, waving her over.

'Hi, yes, I'm looking for Luci Mahon, she said I'd find her here?'

'Yeah, I saw her a minute ago, actually. Stuart?' She called over to a man by the door. 'Where's Luci?'

'Went out to check on Billy, I think,' his Scottish accent laced with beer.

'OK, cheers.' Then turning back to Carla, she said, 'Billy's her dog. She doesn't often stay with us because she doesn't want to leave Billy, so she usually just pops by for a shower and stuff. It was a relief to see her, actually; after Alice she went off grid and we were all worried she was going to spiral out of control.'

Carla nodded, aware of Stuart's eyes on her. 'It must have been very hard on her.'

The woman nodded. 'Yeah, it's hard for us all when one dies.'

'I can imagine.' Although in truth, Carla couldn't. Yes, her work could be hard, but at least she felt she was making headway. Here, it must be like being faced with a tsunami of the worst that could happen to a person, one you didn't have a hope of preventing, let alone managing.

Stuart called over from the door. 'She's outside now.'

'Brilliant, thank you,' Carla called back. She smiled at the woman. 'And thanks for your help.'

'No worries, and tell Luci, Billy owes me a cuddle.'

Outside, Luci was leaning against a wall chatting to a man Carla knew from Facebook as Guy. Billy was sitting between them, wrapped in a dog coat, a thick red collar around his neck. Carla recognised it as one from Dogs on the Street – the homeless charity for street dogs – and, for some reason, that calmed her.

Luci was agitated, cradling her hand as if she'd hurt it. She and Guy glanced over at Carla then away again so, taking a breath and hoping to God they wouldn't attack her, she approached the pair and smiled.

'Hi, I'm Carla, I was hoping to have a talk to you about Alice?'

Luci glared at her from under a tired-looking bobble hat, collar high up against the evening air, pupils wide with drink.

'What about her?' Her tone made Billy start to growl. Guy pushed himself off the wall, taking a couple of steps forward.

'I'm just a friend of hers and I was hoping to get in contact with her family,' Carla said.

'We were her family,' Guy snapped.

'Well yes . . .' Carla kept the smile on her face despite her increasing sense she'd made the wrong decision in going there. 'But also, her biological family? I was hoping, as you were so close to Alice, she might have told you about them. Also, I was hoping to find her phone. It's got lots of contacts on it who I know would like to be invited to the funeral and I wondered if you knew where it was?' As lies went, she'd told worse.

The pair were looking increasingly suspicious and Carla was beginning to regret not leaving it to Nell and Paul, but then Luci asked, 'When's the funeral?'

Carla swallowed, her mouth dry. 'I'm not sure yet, we'll know more when they release her body.'

Luci flinched, but Carla carried on, speaking quickly. 'Would you have her phone? I'd only need it for a little while and then you could have it back, or we could just go through the contacts together and you could help me list who to invite.'

If I Fall

Luci looked uncertain, which only made Carla think she had it, so she said, 'Like this person who'd recently come back into her life? Maybe they would like to go?'

It was the wrong thing to say, she knew it immediately. Luci threw Guy a warning look as she stepped close to Carla, Billy's growl growing louder. When Luci was less than two inches from Carla's face she hissed, 'Fuck off out of here. You're no friend of Alice's.'

Carla tried to take a step back, stumbled. Righting herself, she held up her hands as a car drew up close behind them.

'I'm sorry, I shouldn't have come . . .' Carla heard a car door slam and footsteps making their way towards them. Luci's stare flickered to the side as Guy moved towards her, the dog now barking as the footsteps approached. Carla felt a hand on her shoulder and let out a scream.

'Hey there,' Nell said, looking between Guy and Luci. 'Problems?'

'Jesus, Nell.' Carla's heart rate had soared to a point she wished she had something to grab hold of.

Nell ignored her and continued to stare at Luci. 'Get the dog to shut up, would you.'

'He barks when he smells bacon.'

Nell let out a sharp laugh. 'How original.'

Luci's hand moved to the pocket of her coat.

'Keep your hands where I can see them, please. You too.' Nell nodded to Guy. Luci's hand paused, hovering by the opening.

'Now, what was it you wanted them for, Ms Brown?' Nell

glanced to Carla and she could tell instantly that Nell was furious with her.

Carla shook her head, desperate to leave. 'It's nothing. We should just go.'

Luci threw her a look of disgust. 'Police posing as a dead woman's friend to get her phone? That's lower than even I thought you lot went.'

'I'm sorry, I just wanted to speak to you about Alice and find out more about her.'

'Then why not just ask?' Luci snapped. Carla looked helplessly at Nell, who refused to look at her, and continued to stare at Luci.

'I panicked; I didn't think you'd speak to me if you knew I worked for the police,' Carla said.

'Damn right we wouldn't have.' Guy took another step forward and Nell tensed by Carla's side, as a group formed by the doorway to the hostel, jostling to see what the exchange was about. Carla didn't need Nell to tell her that if they realised they were police, it wasn't going to go their way.

'Why did you want Alice's belongings?' Nell asked. 'What was in there that you wanted?'

Luci looked quickly at Guy and, despite her fear, Carla couldn't help thinking it was a warning shot.

'Nothing in particular, I just wanted her stuff was all.'

Stuart shouted across from the doorway. 'Everything OK Luce? Need a hand?'

'We need to get out of here, now,' Nell said under her breath.

Carla nodded and took a step to go but Luci's hand moved into her pocket. Nell reached to the back of her jeans and pulled out a baton. Flicking it open she held it up, one palm towards the group at the door.

'Everyone calm down. Right now,' she said, then to Luci. 'Drop the knife, now.'

Luci didn't move so Nell pointed the baton further forward. 'Now.'

Luci took a step back but kept hold of the knife – Carla thought of the scars on Nell's body, where a knife had sliced her skin – and it felt as if time stopped, everyone assessing their next move, until Stuart finally started the clock ticking again.

'Luce, drop the knife. Come on, you know how it'll go, they'll take you down the station and then what will happen to Billy?'

Luci glanced down at the dog then back at Nell. 'You going to arrest me if I put it down?'

'No. When you put it down I'm going to walk back to my car with my colleague and drive away.'

Luci watched them, weighing up her options, before leaning down and placing the knife on the floor, eyes on Nell as she did. When she stood back up, Nell kicked the knife to the side and hit her baton on the floor – sound of metal on concrete – closing it. 'Thank you. I appreciate it. Now we'll be off and you all have a good night, OK?'

No reply as Carla and Nell walked back to the car, just dozens of pairs of eyes on them, Billy's incessant barking.

'Get in, lock the door, and don't say a word to me until I tell you to, got it?'

Carla grew hot. She reached for the door handle. 'Got it. Sorry.'

Nell glared at her over the roof of the car. 'Not another bloody word.'

Twenty-two

Nell gripped the steering wheel and tried to breathe through the raging anger she'd felt from the moment she'd got Carla's voicemail, which she'd had to listen to twice in order to believe what she was hearing.

'I mean,' she said finally. 'What the hell were you thinking, Carla? You went into a potentially volatile situation totally unaided and with no backup whatsoever. You then proceeded to lie to a potential witness in a murder inquiry, which not only has the potential to jeopardise the case going to court, but pretty much ruins any chance she'll cooperate if we need her to.'

Carla remained silent.

Still furious, Nell went on. 'And what did you actually hope to achieve? Did you think they'd give you her phone?' She glanced across at Carla but couldn't read her expression from a side profile. 'And if they had, what grounds would you have used to interrogate it? It really is the most absurd thing I've ever come across in all my years in the—'

'OK, OK, I get it. I messed up and I'm sorry. I just panicked and thought if I could find Luci, I'd somehow find the link we needed between Alice and Simon.'

'And you considered going into a group of drunk homeless people was the best way to go about it?'

When Carla didn't reply, Nell let her point sit between them. Jesus, this was all Bremer's fault, taking her out to interviews was always going to cloud her judgement in the end, make Carla think of herself as one of them, rather than the civilian she was: unprotected, untrained, and at risk of attack without any recourse to call for backup.

As the silence and the drive continued, Nell began to calm down. Fair enough, she got that Carla felt invested in Alice, and it was possible she hadn't realised just how dangerous the situation could have been – although Nell was pretty sure she got it now – and she could see how Carla may have reacted, without thinking, when she'd found Luci. After all, Carla had been adamant from the beginning that Simon was linked to Alice's death.

Simon. Of course. She glanced at Carla. 'You know there might be another way to find the link between the two cases.'

'Like what?' Carla asked.

'Laura gave me the passcode to Simon's phone earlier.'

Carla stared at her. 'And you didn't give it to me?'

Nell threw her a look. 'I forgot, and I don't think you're in a position to call me out on that right now, do you? The point is, we have it.'

The look on Carla's face almost made Nell laugh out loud. 'My God, you really are a total phone geek, aren't you?'

Carla was, by now, sitting bolt upright in her seat. 'Where is it now? Do you have it on you? And if so, we need to go and interrogate it now.'

'It's in my pocket, but I'm taking you home, seeing as we had to make a quick getaway and abandon your car, then I'm going to bed. We'll check it out in the morning.'

Carla shifted her whole body round to face Nell. 'Look, we're going to pass HQ on the way back to mine. I just want to take a look. I promise I won't take long but, Nell, I'll go insane if I have to wait overnight.'

Nell tapped her finger on the steering wheel. Carla had a point; it wouldn't take too long. 'God, you must be insufferable to live with, Brown.'

Carla didn't smile. 'You're not the first to say that to me today. But is it a yes?'

Nell glanced over at her. 'It's a yes. But I want to be in and out, got it? It's going to be a long day tomorrow.'

'Got it, and thanks.'

The office was dark save for a light on at the far right of the room, a gentle hum of computers the only noise. Nell went to her desk and pulled out the evidence bag with Simon's phone, a pair of plastic gloves, and the paper with the password. Nell handed them all to Carla.

Carla pulled on the gloves. 'God, I hope we get something after all this.'

'Me too, dude, me too.' Nell perched on the side of Carla's desk, watching as she unlocked the phone and began scrolling through calls made and received. 'Anything?'

Carla didn't look up. 'Man, give me a minute!'

Nell looked at the clock. Ten fifty. Great. Another evening ruined by the job.

'Oh my God, I've got something!' Carla looked up, held up the phone, and gestured for Nell to come over. 'Look.' She held up the screen. 'Simon's phone called someone listed as Ash, and someone listed as Hannah, the night before Alice died.'

Nell peered at the screen. 'Call length?'

'Between five and seven minutes.'

'So, the calls definitely were answered?'

'Can't say for sure, but I'd imagine so, yes. Otherwise would have gone to answerphone.'

'What about this call?' Nell pointed to a number called between the calls to Hannah and Ash, but which had no name assigned to it.

'Well, that's where it gets interesting,' Carla replied. 'If Simon was calling someone between calling Hannah and Ash, it's likely it's connected, no? I mean, it was probably about the reunion at The Varsity Club, yeah? So, we could assume, for the moment, this call was also about that. Therefore, this number –'

Carla pointed to the phone – 'is important enough to take place midway through that discussion.'

'You think it's Alice?' Nell watched Carla consider this.

'Well, we won't know until we do a check and, even then, if it is, it may well have no registration details. If a homeless person buys a phone, how can they put a home address?'

Nell hadn't thought of that. 'Good point. So how will we know?'

'Either we work it out from phone bills, try to link it to one person and then trace the activity from that or' – Carla clicked on the Google button – 'we do what every good analyst does, late at night and with limited resources, and run an internet search on it.'

Nell pulled over a chair. 'Think we'll get anything?'

Carla pointed at a Facebook hit. 'Looks like it.'

Nell watched as Carla opened it. A picture of Luci's dog popped up, under which a post said, 'Call if you need me,' listing the number on Simon's phone.

Nell leant back. What the hell? 'So it's Luci's phone he was calling, not Alice's?' But why the hell was Simon contacting Alice's friend, Luci?

Carla looked back at the computer. 'I think it's a solid starting point. But Alice could have been using it? I mean, we can't find a phone for her, so maybe she and Luci shared one?'

Nell considered that for a moment. 'But that means Simon knew Luci's number – how, why? Had he called it before?'

'Not in the recent phone history, but the phone bills will tell me that.' Carla turned back to the Facebook post. 'Surely Luci can't be involved?'

'Why?'

'Because she loved Alice.'

Nell leant forward. 'Luci is also homeless and penniless, Carla. We've no idea what she and Simon discussed, but what we do know is that they discussed something, and shortly after that Alice was dead.' Nell pointed to the phone. 'Anything from or to Luci's phone on the night Simon died?'

Carla scrolled through the rest of Simon's call history. 'No, nothing.'

'So just one call, the night before the reunion?'

Carla nodded.

'And now we know,' Nell continued, 'that Rachel's assertion that Simon had had no contact with Hannah or Ash for years is manifestly untrue. Whether she lied, or didn't know, remains to be seen.'

Carla looked across at her. 'So, what now?'

'We bring them all in: Hannah, Ash, Luci and Rachel.' She clocked Carla's look of doubt. 'Come on, man, you've done it, you've found the link between Simon's murder and Alice's death. Isn't this what you wanted? Simon was in contact with Alice – either directly or through a friend – which means they're all involved, and all now potential suspects. Surely that's what this whole nightmare evening has been for, no?'

'I guess so . . .'

Nell saw her pause. 'What?'

She looked over at Nell. 'What's Bremer going to say about me tracking Luci down?'

Nell contemplated her. She had a point. That wasn't going to be an easy one to brush over. 'OK, the story is, you found Luci via a Facebook picture, you called me – which isn't a lie – and we went to speak to her. It all went horribly wrong, so we came back here and found the link – also not a lie. Job done.'

Carla looked doubtful. 'You think he'll go for that?'

Nell had no idea, but it was all she had, that and a desperate need for her bed. 'Yes.' She tried to sound convincing. 'If we stick to the story, who's he going to believe? Us or Luci?'

Carla looked as if she was about to speak but Nell cut her off. 'Dude, get into the morals of that on your own time. You fucked up, I pulled it back, and now we have a really good lead. Let's just go with that, OK?'

'OK.'

'Come on. I'll drive you home.'

Carla switched off the computer and picked up her bag. 'Maybe I should get in super early, and make it look like I'd just found the calls?'

Nell pulled out a Marlboro, ready to light up the minute they hit the back yard. 'Sure, whatever you think.' It didn't matter to her either way, so long as they got the lead. But seeing Carla's face – a mixture of worry and doubt – she relented.

'Come in early, I'll do the same,' and silently cursing the lack of sleep, Nell added, 'I'll even pick you up, seeing as your car is probably on fire, right now, outside that hostel.'

Carla grinned.

'But the coffee is on you.'

'Deal,' Carla replied.

Twenty-three

My face is throbbing. It's not an unknown pain but one I know will leave a mark. How will I explain that to the police? I start to panic, growing hot, pacing the room thinking of explanations. 'Come on, Rachel, you're good at this, it's what you do – hiding the truth,' but I can't see a way out, the panic is too great.

I ring Ash. 'Ash. I need your help.'

'What's happened?' He sounds sleepy and I suddenly realise he doesn't know about Simon. There had been no name released in the news and I was pretty sure the police hadn't connected his death to the reunion – not yet, anyway – so Ash wouldn't be linked to the murder. I press on the bruise around my eye, feel pain like a shard of glass, and tell him about Simon.

When I've finished, all he says is, 'I'll be right over.'

*

Ash makes coffee while I explain about seeing Luci. 'I just don't understand why you'd do that. Not on the day you find out Simon is dead. Do you know how that is going to look to the police?' He hands me a mug and I wrap my hands around it.

'I wanted to see if she was OK.'

'But the police will want to know why you were thinking of Alice and not your husband.' He looks exasperated but I know, really, he understands.

'Now Simon is dead, I could go and find her. I couldn't before.'

He sits down across from me, the kitchen island between us. 'What are you going to do?'

'I'm not going home, I can't, not again. Not ever.' The force with which I say it obviously takes him by surprise, because he sits back, contemplating me.

'They won't let you stay here – your parents, I mean.'

'I know that.' I stare down at my coffee. 'Do you remember that summer? The way we felt when we drove up to the front door, so full of excitement and hope?' He doesn't reply. 'Do you hate me for it? For letting you go there when I knew what would happen?' I look up at him and he's staring into the distance, as if he hasn't heard me, but I know he has.

'I didn't know what to expect,' he starts, hesitantly. 'But I was willing to give it a go. I was desperate back then; terrified of losing my family, of always being the man I shouldn't be, and I would have tried anything to make it right.' He gave a small smile. 'And at first it was lovely. I felt loved, welcomed, embraced even. I loved hearing the Bible stories, being told how much God loved me.' He reached out and squeezed my hand. 'I loved spending the days outdoors with you, lying on the grass, making stories out of clouds.'

I allow myself a second with the memory, take my hand back. 'But that was the beginning.'

He frowns, takes a sip of coffee. 'Yes, the beginning.'

'And after it began?'

He shook his head. 'I didn't like that so much. I hadn't realised God's love came at a price, and so it felt like being given this beautiful gift, only to have it snatched away.'

I nod.

'You know what I remember the most? It's the hunger. I've never known anything like it, the way your head plays tricks on you, the way it dominates all thought, until you'd do anything for food – any food at all.' He stares at me. 'Was it always like that for you, growing up?'

'No. There were good times. Not many, but some. It's just God always came first. I don't think they see what they did as wrong. They wanted the best for me. And the best is God.'

'Do you believe that? Do you believe in a God, even after everything they did to us to change who God made us?'

I don't dare say I don't. The fear and guilt are too strong, so instead I just say, 'I now think God is not my jailer, but my guide.' I want to tell him it isn't God's fault we are sinners. God doesn't want me to sin, yet the devil makes us believe we deserve to be who we want, not who we should be. But I know he'll just pity me, believing my parents beat that into me, which the scars on my body attest to – yet I do believe you can be the person God wants, you can turn from sin and be held up to his glory, and when you do you earn the right to be forgiven, just as God has forgiven me for loving Alice.

'Do you believe I am a sinner, Rachel? Because I chose to be who I am and marry a man? Am I going to hell because of it?'

He's never asked me that before and I instinctively reply, 'No, of course not,' because I can't conceive of any God not loving a man as good as Ash.

'But your parents' Bible – the one they made us hold above our heads for hours on end to prove our love for their God – says I will.'

I don't know what he wants me to say – yes, you and Eric will burn in hell for eternity? Because I can't and I won't.

'If I won't go to hell, Rachel, why would you?' His tone is soft, and I look across at him.

'Because God will forgive you. You are the person you were meant to be. But I'm not supposed to be this person; I'm supposed to love men. To love Simon.'

Ash looks at me with such pity, I stand; taking my mug to the sink, I wash it out. 'It's just how it is, Ash.'

'And did you love him – Simon, I mean?'

I turn on the hot tap, running my fingers under it until they scald. 'Yes.'

Ash lets the lie stand. 'How does it feel without him?'

On safer ground, I relax a little. 'Strange.' I turn to face him, wiping the washing-up liquid off my hands. 'It's silent here. I keep having to remind myself I can do what I want now.'

'Can you, though?'

'Ash, I'm not going home. I've told them I am, but I won't.' And I mean it. 'I'm going to ring them and find some excuse to stay here, and then I'm going to figure out what to do.'

Ash rubs his hand across his chin. 'OK. Then what do you need me to do? I'm going to help. I'll not have you go back home, and I'll do whatever you need me to do in order to prevent it.'

I look at his face – earnest, truthful – and ask, 'Anything?'

'Anything,' he confirms. Which is just what I needed to hear.

Twenty-four

Carla hadn't slept for worry that Bremer had found out what she'd done. The more she thought about it, the more she couldn't believe she'd been so stupid; shame had stopped her waking Baz to tell him about Luci, that and the fact she wasn't in any position to ask for his understanding, not when she'd lied and deceived him about trying for a baby when really she'd been taking the pill all along. She'd ruined their relationship, and now it looked as if she'd ruined her job, all in under six months; pretty good going when you thought about it.

Giving up on sleep, she had scribbled a note to Baz to say she'd gone in early – conscious that would make it two days since she'd properly seen him – and was at her desk two hours before Nell rocked up, looking murderous, two takeout coffees in hand. Banging one down on Carla's desk, Nell said, 'Just give me twenty minutes to wake up and then another ten to forgive you for dragging me in here at this ungodly hour.'

Carla grinned and took the lid off the coffee. 'Thanks, dude. Want to know what I've found?' she asked, knocking a sachet of sugar on the desk before pouring it in.

Nell grimaced. 'Do you ever listen to a word I say?'

'Absolutely. Now, I've run the number Simon called, the one we connected to Luci, and guess what?'

Nell stared at her, slowly stirring her coffee with a wooden stick.

'It's definitely registered to her,' Carla went on. 'But what's more, it's registered to a home address in Birmingham, so probably before she was made homeless.'

Nell frowned. 'Luci's from Brum?'

'Looks like it.'

'Didn't sound Brum.'

Carla folded her arms. 'Well, maybe that's just the last address for her. Does that matter?'

Nell shrugged. 'Probably not.'

Carla swivelled her chair back round to the screen. 'Anyway, I've run Luci through the computer and she's been arrested twice for dealing, once for shoplifting. The former got her eighteen months, she's still on licence for it, and the latter she's still out on bail for.' Carla paused to take a sip of her coffee, then continued. 'But that's where it gets interesting,' she said, swivelling back round to face Nell. 'I decided to check Simon's incoming call log on the phone against the date Luci was arrested, and guess who called it the day after?'

Nell sat up in her chair. 'Luci?'

Carla shook her head. 'Alice.'

Nell sat, mouth open. 'What?'

'I know, I was like that when I found it. It was another number with no name but, when I checked it, it came back to Alice. Registered to her address at Oxford Brookes.'

Nell leant forward, hands around the coffee cup. 'So, let me get this right. Alice called Simon's phone the day after Luci was arrested for shoplifting?'

'And got bail,' Carla added. 'That's the crucial point. Luci got bail while on licence for another offence, which we both know is almost unheard of, especially for someone with no fixed abode.'

'What were the bail conditions?' Nell asked.

'I'm waiting for a call back, but any bail in her situation suggests an expensive lawyer, and how is a homeless person going to be able to afford that?'

'But Simon could.'

Carla nodded. 'Exactly.'

Nell put her coffee on the desk. 'But why? Why would Simon help Alice, a homeless woman he made a complaint against, and why the hell would she ask him for it when he's indirectly the cause of her being on the street?'

Carla agreed it made no sense, but the calls were right there in front of them, so there had definitely been contact. Why, was another matter entirely.

'You know Bremer is going to want to call Luci in now, don't you?' Nell said, her face filled with all the implications that could bring.

That thought had been nervously gnawing at Carla's stomach. But Nell was right, he would want to bring Luci in for questioning, and so he should. 'I'll just tell him I fucked up,' she said.

Nell nodded. 'Good idea. Then he can just fire the both of us.'

'You don't think I should?'

Nell stood and shrugged off her jacket. 'No, you idiot, I don't think you should. Let's just hold our nerve and see what Luci says first, OK?'

'But—'

Nell held up her hand. 'No. That's the plan. Live with it. Now as soon as Paul and Bremer get in, we'll brief them on what we know and go from there.'

The feeling in Carla's stomach intensified. She was a terrible liar, they'd established that last night, so how the hell was she going to manage with Bremer looking her in the eye? Carla heard footsteps on the stairs; looked like she was going to find out sooner rather than later, and as Nell threw her a warning look, Bremer walked in through the door.

'Meeting in five,' he said, walking across the room. 'Where's Paul?'

Nell glanced at the clock. 'Almost here.'

'Right, well call me when he's in,' he said, then slammed his office door.

Nell gave her a pointed look. 'Still want to tell him when he's in that mood?'

Carla turned to her computer screen and didn't trust herself to reply without crying. Why the hell had she gone to O'Hanlan House? It was all Bremer's fault, muddying her role, and now see where it had got him. But just as her anger convinced her to confront Bremer, Paul burst in through the door looking as though he hadn't slept.

Nell didn't bother looking up. 'We've got a meeting now.'

'Great, just what I need.' Paul threw his bag on the floor and slumped in his chair.

'What happened?' Carla asked.

'Debbie from HR had me up all night, and not in a good way.'

Carla smiled; there was always a sense of karma when Paul relayed his women trouble. 'What's she done now?'

'She wants to get serious.'

Carla laughed but then stopped at Paul's expression. 'Sorry.'

'Do you not think I'm relationship material, is that it? Because Debbie made it pretty clear last night that's what she thought.'

'Oh, for the love of God,' Nell interrupted. 'Please stop before I make you. This is a murder inquiry, not a relationship therapy session.'

Bremer appeared at his door. 'Ready?'

Nell stood. 'Yes. Carla, go through what you found this morning.'

As Bremer and Paul listened, Carla felt calm return, now that she was able to control the room with facts.

Bremer folded his arms. 'You're telling me Luci and Alice had some form of contact with Simon prior to death?'

Carla nodded. 'Yes.'

He held her stare. 'Good work,' then turned to Nell. 'You and Paul, go and speak with Hannah and Ash. We'll deal with Rachel later this afternoon when we know more. Carla, you and I will bring Luci in, if we can find her, that is.'

Carla glanced at Nell, who ignored her. She was on her own then. 'OK. I think she was at O'Hanlan House last night, from what I saw on her Facebook.'

'Right, well, good enough a place to start as any.' He turned to Nell. 'Let me know what you get from Ash and Hannah, OK?'

Nell nodded, picking up her car keys and gesturing to Paul to follow, leaving Carla alone with Bremer.

He remained seated on the edge of her desk. Carla clicked open the telephone units email – call data for Ash, Hannah, Simon, Luci and Alice – and felt her heart beat a bit quicker. Not only was this good for the case, but maybe it would get her out of talking to Luci again.

Carla looked up at him. 'I've got some phone bills through; wouldn't it be more useful if I stayed and analysed those before Ash and Hannah get here?'

Bremer crossed his arms. 'Possibly. What are you expecting to find?'

'I don't know if expecting is the right word, but I'm hoping I can find a pattern of calls which prove Ash and Hannah were more connected to Simon than we thought, as well as linking that group to Alice.'

He frowned. 'You know what's bothering me, Carla?'

She looked at him, surprised, 'No?'

'The one thing we have yet to establish is, who set up the reunion in the first place?' He walked over to her desk. 'We've got invitations sent to Simon and Alice and a Facebook post suggesting Ash and Hannah will have had one too. So, who set it up and why are we no closer to finding this out?'

'Because maybe whoever set it up isn't our killer? Maybe the reunion is a red herring, or it's a lot more complicated than just a simple university reunion?' Noting the expression on his face, she said, 'Maybe the motive for setting up the reunion is more nuanced. I mean Simon's death looked pretty staged and Alice's looked like a suicide. What if we are looking for someone who is making all these people act in ways they wouldn't usually? Some sort of puppet master. The Facebook page would suggest that. We wondered why it was there, when the invites had been sent by post, and the only reason I can come up with is that whoever set it up wanted them to know it was about them – to make them attend even if they didn't want to.'

Bremer looked thoughtful. 'And the reason it's still up?'

'I think they're going to use it to post again – whether that's for the benefit of us or Hannah and Ash, I don't know.'

Bremer contemplated her computer screen. 'If it's not our killer who set up the page, that's all fine and good, they can shoot warning shots about secrets all they like. But if it is the killer who created this page, and I for one think it is, there is only one reason to keep it up there, Carla, and that's because they're not done yet.' He turned to look at her. 'I don't want this to turn into Oxford's next big serial killer.' He pointed at her screen. 'Do the phone bills. I'll get uniform to go to the hostel.'

'Will do.' Carla tried to hide the relief she felt. She was likely to have to confront Luci at some point, but at least for now she was out of the woods, or at least on the very edge of them, and she'd take that for now.

Twenty-five

The next morning, Nell and Paul pulled up outside Hannah's house in Headington. Looking over at the ex-council house with its garden full of weeds and walls of cracked paint, Nell's first thought was to wonder if it was lack of imagination that resulted in Hannah living only a short distance from where she'd gone to university. Her second thought was that the outside of Hannah's house suggested her vet practice wasn't doing so well.

Nell knocked on the front door. It opened slightly, and a child Nell guessed to be about eight years old peered up at them.

Paul leant down. 'Hey, is your mum in?'

The girl looked uncertain before calling, 'Mum,' over her shoulder, without taking her eyes off Paul.

'Even the young ones have got you figured,' Nell muttered.

Paul threw her a look over his shoulder as Hannah appeared behind her daughter.

'Eloise, I've told you before about opening the door without asking.' She gave an exasperated shrug to Nell and Paul as Eloise scurried off, then pulled the door open. 'Hi, how can I help?'

Nell showed her warrant card, as did Paul.

'DS Jackson, we wondered if we could come in to speak with you about an incident that occurred two evenings ago.'

Hannah had paled. She opened the door wide, 'Of course, come in.'

The interior of the house was a significant improvement on the outside. They walked through to a living room neatly accessorised with delicate china objects, vases filled with pungent lilies, all focused around a cream sofa dotted with brightly coloured scatter cushions. Hannah was clearly not the sort to have the girls over for red wine because, if Nell's friends were anything to go by, this place would look like a murder scene by morning; the sort of house she felt she was dirtying by just sitting down. She perched on the edge of the sofa. 'Hannah, two nights ago, did you spend the evening with Simon Morris?'

Hannah looked between Nell and Paul. 'Yes, why?'

'Can you recall what you did that evening?' Nell asked.

Hannah looked confused. 'Well, yes. We went to The Dewdrop in Summertown.'

'What time would that have been?'

'We met at seven thirty and left at closing time.'

The Dewdrop Inn was about a fifteen-minute walk from

Simon's house on the Woodstock Road and the opposite direction from the University Parks. 'Did you go on anywhere afterwards? Maybe into Oxford?'

'No, we said goodbye and went home. Why?'

'Simon was found dead in University Parks and we believe you may have been the last person to see him.' Nell let it sink in. Hannah's shock was palpable, pale, wide-eyed, she wrapped her arms around herself like some sort of shield from the news.

'Dead, how, like an accident?' Hannah finally asked, and Nell couldn't help but think that's the question she'd expected Rachel to ask.

'I'm afraid we believe Simon was murdered.'

'But that's impossible. We were together that night, and everything was fine.' She paused. 'Why was he in the University Parks? We said goodbye and he turned to go home, which is away from the Parks, not towards it.'

'Well, that's what we were hoping you could help with.'

'But I can't. I can't because he went the other way.' Hannah's voice was rising; Nell knew she needed to calm her down or they weren't going to get anything out of her. 'Do you recall attending The Varsity Club two weeks ago with Simon and a man called Ash?' It worked. Hannah took in the question, visibly calming.

'Yes.'

'A woman died that evening.'

'I know that,' Hannah snapped. 'It's not something you forget.'

'Did you know the woman who died?'

'No, of course not. She was just some random homeless woman.'

If I Fall

There was an edge to Hannah's voice that Nell didn't like – arrogant, dismissive, patronising. A rapid shift from the distraught women only seconds ago.

'We are looking to see if there was a connection between that woman's death, and Simon's.'

Hannah's voice rose. 'Well, that's ridiculous. How could a homeless girl be linked to Simon?'

'We found an invitation to the reunion in her belongings, and we found the same one at Simon's house. We also found a Facebook page where you, Simon, Ash and Alice were the only ones invited to join. It was also called The Reunion.' From the look on Hannah's face, Nell fully expected her to pull the 'I need a lawyer' card, but instead she said, 'What's Rachel said?'

Nell frowned. 'Sorry?'

'What's Rachel said about Simon's death?'

Nell caught Paul's look and nodded to him.

'She's devastated,' he said, 'as I'm sure you can imagine.'

Hannah gave a short laugh. 'Yes, I'm sure she's quite the perfect picture of a grieving widow.'

'Do you not get on with Rachel?' Paul had leant forward, his face concerned. Nell had to give it to him, he was a good copper when he wanted to be.

'She had issues about my friendship with Simon. Ridiculous really. But she'd come over from her university in Liverpool almost every bloody weekend to check up on him while we were at Brookes. She had a terrible upbringing, you see, no love there at all, so she clung to Simon like a limpet.'

Paul nodded his understanding, waited for her to continue.

'And he always said he didn't mind, but you could tell she was a millstone around his neck. If it hadn't been for the money, I doubt he would have stuck it out.'

'Money?' Paul asked, totally focused on Hannah.

'Yes,' Hannah said, surprised. 'Rachel is absolutely loaded. Her parents probably thought it made up for her terrible upbringing.'

'What was so terrible about it?'

'I don't know, but it was definitely bad, whatever it was. He said she'd still wake having nightmares years after she'd left home. I think they are overly religious, so it was probably a strict upbringing, but Simon wouldn't say.'

'That must have been bad,' Paul said, voice full of concern. 'To have nightmares after all that time.'

'Exactly,' Hannah confirmed.

Nell decided to get back in the game. 'Rules her out as a suspect I suppose, though, seeing as money couldn't be the motive.' She'd hoped it would rile Hannah and she was right.

Hannah turned to face her. 'There are plenty of other motives, though, aren't there? Like jealousy, for example.'

Nell gave a slight shrug. 'You're right, of course. Do you know if she had a reason to be jealous?'

'God no. Simon could be an arrogant prick, but he wasn't having an affair, if that's what you mean.'

'Not even with Alice?'

Hannah wrinkled her nose in disgust. 'Are you serious?'

'Well, maybe they'd been having an affair and he broke it off, and she couldn't bear a broken heart, so decided to take her own life in front of him.'

'Makes sense,' Paul said lightly.

'No it doesn't, because that would presume Simon would fall in love with a homeless woman and that's just ridiculous. He'd be more likely to fall for . . .' She stopped, so Nell filled in the blanks.

'Someone like you?'

'Someone more on his level,' Hannah snapped back. 'And anyway, if that was the case, it still doesn't explain who killed Simon.'

Nell pictured the body on the floor, the staging of the scene, perfectly crafted to look like a random murder and, except for the religious implications, they probably would have thought it was. Nell was beginning to wonder if this had more to do with Rachel than they'd thought. Rachel, or her parents. 'Have you ever met Rachel's parents?'

'Only at their wedding. They seemed nice.' Hannah gave a slight shrug. 'The mum was this little speck of a thing, perfectly blow-dried hair and enough diamonds on her hands to pay off my mortgage four times over. The dad . . .' Hannah paused, looking out through the window, thinking. 'Was large, tall. He seemed serious and Rachel was quite jumpy around him.' She turned back to Nell. 'He gave some rambling speech about sin at the reception, which was totally inappropriate if you ask me.'

Knowing it was a long shot, she asked, 'Can you remember specifically what he said about sin?'

'Oh yes. Well, the gist of it anyway. I was so amazed I'd almost laughed, and I'd turned to Ash because I assumed he'd find it funny too but he just looked horrified. The dad went on about how Simon was Rachel's protection, thanking him for saving his daughter, then he quoted some Bible verse, all about how if you discover a person is a sinner you can gently "restore" them, but you have to make sure you protect yourself so you don't get dragged into the sin with them. He was all but saying Rachel was saved by Simon. All quite absurd, especially to say it at your daughter's wedding. I mean, he basically called her a sinner in front of us all.'

As Hannah shook her head at the memory, Nell noted it down. If Simon's death had been about justice and punishment in the eyes of God, she certainly wanted to get hold of that verse about sin. Might be something, might not. She looked across at Hannah. 'Thank you, that's very helpful.' She closed her notebook. 'I think we have everything we need for now.' She stood. 'Thank you for your time, especially after such upsetting news. About Simon,' she added, when Hannah looked confused.

'Oh yes, well, I'm sure the shock will hit me later, might have a whisky in anticipation.' She gave a little laugh.

'Good idea, you can never be too careful, and thanks again,' Nell said as they got to the front door.

But as they walked back to the car, Nell let vent. 'Have you ever seen someone who says she's a friend of a murder victim look less upset? I mean, she put on a good show to start with, but then the woman was more obsessed about Rachel, than

Simon being dead. If you ask me' – she pulled open the car door and pointed at Paul over the car roof – 'it's her we should be looking at.'

'Were you serious about Alice and Simon having an affair?' he asked as they got in.

Nell clicked in her seatbelt. 'I was just thinking out loud, because obviously Alice was a lesbian, so . . . But that doesn't mean he wasn't paying her for sex. It might explain the argument with Rachel's parents over money – maybe he needed help to keep up his rendezvous with Alice.'

'But why would he? I mean, I'm sure he could have gone a bit more upmarket?'

'I don't know,' she snapped. 'I have no idea what perversions men have, it's why I don't shag any of you.' She was irritated. They'd come away with more questions than answers and it was getting to that point in an investigation where trying to gather up ideas felt like herding kittens.

'You don't know what you're missing, us men are a delicacy,' Paul said, pulling the car out of the drive.

Nell didn't reply, just stared out of the window as they pulled onto the ring road, thick fog swallowing cars ahead of them.

She thought about sin and punishment and the contradiction between the two. What sins could Simon have committed which would justify murder as a punishment? And what had Alice done to make her think her sins were worthy of taking her own life? Did she even take her own life? Because, despite all evidence to the contrary, Nell was starting to think Carla had a point; there were ways to get someone to jump off a building, other than just pushing them, and what if Alice had been made to believe she had no other choice?

She turned to Paul. 'After we've checked on Rachel, we need to speak with Luci. Guy said Alice had been spooked by someone coming back from the past. We need to find out just how spooked she was and who that person is. Because I'll bet you my pension that's the person who set up the reunion, and whoever it is, is also our murderer.'

Twenty-six

I ignore the calls from my parents and Laura the police officer, and ring Hannah. I know time is running out, but I tell myself not to panic, everything is going to be OK.

'Hannah, it's Rachel. We need to meet.'

There is silence.

'Please. It won't take long. Nine a.m. at Costa in Summertown?' It's busy enough so we can hide at the back amongst the writers and freelancers.

'Why do you need to see me?' She sounds tired and I wonder if she's been up all night crying over Simon. I feel a stab of something – not jealousy; I'd always known Simon had wanted to be with her not me, and I'd long since buried my anger that he hadn't had the courage to be . . . I think it's pity; pity that Hannah spent her life wanting a man she couldn't have and now never would. It's why she hates me, I know that, and I think she assumes I feel the same, which I do, but not for the reasons she thinks.

'I just want to speak about Simon. Please, Hannah, I'll keep it short.'

She agrees and I get ready, carefully covering the bruise on my face left behind by Luci. This will be the last time I see Hannah, God willing, and I need to focus: no time for niceties, this is my time for answers.

The coffee shop is, as I predicted, packed. It takes me five minutes to get my coffee and another two to find a seat. I pick the last one at the back by the toilet, pressed against a wall, just two seats across from one another; when Hannah joins me, I don't bother to stand to greet her.

'What do you want, Rachel?' She looks tired, older than her twenty-nine years; her hair is unwashed and I can see the edges of it tinged with grease.

'I want to know about Alice.' I can tell from her expression that's not what she was expecting.

'Alice?'

'Ash told me you saw her, and I want to know why you told Simon, and if he told my parents she was back.' My heart is racing now. 'I want to know what they said and what you did for them.'

'What I did for them?' She laughed. 'I didn't do anything for them.'

'Did they pay you?'

'Pay me to do what?' She's wearing a mock amused expression and I know it's designed to bait me. I take a breath.

'When you saw Alice, did you tell Simon?'

'Yes.'

'And what did he say?' I refuse to lower my eyes; she holds them for a second, then another, until finally she says, 'You know what, Rachel, you're madder than I thought. I mean, I've always known you were pathetic, hanging around at Simon's university with his friends every other weekend, when you should have been at your own. But Alice, after all this time, you're still fixated on her? It's embarrassing.' She leans back in her chair and contemplates me. 'I'm embarrassed for you, Rachel.'

I say nothing, so she continues. 'Nothing even happened between you, did it? You are so pathetic, you fell in love with a woman and you didn't even have the courage to do something about it. You just let your parents bully you into marrying a man who only wanted you for your money.' She's breathing heavily and I feel strangely light – as if having the truth out in the world has taken some pain away.

I smile. 'A bit like you and Simon then. You, hanging off his every word at university, staying in Oxford so you could be near him when he was never going to love you like you loved him. Is that the sort of pathetic you mean?'

She opens her mouth to speak but I'm not finished. 'Simon was never going to love you because he was incapable of love. He was a selfish, bitter man, who never got over the fact his family came from nothing and mine had so much. He couldn't make it on his own so he took from my parents, telling them and himself he was doing the work of God, when he never had any concept of who God was or what his love meant. He was a fraud and a failure, and what does it say about you that you loved him?'

'At least I didn't pine after a woman who slept on the street.'

I almost launch myself over the table. 'How dare you say that? It's your fault she was there. Simon's vindictive complaint against her, that she made sexual advances towards him, when the exact opposite was true. She lost her job and had no home to go to, so no wonder she ended up on the street, all because Simon wanted to get rid of her to make sure I'd marry him and he'd get to live the life he thought he deserved.'

'But it wasn't our fault, was it?' She's angry now, her face flushed with it. 'You're the one who could have stopped it. You're the one who turned your back on Alice when he made the complaint and yes, I did provide a statement to support him, because I loved him. You loved Alice, and what did you do to support her? So don't judge me when it's you who should be judged.'

My heart is beating too fast, my head feels light. I need to focus, I need answers, not recriminations. 'What did Simon say when you told him about Alice coming back?'

Hannah leant over the table. 'He said, "Cash cow, ker-ching."'

I ignore the anger, the hate I feel right now, and instead ask, 'So he did tell my parents, and they paid him to get rid of her?'

Hannah leant back, shrugged. 'You've got to do what you can to get ahead, Rachel. But you wouldn't know anything about that.'

If I Fall

Her tone – bitter, snide – makes me wonder if she's struggling financially, if that's the reason she sold Alice out for a second time.

'She killed herself, Rachel. No one made her do it, she chose to do what she did, we didn't kill her.'

'But you spoke with her? You warned her off?'

Hannah raised her hands. 'What does it matter now? It's over, finished.'

I watch her, all puffed up and full of self-importance. 'Is it, though?' I say, 'Or are you and Ash next?'

Twenty-seven

Carla began to go through the call data she'd got from the telephone unit, trying to track Hannah, Ash and Simon's contact levels, as well as to see if anyone other than Simon had been in contact with Alice or Luci. Hannah appeared to call and message Simon pretty regularly, but Ash hardly at all, other than a flurry of calls around the time of the reunion. But the only calls to or from Luci's phone were limited to those Carla had already identified on Simon's phone. So, no evidence Alice was in anything like regular contact with the group, and there was no unknown number which linked them all – a potential suspect for the organiser of the reunion; in fact, nothing much at all to suggest any of them were leading anything but very ordinary lives. A waste of time then. Maybe she should go to meet Ash, like Bremer wanted.

Annoyed with herself, she opened up The Reunion Facebook page. It took a moment for her to register what she was seeing – staring back at her was a picture of Simon, his body on the ground, hand, foot and eye missing. And next to it was a picture of Alice, back against the ground, eyes open, mouth wide.

Bile rose in her throat; she couldn't look away and it took a second for her to be able to call for Bremer.

When he didn't reply, she called again, shouting this time. 'Bremer.'

He appeared at his office door. 'What's wrong?' Then, seeing her face, he jogged over. 'What have you ... ?' He stopped speaking when he saw the picture on the screen. 'When the hell did that appear?'

Carla checked when the picture was uploaded. 'This morning at 01:03, by Admin.'

Bremer stared at the screen.

'It's a warning,' Carla said. 'To the others.'

He was still staring at the screen. 'And you can't find out who posted it or where from?'

'Nope. I can get Tech to take a look, but the page has no markers so I don't see how they will get anything from it.' Carla looked back at the screen – it felt as if this was the start of a new stage, the next step in the killer's plan, because who would post a picture like that on social media if it wasn't meant to scare?

'Did you get uniform to bring Ash in?' she asked.

'He wasn't in.' Bremer glanced at her. 'I know, I'll get them to go back now and check, look in the windows, break in if they have cause. And I'll ring the Technical Support Unit; we're going to need them to risk-assess Hannah and Ash's home addresses.' Bremer stood. 'Can you check his work? See if he's there?'

Carla nodded and, after Bremer had gone back to his office, she dialled the Oxford University switchboard. 'Hi, this is Carla Brown from Thames Valley Police. We're trying to locate a member of your staff, Ash Desai, as a matter of urgency.'

'OK, please hold.'

As she waited, she watched Bremer pace his office. She knew him well enough now to know he was thinking, working his way ahead; she just hoped it didn't involve her coming face to face with Luci.

'Hello?' the receptionist said. 'I've checked and Mr Desai has been in but he's popped out again. I'm afraid the department didn't know when he would be back.'

'Thank you. But he is due back in?'

'Yes,' the receptionist confirmed. 'Although his department did mention he left after he got a call direct to his mobile, and he seemed unnerved by it. They wanted me to pass that on, seeing as you are the police.'

Carla made a note, thanked her and hung up. 'Ash got a call to his mobile and apparently it caused him to leave work early,' she called.

Bremer came to his door. 'A call? From who?'

'They didn't say. Maybe he's on his way home?'

'Right, I'll get uniform over there ASAP, tell them to kick the door in if they have to.' He was agitated and Carla got it; things were moving too quickly for them to keep up – to keep people safe.

'What do you want me to tell Nell? Go back to Hannah and speak with Rachel later, or just let Tech Support deal?'

'She's of more use at Rachel's. Uniform can accompany Tech. I want to get to The Varsity Club, see if they saw anyone taking photos on the evening Alice died. Noticed anything suspicious in the time leading up to her death or in the days before it. Whoever planned the reunion is thorough; strikes me they'd want to do a recce of the venue, which means someone will have seen them.'

Carla knew better than to argue when he was in this mood. She pulled on her coat. 'Have we checked CCTV from there yet?'

Bremer was out the door before she'd finished the question. 'CID didn't pull it because witnesses made it clear Alice's death was a suicide.' He jogged down the stairs. Carla followed him, missing a couple of steps to catch up. 'Understandable.'

Bremer stopped and turned to her. 'Slack, Carla. They didn't know it was suicide and they should have bagged it.' He began back down the stairs. 'We'll do The Varsity Club and, as we'll be in Oxford, we'll see if we can locate Luci. Two birds and all that.'

She didn't reply, just hoped she'd have time for a cigarette before the car ride, because the stress coming off Bremer, coupled with the reference to Luci, was making her crave nicotine.

'We're making progress,' he said, unlocking the car door and clearly mistaking her silence for downheartedness rather than stone-cold fear that he'd find out what she'd done.

'Yeah, I know.' Carla clicked the seatbelt and blew on her hands. Bremer cranked up the heating. Waiting for the screen to clear, she dug out her mobile phone as she realised she hadn't heard from Baz – giving up on her, maybe? Well, she couldn't blame him – and an envelope fell from her bag into the footwell. She caught Bremer's eye, before reaching down to retrieve it. Sitting in silence, Carla held it on her lap, heart racing.

When Bremer spoke, his tone was deliberately light. 'Gerry sent you a visiting order then?'

Carla looked down at her name on the envelope, written in Gerry's familiar scrawl. Police officers had terrible handwriting. 'I haven't replied yet.'

Bremer nodded, clicking on the windscreen wipers in an attempt to clear it faster. 'And will you?'

Carla watched the window slowly demist from the bottom up. Would she? Gerry had been the closest thing to a father she'd ever had – closest thing to a parent, given her mother's failed attempts – but what would she say to him? Nell had almost died, for God's sake, and how could she look him in the face after what he'd done to Joanna? 'I don't know,' she said finally. 'I want to because I miss him, I liked him being in my life, but I'm not sure if the person I loved is there any more.'

Bremer held the steering wheel, ten to two, eyes straight ahead. Carla looked at him. 'You think I should, do you?'

'I didn't say that.' He looked at her, face serious. 'I just don't want him to hurt you again.'

There was something in the way he said it, or maybe it was just hearing kind words after weeks without, that made Carla want to cry and, as if sensing that, Bremer looked away. 'Come on, let's see if we can get anything from The Varsity Club. There has to be something we are missing. Whoever organised the reunion must have checked out the venue beforehand, otherwise how would they know Alice could jump from that exact spot?'

'Or know how to orchestrate it so she did,' Carla added. And despite Bremer's silence, she knew he was starting to believe her – Alice's death wasn't a suicide and Carla had no doubt Hannah or Ash were intended to be next.

Twenty-eight

I sit and wait for Hannah to return from the toilet, keen to get home before policewoman Laura tracks me down. She's rung three times since I've been at the café, and there's only so long I can avoid her.

Hannah walks back to the table and I immediately know something is wrong.

'What is it?'

'We need to call Ash,' she says, face almost grey. Then hands me her phone.

Simon is lying on his back, naked, I can see a stump where his hand should have been, a hole where once was his eye, but it's the picture of Alice which makes me retch. Hannah snatches it back from me, I retch again as Hannah propels me towards the toilet, pushing me through the door as I fall to the floor and reach the toilet bowl just in time.

I stay like that until my stomach stops constricting, until the stench of urine forces me from the floor. I wash my face, rinsing my mouth until only a hint of vomit remains, and open the door. Hannah grabs my arm. 'Come on, I've called Ash, he's meeting us by the leisure centre. Come on.' She tugs hard at my coat, but I hold back.

'Why do you want me to meet Ash?'

Hannah looks around the café. 'Jesus, Rachel,' she hisses. 'Did you not see the picture of Simon and Alice? Who do you think posted them and why?'

When I don't reply, she carries on. 'It's a message. We're next. Don't you see that? This all started with the reunion. It's about Alice. She got us there and now she's paying us back for what we did. Picking us off one by one. And don't think she'll leave you off the list; she'll be saving you for last.'

I stare at her, unable to think she's being serious, but knowing she is. 'Alice is dead. How can she have killed Simon?'

'I don't know, Rachel,' Hannah snaps, loudly now. 'But that's the only explanation for all this. Why else would we all be gathered together if it wasn't to do with what Simon did and what we all ignored?'

'The complaint?'

Hannah looks exasperated. 'Not the goddamn complaint – what happened before it.' And dragging me through the café, she pushes me out onto the street and towards the Ferry Leisure Centre.

Ash is sitting on a low wall, adjacent to the car park. He stands when we arrive and pales as Hannah passes him her mobile phone. 'Alice is doing this. She's doing it to punish us.' When none of us replies, she sits on the wall, head bowed.

'You don't actually think Alice would have left over a complaint alone?' she starts. 'I mean, that's what you all thought, wasn't it? Alice had left rather than face a complaint of sexual harassment.' She stopped speaking before looking up at us.

'There were pictures. Pictures of Alice and Simon. Together.'

Rachel didn't understand. Together like how?

Ash was looking down at Hannah, confused, worried. 'I thought the complaint was fabricated. Are you saying Alice sexually harassed Simon?'

Hannah let out a short laugh. 'She was a lesbian, Ash. Of course she didn't. But we had to make the complaint rock solid; there had to be evidence.'

Ash stares at her. 'What did you and Simon do, Hannah?'

'We made sure it would stand up to scrutiny. A complaint on its own was just his word against hers, and we needed to make sure we had more.' Hannah looks at me and I don't want to dwell on what's in my head, the pictures which are starting to form.

'You know you said Simon was selfish and bitter and he couldn't love?' she asks me. I nod.

'Well, that's not the half of it. He was cruel. He would fantasise about ways to hurt people, emotionally and physically. So when your parents told him to get rid of Alice, to make sure she didn't threaten your marriage, your heterosexuality; to make sure you didn't go to hell,' she spat, 'Simon thought he'd have a bit of fun with it.' She gives a short laugh, devoid of humour. 'I didn't think he'd do it, I really didn't.' She stops speaking, staring out across the car park.

'Do what?' Ash asks, his voice so quiet it's hard to hear. 'Tell me what you did to Alice.'

Hannah looks at him, pale hands clasped in front of her. 'We just paid her a visit one night. To make sure she didn't try to challenge the complaint. I thought we were going to just stage a few things, steal some underwear, that sort of thing. To say she'd sent it to Simon, that she was harassing him. But when we got there—' She stops speaking for a second before continuing. 'When we got there, Alice was home. She wasn't supposed to be there, you see,' she says to me. 'Simon said he was sure she was out.'

I stare down at her. 'What did Simon do?'

Hannah sighs, as if giving up. 'At first they argued. Alice didn't understand why we were there and she wanted us to leave. But Simon wouldn't, and when she reached for her phone to call security, he grabbed her arm and pushed her onto the bed.' She looks at me. 'He raped her, like he raped you, like your parents paid him to rape you in some warped way of keeping you safe.'

I want to throw up but my stomach has nothing left to give, so I just sink to the wall.

'And you took photos?' Ash's voice is disbelieving. 'Instead of stopping him, of helping Alice, you took photos and used them against her?'

'I was scared, Ash. I couldn't have stopped him, and he was yelling at me to take them, like the idea turned him on even more. And when it was done, I had to get you to support the complaint. There had to be more than just me to give a statement to say Alice had been harassing Simon; there had to be enough for her not to try to report it.'

Ash is silent. I stare at the ground, head void of thoughts or words.

'Whatever you think of me,' Hannah says eventually, 'we have to work together to make sure none of us are next. Because we're all to blame for this, even you, Rachel, for not standing up for her when you knew the complaint couldn't be true.'

I stand.

'Rachel, you can't ignore this. They've killed your husband and you might be next.'

But I just turn and walk away.

Twenty-nine

The Varsity Club was almost empty. The manager indicated the move to the terrace, the only bar open being the one below it. 'I really can't be of much use,' he said as they climbed the three flights of stairs. 'I've dug out the CCTV but I'm afraid it's not the best quality and I'm not sure it even covers the areas you need to check, but I'll have it for you by the time you leave.'

As they reached the terrace, Carla pulled her coat around her to ward off a sudden slap of wind. The manager gestured to the benches.

'They're heated. And we have blankets.' He pointed to the neatly folded grey wool squares on each seat. 'Why don't you sit down and get warm?'

Carla looked to Bremer, unsure, but a gust of wind convinced her to take up the offer. Once tucked up beneath the blanket, the feel of heat from the bench gradually warming her, she gestured for the manager to join her. When he perched on the edge of the row, under a glowing overhead heater, she asked him about what he remembered from two nights ago.

'Do you remember them? The group from the VIP section?'

'It was busy, you know? I mean, I'm rushed off my feet on the weekends, so it's hard to remember any one set of people.'

Carla waited, sure something was coming.

'But I do remember three, maybe four people, huddled around about there.' He pointed to the place Simon and his group had been standing, Carla just in front of them.

'I remember being irritated by them,' he continued, 'because someone had stuck up this sign saying it was some sort of reunion, without asking for permission, and they were just taking up space but not really buying drinks, you know?' He looked apologetic. 'I mean, we want everyone to have a good time, but we still need to make money, and the roof terrace isn't that big so . . .' He trailed off. Carla got it. It was a business not a social club, or at least not one where you got to stand around for free.

'They didn't buy many drinks?'

The manager shook his head. 'I don't think so. They seemed to sip at the ones they bought when they arrived. Like they were unsure of something. I know a few of my staff mentioned it. We like a good turnover,' he offered by way of an explanation.

'And how did they seem to you? Were they relaxed? Tense?' She stopped speaking, aware she was leading him to an answer.

'Distracted. I remember wondering what they were waiting for, or who, I suppose.'

'And what was their reaction when the woman' – she decided to choose her words carefully – 'fell off the terrace?'

The manager looked across to Bremer then back to Carla. 'Well, it was all mayhem. Screams and people running to look. It was all mad and the police were called and they took over, but that little group just stood there, like they were cast into stone. And when they had to speak to the police they seemed' – he looked into the sky – 'I don't know. Speechless. No, not speechless, like they were trying not to speak, as if they were holding something back.'

'Did you recognise any of them?' Carla asked. "Did they come here often or in the days leading up to that evening? They may have just popped in for a look around, something like that.'

The manager frowned. 'I can't say they had, sorry. I mean, they annoyed me, as I said. I got a good look at them but they didn't appear familiar.'

Carla nodded. 'How about anyone else? Can you recall any-one else coming and just seeming to look around, in a way you didn't consider normal? Or anyone doing anything strange that you may have noticed, maybe watching the group, speaking to the woman before she died?'

The manager looked apologetic. 'No, sorry, just business as usual.'

Carla watched Bremer as he walked the perimeter of the ter-race. Turning back, she said, 'Did you see anyone with a camera? Anyone taking pictures of people they didn't seem to be with?

So not like the usual selfies or group shots, but people taking pictures of people they weren't with?'

'No, nothing.' He looked almost embarrassed.

Carla smiled. 'It's OK. If you didn't see anything, you didn't see anything. That's just as helpful as seeing something.' She watched him relax before asking, 'What about the girl who died. Anything about her you thought was odd?'

'Other than the totally inappropriate dress code and the obsession with a pot plant?' He gestured to the large palm-type tree in a big grey pot. 'No, not really.'

'When you say "inappropriate dress code", do you mean you knew she was homeless?'

The manager gave her a look. 'Obviously. This is Oxford. Tourists and homeless. One pays, the other doesn't. But the latter are residents. The former are in transit. We don't make a fuss about homeless coming in as long as they don't cause trouble,' he added.

Carla was impressed. She'd assumed the knee-jerk reaction would be to kick them out.

'Problem?' Bremer asked, mistaking her expression for one of concern, and sitting down. Carla was looking at the pot plant – the height of a child, it stood at the far end of the terrace. Why was Alice bothered about a plant?

'Carla?' Bremer asked.

'She was there' – she pointed to the plant – 'as if she was hiding behind it. Numerous witness statements said, so I didn't give it another thought.' She looked to Bremer. 'But what if she wasn't hiding?'

Bremer looked at the plant. 'What did the other witnesses say exactly?'

'Just that she'd been hanging around the plant, crouched down for a while, before making her way to the wall.'

Bremer stood, pulled the blanket off her and handed it to the manager. 'Let's take a look.'

They walked to the plant and Bremer crouched down by the pot, running his hand around the edge and down to the bottom. Carla knelt down next to him. 'I don't even know what we are looking for.'

Bremer moved some of the soil aside, then a little more, nothing. Bremer sat back on his haunches. 'Let's empty out the pot?'

The manager hovered next to them. 'I don't think that's really possible; it's a large pot and the soil will go everywhere. We have customers to think of . . .'

Bremer smiled up at him, grabbed the edge of the plant pot and tipped it over. Soil spilled over the wooden flooring. Ignoring the manager's look of horror, Bremer started to dig through it, Carla following.

'What are we looking for?' she asked, aware of the manager watching them, the soil hand-deep beneath them.

Bremer glanced over at her. 'People who kill themselves don't spend time hesitating behind a pot plant. They come, ready, convinced about doing what they want to do. Any hesitation in implementing their plan risks letting back in the world they want to put behind them. Alice was doing something deliberate here, we just need to find out what.'

Carla started to dig. 'Like leaving behind a message?'

Bremer was intent on the soil and ignored the question; thirty seconds later he pulled out a mobile phone. 'And here's our message.'

Carla sat back on the ground as Bremer held it out to her. She looked over at him, the shabby old iPhone between them. 'Why would she hide a mobile phone? I mean, we can just get call data from the company, it doesn't make sense.'

'Maybe there is something on there we can't see from call data alone? We can't see WhatsApp messages, can we? Maybe she's got a conversation on there she wants us to see?'

Carla agreed that was a possibility. Bremer stood, holding his hand out to help her up. 'Let's get the CCTV and go back to the office. If there's something Alice is trying to tell us, we're not going to find it sitting here. This is the best lead we've had in the whole case, but we're going to need Tech to break the passcode. No time to waste,' he said, pulling her up and handing her an evidence bag for the phone.

'There is one way to get into the phone without Tech.' Carla didn't want to say it but then if there was something on the phone, they needed to get access as soon as they could – Tech could take hours or days.

'Yes?' Bremer asked.

'Luci. I bet she'll have the passcode. If we can find Luci, we can get in today,' and Carla would just have to hope Luci would keep her mouth shut when they did.

Thirty

Laura is waiting for me when I arrive home. I don't bother to greet her; I am numb, light, absent almost, as if a part of me is walking into my house while another part of me is left behind.

'Would you like some tea?' Laura asks.

'Yes please. But I'm just going into Simon's study for a moment, there's something I'd like to find. I'll be out in a few minutes.'

She's studying me, I see her eyes rest on my cheek, and I turn to go.

'OK,' she calls after me, 'see you in a minute.'

I close the door to Simon's study and open up the laptop he kept in the top drawer of his desk – the one I'd hidden from the police. The room smells of his aftershave, the one I hate, the one he insisted on wearing. I scan the files, and seeing one file titled, 'M and H', I click on it to display the payments made into his account – the account I haven't told the police about – the one he didn't think I knew he had.

There are eight entries, one for each year of our marriage: £35,000 deposited by my parents into his account on the same date every year – our anniversary.

I lean back on the chair. My parents are nothing if not generous, and at least they felt me worthy of the price. Shutting down the file, I scan more documents. It's been a while since I'd sifted through his life like this, always making sure I left everything exactly as I'd found it, always looking for evidence of what my parents were doing to control me.

There are files of photos, our birthdays, holidays, files from our joint bank account and files to do with his work. Finding nothing of interest, I open up his emails. The first one is from Hannah. I open it to find a picture of a dog with the message, 'You should get this cutie.' I move it to the trash.

Scanning the sidebar, I see files Simon had set up to save important emails. One is titled H and M – Hilary and Malcolm, my parents. I open to find twenty or so emails filling the screen, the first an email from Simon to my parents, dated two months ago.

Dear Hilary and Malcolm

I hope this email finds you well. I am in the process of reviewing my accounts and I noticed the amount you enter into my account per year has remained the same throughout the last eight years. Rachel is, as I'm sure you

are aware, a lover of shopping and therefore I request
that you increase this amount to £40,000 to take into
account inflation and Rachel's refusal to find paid work.

> *Yours,*
> *Simon*

The anger I feel is so sudden that I practically slam the computer shut in fury. How dare he? It was Simon who didn't want me to work, wanted the house to be clean, the household bills to be paid on time. I'd asked time and again to be able to find a job, even a part-time one, but he'd been steadfast. And shopping? The clothes I bought were from expensive shops but second-hand, because he wouldn't let me go further than Summertown, and even the charity shops there charged more than most.

The injustice of it burns, made worse by him not being here to challenge – although would I have done so, even if he had been? Regardless, the reality was that – from now until my death – all Simon had done to me was going to go unchecked, unpunished. Even his dead body on the mortuary slab does nothing to quench that anger.

I open up another email, a reply from my parents. In it they decline to increase the amount, offering instead to issue a prayer every night asking God to make me a better person. That washes off me. I'd had years of guilt-laden prayers sent on my behalf, a few more wouldn't hurt.

Emails were exchanged, for three more weeks, in which the

price of me was haggled over. My parents were, as I always knew them to be, utterly intransigent. It gives me a little bit of joy to feel Simon's anger and frustration pouring forth through his words, that he got to feel a little bit of what I do.

As I read, I wondered why he might need the money. On top of the bounty on my head, I get far in excess of what I need to live on, and Simon's job is well paid. Was he being greedy, or had he done something stupid that he needed a payout to rectify? Or maybe he really was having an affair with Hannah and needed money to wine and dine her in a way he never bothered to with me. But no, she would have told me; it's not as if she had anything to lose, not now.

I open an email dated two weeks ago.

Dear Hilary and Malcolm

I have news which might break our current impasse. Hannah has seen Alice. It's a long story as to why or how, but the upshot is that Alice is back in Oxford. Homeless. There are two issues here: one, Rachel may well see Alice if she goes into Oxford. Two, and this is of far greater concern, Alice may have returned to retaliate after what we did to her.

Regarding point two, I would remind you I did that at your behest. Regarding point one, I can do all I can from my end, but it will obviously entail time away from work to keep her occupied and away from Oxford. It doesn't

bear thinking about, should Rachel see Alice, and all your
hard work and dedication to her over the intervening
years go to waste.

I therefore request the amount rise from £35,000 to
£50,000 per year in order to take into account this new
development. Hannah is willing to assist again, should
you wish her to become involved, for a nominal amount.

> *Yours,*
> *Simon*

I stare at the screen. So many thoughts wrestling to be heard. It was an open secret that Simon had been paid to marry me, there was no shock in that, but here was proof Hannah played a role too – proof she was complicit. Proof, as well, that my parents knew what happened to Alice and did nothing. What kind of God allows that to remain unpunished?

I read the email again, pick up my mobile, hands shaking with anger, and call Ash.

'I've got proof my parents knew Alice was back in Oxford, proof they knew what Hannah and Simon did to her,' I say, before he even has a chance to say hello. I explain what I've found and wait for his reply while he considers it. I can hear cars in the background, a shout, the beep of a horn, and wonder where he is.

'It's not really proof, is it?' he says finally. 'If Hannah hadn't told us what she did, it could mean anything.'

My head is spinning, thoughts bashing against each other,

none making sense, and all I know is the anger I feel has to come out. 'Should I go to the police? Tell them about what Hannah said? What if she did something to Simon and Alice; what if it's not Alice who set up the reunion, but Hannah?'

'But why would she do that?'

'I don't know,' I almost shout, but then remembering Laura, I lower my voice. 'Maybe she needs money. Simon said she wasn't doing so well with her practice; maybe she decided to blackmail him or my parents for money?' I have no idea if I think this is true or not but the words just form themselves. 'Or what if my parents are in on it with Hannah? What if they were sick of giving him money and it was cheaper to give a one-off payment to Hannah, to kill Alice and Simon, rather than keep paying him for the rest of my life?'

He is silent, so I say, 'You know what they are capable of, Ash.'

'Yes, but murder. That's way beyond . . .' He trails off, but I don't stop.

'It's Hannah, my parents, or both, Ash. I know it. I just need proof they've paid Hannah.'

'But how are you going to get that?'

I take a breath. 'I'm going to go back home.'

Thirty-one

Nell pushed her phone in her jacket and turned to Paul. Parked outside Rachel's house, rain pounded the roof. 'Bremer says they've found a phone for Alice; they're going to try to find Luci to get the passcode.'

Paul stared out of the windscreen. 'Good luck with that. She's probably miles away by now.'

Nell unclicked her seatbelt. 'You're a bundle of joy this evening. Debbie from HR still getting you down?'

'Yeah. It's hard to juggle it all sometimes, isn't it?'

Nell knew what he meant, which was why she was still single. Even when you weren't physically at work, you could be mentally there. Sure, there were people who worked out a way to separate the two, Nell just couldn't work out how they did it. It suddenly occurred to her, in all the time she'd known Paul, she'd never seen him bothered by a woman – he was more a love-them-and-leave-them type – but maybe that's because he'd just never let himself be. 'You like this Debbie, then?'

He sighed and pulled his phone from the dashboard. 'Yeah, I do. But I'll probably mess it up, as usual.'

'She's stuck around for this long, what is it, almost eight months?' Paul nodded.

'Well there you go. You're obviously doing something right.' She looked up at the house, blurred by rivulets of rain running down the window. 'Come on, let's go and see how Rachel is doing.'

Laura opened the door and ushered them in. 'She's in the front room.'

Nell shook water from her collar. 'How does she seem?'

'Quiet. She was in Simon's study for a while, and I'm sure I heard her talking to someone, but when she came out she just went straight to her chair and curled up like a lost cat.'

'Did she say where she'd been?'

'Not a word. And I didn't want to ask.'

Good call. Laura was there to support, not interrogate, although if she managed to happen across a bit of intel while she was there, so much the better.

Walking into the living room, Nell felt a blast of heat from the fire, but Rachel was still covered in a blanket as if it wasn't even on. Shock maybe, or tiredness, Nell thought it could be either and, taking a seat on the sofa, she smiled across at Rachel. God, the woman was beautiful. She reminded Nell of a fairy in one of her childhood books, the one she'd read every night before bed, sleeping with it under her pillow; it struck her now that fairy was probably the first woman she'd ever loved.

'How are you, Rachel?' she asked.

'Fine, thank you.' She gave a little shrug. 'Well, you know, sort of. I think I'll go home to my parents in the morning.'

Nell was surprised. The impression she'd got from Laura was that Rachel would rather do anything but that, and Rachel herself had seemed fearful of the idea the last time they'd met. 'We can have Laura drive you, if that would help?'

'Oh, I don't want to be a bother.'

'It wouldn't be a bother.' Truth was, Nell wanted Laura to have a poke around, see what Rachel's parents were like, if anything didn't feel right. 'And we'd quite like Laura to stay with you for a while, if that's OK, just for safety.' She was about to bring up the image of Simon on Facebook when Rachel said, 'I've seen it. His picture. It made me throw up.'

Nell was sure it did.

'So you think I'm in danger too?' Rachel asked.

Nell frowned. 'Who has told you you're in danger?' She doubted Laura would be so stupid as to say that, but she'd kill her if it was.

'Oh, no, I didn't mean anyone has said that. It came out wrong.' Rachel gave her an apologetic smile, eyes holding Nell's for what felt like a beat too long. Nell shifted in her seat, suddenly hotter than before; she pulled off her jacket.

'Did you meet with someone today? Someone who had also seen the picture?' It could only be Hannah or Ash and, as uniform seemed unable to locate either, it was a distinct possibility Rachel had been with them. But why meet them when she'd said she wasn't friends with them?

'Maybe you wanted to discuss the image of Simon, with people who also knew him well?' She smiled. 'That would be totally understandable.'

Rachel stared at her. 'I don't have any friends, so I have no one to meet.'

Nell felt a surge of sympathy; this small fragile woman, who'd just lost a husband, had no one to speak to except parents she obviously feared. How did someone end up with no friends? Especially someone like Rachel – people usually fell over them-selves to associate with a beautiful rich woman like her.

'We're going to send Tech Support out to check your house, is that OK?' Nell asked. 'It may be in the morning as we also have to check Hannah's and then Ash's, but Laura can stay with you overnight if you wish.' Nell hoped Bremer's overtime budget could cover that offer.

'Do you think the killer is going to go after one of them?' Rachel's face darkened.

'It's just a precaution.'

As Rachel studied Nell's face, Nell felt a flush begin at her neck; giving a cough, she ignored the look Paul was throwing her.

'What if one of them is the killer?' Rachel asked.

Nell hid her surprise. 'Do you think one of them is?'

'Simon told me Hannah was having money worries and I wondered if maybe they'd argued and she'd killed him.'

Nell frowned. 'Like an accident.'

Rachel nodded, brown eyes bright. 'Yes, it happens, doesn't it.'

Nell couldn't tell if Rachel actually believed what she was saying or was just trying to distract herself from the knowledge she might be in danger. 'You have seen the picture of Simon, the one on Facebook. Did that look like an accident to you?' She said it as gently as she could, but Rachel still shrank back into the chair, pulling the blanket further across her shoulders.

'Yes, sorry, it was a silly thought.'

'Not silly at all. All thoughts are useful at this stage in an investigation.'

Rachel smiled gratefully at her and Nell felt a pang of something – pleasure that she'd made Rachel feel better? Jesus, she needed to get out of there and back to the office. This house must be driving her insane. She stood. 'I'll send Laura to get you mid-morning. She'll stay this evening for as long as you like, and if anything happens between her leaving and coming back, you have my number.'

Rachel unfolded herself from the chair. Standing, she was a little shorter than Nell, as thin as Nell had imagined. She smiled up at her and held out her hand. 'Thank you, Sergeant, for being so kind to me. And I'm happy for Laura to leave now. It's a kind offer but I'd quite like to be alone.'

'Of course, and it's Nell, please,' she said, trying to ignore the feel of Rachel's hand as she took it.

Thirty-two

Nell was sitting on the edge of Carla's desk, Paul slumped in a chair to the left, Laura in one to their right, as Bremer stood by the wipe board, pen in hand.

'OK, so we have two deaths,' he wrote down *Alice* and *Simon* and a line between the two. 'Both connected by an invitation to a reunion and a complaint made years earlier which seems to have resulted in Alice becoming homeless a few years later after she failed to secure another job.'

Carla took a sip of her coffee and watched as he drew another line from each name.

'Simon was murdered,' he wrote. 'And initially there was nothing to suppose Alice's death was anything other than a suicide.' He underlined the words 'murdered' and 'suicide' and turned to the group. 'But we now have the possibility that she

was enticed into taking her own life by one of the group or whoever organised the reunion – which of course could be one and
the same. The motive behind that remains unclear.'

He turned back to the board and wrote, *Rachel, Hannah, Ash,
Luci* in a row underneath *Simon* and *Alice*, then tapped Rachel's
name. 'Let's go through them. Rachel, what's her motive?' He
looked to Nell.

'Well, despite what she says, I'm not convinced hers was a
happy marriage. But then if every unhappy marriage ended in
murder, we'd never have time for any other crimes, so that's not a
definite motive. Also, she's self-sufficient, financially, so I can't
see financial gain being a motive the CPS would want to run with.'

Bremer nodded. 'So you think we rule her out for now?'

'I'm not sure. There's something about her which unsettles me
but I can't put my finger on it.'

Carla looked up, surprised. She didn't think she could remember a time when Nell had volunteered information which alluded
to any vulnerability.

'I think it's something to do with her parents,' Nell continued.
'There's almost a fear in her face when she speaks of them, and
I got the impression they were the source of her financial solv-
ency.' She looked to Paul. 'What did you think?'

Paul nodded his agreement. 'I think the parents are definitely
an angle to look into.'

Carla flicked open her notepad. 'Because if they are the
source of her money, then she's not financially independent, is
she? So money could still be a motive?'

Bremer nodded. 'Exactly. OK, make a note to start on the parents tomorrow, Carla. Good work, Nell.' He wrote 'parents' next to Rachel's name and then turned back to the board, pointing to the next name.

'Hannah. Thoughts?'

Paul spoke first. 'There's definitely a jealousy there, towards Rachel. Seems a long-standing one, but I'm not sure how that would be a catalyst for her to murder Simon rather than Rachel herself. If she loved Simon, surely she'd kill his wife, not him?'

'Maybe Simon promised her he'd leave Rachel and when he wouldn't she killed him in anger?' Nell said.

Bremer frowned. 'But the scene was more carefully staged than that, wasn't it? And then we have the biblical references – what was it again?' He turned to Nell.

'An eye for an eye, tooth for tooth, hand for hand, foot for foot,' she replied.

Bremer nodded. 'And each of those was removed – Simon's eye, tooth, hand and foot, all severed. Which means the murder was his punishment?'

Carla had opened up Google and was reading the Bible passage. 'It's all about punishment; the whole of Exodus 21 seems to be a how-to guide to punishing people who have done wrong. But the "eye for eye" bit is in specific reference to wives.' She began to read. 'If people are fighting and hit a pregnant woman and she gives birth prematurely but there is no serious injury, the offender must be fined whatever the woman's husband demands and the court allows. But if there is serious injury, you are to take life for life, eye for eye, tooth for tooth, hand for hand, foot for foot, burn for burn, wound for wound, bruise for bruise.' She looked up. 'Was Rachel pregnant?'

Nell shook her head, 'Not that she told me.' She turned to Laura. 'Did she tell you anything which would suggest a failed pregnancy?'

'No, nothing at all. She made reference to trying for children but said they'd been unable to.'

Bremer was frowning at the board. 'But if the punishment meted out to Simon was one the Bible links to a wife, we have to consider Rachel is back in the running, no?' He turned to Carla. 'Let's find out if she has had any pregnancies which have resulted in miscarriages.'

Carla nodded and made a note to contact Rachel's doctor in the morning.

Bremer turned back to the wipe board. 'What about the affair angle? We have the phone calls between Simon and Hannah which could support the possibility, but do we think Hannah is capable of planning a murder?'

'Maybe Hannah was the one who lost a baby and blamed Simon? Do we have any inkling she is religious?'

Nell shook her head. 'None at all, and frankly, she didn't strike me as the religious type. But Hannah could have used that to distract us from the fact she's our killer? Have you run a criminal records check on her; anything to suggest prior history of violence?'

Carla shook her head. 'No, she's totally clean.'

'OK.' Bremer wrote 'revenge' next to Hannah's name. 'Let's keep that as a possibility. Now, Ash.' He looked at them each in turn but no one spoke. 'OK, well that's our intelligence gap right there. We need to find out more about him. We know he's a lecturer at Oxford Uni, right? But what level of contact he'd had with Simon and Hannah over the years, what his relationship was like with them at university and what he's doing now, we don't know. If he's been in Oxford all this time, at the same time they were, strikes me as implausible they wouldn't have had some contact.'

Carla scribbled notes in her notebook. The notion that the silent ones were always the ones to look out for might be a cliché, but clichés were clichés for a reason. Ash's anonymity so far in the case could mean he was just better at hiding than the rest of them. Which then begged the question – hiding from what?

'And what about Luci?' Bremer asked. 'Motive?'

'Anger,' Nell said. 'There's something there she knows and isn't saying and it's linked to Alice and the group.'

Bremer looked across, surprised. Carla threw Nell a warning look.

'Why do you say that?' he asked.

Nell glanced at Carla before continuing. 'Carla and I made an impromptu stop at the hostel last night. We hadn't got around to briefing you on it yet. But Luci seemed keen to blame them for Alice's death; whether that was because the complaint they made about her resulted in Alice becoming homeless and then subsequently taking her own life, or because of something more direct, I couldn't tell.'

Bremer turned to Carla, 'Do you agree with that assessment?'

Her heart was beating so fast she felt as though Bremer must be able to see it, but he seemed to have glossed over the fact they'd visited Luci without his permission.

'I do, yes,' she said. 'She was obviously in love with Alice, or at least very attached, and is angry that their return has resulted in Alice's death.'

'Angry enough to kill Simon?'

Carla thought for a moment but the timeline didn't stack up. 'I just don't see how Luci would have known about Alice's death, connected it to Simon, and been able to murder him within the time frame. How would she even know what he looked like?'

Nell tapped her pen on the desk. 'Maybe she followed Alice to The Varsity Club, saw Alice fall, and realised Simon was there too. She could have heard them speaking, identified him, followed him to the park and killed him.'

'The other possibility is the contact between Simon and Alice around the time Luci was in custody. If Simon paid for the lawyer, maybe he turned up and Luci met him then. Carla, check custody records and see if it mentions people who attended that night.'

Bremer looked at the board. 'This is all good but what are we missing?'

'The complaint,' said Nell. 'Alice is connected to the group because of a complaint they made about her at university. Everything seems to stem from there, so we need to know what that was about and how it is connected to the reunion invitations.'

'Agreed.' Bremer wrote 'complaint' in the middle of the board and drew a circle around it before glancing at the clock. He put the lid back on the pen. 'That's enough for today, it's late.' He turned to Nell. 'In the morning I want Luci in. We need her to access Alice's phone and I'd like to hear what she has to say about Simon. Then we'll take a visit to Rachel's parents. Carla, start digging on them in the morning. Laura, you can cover the pregnancy angle for both Hannah and Rachel, and I'll try and use my elevated status to get Oxford Brookes to release the complaint details.' He smiled. 'Sometimes rank is useful, although I know you think it's just an excuse for me to swan about looking like I'm in charge.'

Carla laughed. 'We don't think that,' she said, ignoring the look from Nell which suggested they did.

Thirty-three

Nell wanted a glass of wine but didn't fancy drinking one alone in her flat. She caught up with Carla, walking across the back yard, coat pulled high around her neck to ward off the bite in the night air.

'Fancy a glass of red? I can drop you home after.'

Carla looked hesitant, so Nell beeped open the car. 'Warm car,' she said, 'comfy seats . . . I'll even put the seat warmer on for you.'

Carla grinned. 'Go on, then, we can stop in Witney and then I can just walk home.'

'Deal.' Nell nodded to Laura who was leaving the station. 'Mind if we invite her?'

'Go on then, but if you start swapping police war stories, I'm off.'

'When do I ever do that?' Nell asked.

'Every time you meet a copper, Nell.'

Nell laughed, gesturing over to Laura to join them. 'OK, I promise. Now get in the car before your feet get frostbite. Christ only knows how you can wear ballet shoes in weather like this.'

They parked up at the back of The Fleece, just off the green in Witney, the end of which was dominated by an impressive church. Taking their drinks to a corner table, they peeled off their coats, the heat from the fire a wall of warmth. Nell took a sip of her wine and looked out of the window, trying to decide if her need for a cigarette outweighed her need for warmth. What she'd give to bring back the days in pubs where you couldn't see two feet in front of you for the smoke.

'Rachel seemed quite taken with you, though.'

Nell turned back to Laura, ignoring Carla's interested look. 'What?'

'Well, she was different around you. You must have noticed? She paid more attention to you than me. It was like she wanted you to like her, whereas she couldn't care less if I did.'

Nell frowned. What was Laura implying? Carla looked about to say something so Nell said it for her. 'You can't be saying Rachel fancies me! She was married to a man.'

Laura shrugged. 'Doesn't mean she liked being that way. People marry for all sorts of reasons besides love. Rachel strikes me as someone who could have been in that camp. It's not like she seemed bothered at the idea of her husband screwing someone else, which suggests she didn't bother screwing him herself.'

Carla looked at Nell.

Nell felt annoyed, but wasn't sure why. 'That doesn't make her a lesbian, though, does it? From what I can tell, if every woman who didn't want to have sex with her husband was a lesbian, we'd be over half the female population by now.'

'Maybe. But I'm just saying what I saw, that's all.' Laura took a sip of her pint and gave a shrug of one shoulder. Nell pulled out her packet of cigarettes; she was beginning to regret having invited Laura, especially when Carla started to speak in a tone which told Nell she'd got hold of an idea.

'What if she is a lesbian?' Carla was saying. 'What if she killed Simon so she could get out of their marriage?'

Nell stared at her. Even for Carla that was quite a theory, and she told her so.

Carla's face was flushed from heat and wine. 'But it could be a potential motive, no? And maybe the connection with Alice is Rachel meeting her at Oxford Brookes and Simon felt threatened and got Alice sacked?'

Nell didn't buy it for a second, but she was tired, and the wine felt good, so she said, 'OK, but why now, after all this time? Rachel must have known about the complaint if Alice was thrown off campus, so why suddenly want to take revenge on Simon? And if she loved Alice, or had even just cared for her, why would she push her to kill herself? Wouldn't Rachel be thrilled to have found her again?'

'Maybe she didn't know,' Laura said, putting her pint on the table. 'She found out Simon had been in contact with Alice but hadn't told her, and was so angry when she did, she killed him?'

Carla was nodding as Laura spoke. 'We know Simon and Alice had contact and we've assumed it was to do with Luci being arrested, a sort of blackmail to help get her out of custody, but what if it wasn't and Simon was actually in contact with Alice to warn her off Rachel again?'

Nell pictured Rachel sitting on her sofa, surrounded by luxury, cradling a coffee cup edged with a gold rim; she didn't think she'd ever seen anyone less likely to be a murderer, and Nell had seen her fair share. 'I think you both have a point—' she started.

'But?' Carla interrupted.

'But, I think we need a bit more to go on than a wine-fuelled theory session in a pub.'

Laura took a sip of her pint, eyeing Nell over the glass, while Carla took out her tobacco pouch and started rolling a cigarette. Nell sensed the hostility.

'Look, I'm not saying it's not a possibility,' she said, 'just it all hinges on whether Rachel is a lesbian or not, and you have to admit that has come slightly out of nowhere and is off the back of an observation you made, Laura, from a couple of interactions between me and her.' She looked to Carla. 'You have to admit that's not the best basis for a murder case.'

'I know what I saw,' Laura said, downing her pint and putting it down heavily on the table.

'I know, and I wasn't suggesting it wasn't something we should look into,' Nell said, keen not to dampen Laura's enthusiasm, but equally keen to stick to the facts. 'It's just I know how Carla gets and I wanted to stem the excitement a bit.'

Carla stared at her. 'What do you mean, "how Carla gets"?'

Nell sensed the night go rapidly downhill. 'I just meant you like a good "theory", that's all.'

Carla picked up her lighter. 'Yes, I do. But only one I can work with, and this theory has the potential to pinpoint a motive for Simon's murder.' Carla stood and pulled her coat off the back of the chair. 'I'm sure it's great to have another cop to explore these "theories" with, but I'd hoped you'd known me long enough to trust my judgement.'

Nell knew she needed to shut up, that Carla felt threatened and she needed to reassure her, but she was unable to. 'I thought you preferred facts to theory? You're always the one who says motive doesn't matter and all we are here to do is join all the facts to prove who the killer was, not why they were one.'

Carla was standing by the table, rolled cigarette in hand. 'Yeah, well, the facts are, Laura thinks Rachel is possibly a lesbian. That means she could have had reason to kill Simon.'

Nell laughed. 'It's not a "fact". Laura thought she saw something between Rachel and me and I can tell you, as an actual lesbian, she's wrong.'

Laura glared at her across the table but Nell didn't care. She was sick and tired of hetero women thinking they knew everything about gay women and making wild assumptions about who they did or didn't fancy.

'Fine,' said Carla. 'I'm going for a cigarette and then I'll walk home.'

'Fine,' Nell replied, the realisation she'd now have to wait until Carla had finished her cigarette before she could have one annoying her further.

Laura looked between them both. 'Well, guys, this has been *fun*. We must do it again sometime, but meanwhile, I'm going to get me a taxi and a kebab.'

Nell took a swig of her wine. At least she wouldn't have to give her a ride home and have her car stunk out with the smell of dead dog.

'I'll walk with you,' Carla said, before pausing and looking back at Nell. 'Fancy a kebab?' It was an olive branch and Nell knew she should take it but she couldn't bring herself to.

'No, but thanks, I'm going to head off.'

After they'd gone, Nell sat staring at the table as the fire next to her spat and hissed. Why had she got so angry? Why had she rubbished what was actually a reasonable theory which could throw the case wide open? Guilt, that was what. Guilt and pride because Nell knew full well Rachel had thrown her off balance and that her professionalism had been compromised because of it.

Nell pulled on her coat and grabbed her bag. Walking into the car park she lit up and took a long drag. Leaning against the bonnet of the car, she thought about Rachel. Tomorrow she'd go back and see if it happened again, see if the feeling had been because she'd wanted to feel it, or whether Rachel had hoped she would. If it was the latter, she'd apologise to Carla and Laura for being a pig-headed idiot. If it was the former − if she'd just imagined it? − well, she'd damn well get a grip on herself and go out and have a damned good lay.

Thirty-four

The next morning Carla sat at her computer, determined to lose the irritation she still felt with Nell, by researching Rachel's parents instead.

She put all the information she held about Rachel into the relevant databases but found no mention of them. Flicking through her notepad she found the car Rachel had been driving – a ten-year-old Mercedes, compared to Simon's 2018 one – and put it through the DVLA database, checking the address it was registered to:

112–128 Windsor Court, London Road, Liverpool.

Liverpool? Then Carla remembered, Rachel had been studying there, only travelling to Oxford at weekends. She must not have remembered to re-register the address.

Carla googled the address and determined it was a rental

property not far from Liverpool University. Several complaints listed against its name on a student housing forum told her it was run by a letting agency. Picking up the phone she dialled the letting agency, tapping her pen on the notepad, she waited for them to answer.

'Hello?' The voice was cheerful, young, Carla took that to be a good sign, an eagerness to help.

'Hi, this is Carla Brown from Thames Valley Police and I was hoping you could help me with an address I believe you manage?' she said, reading it out.

'Well that is one of ours, yes, but all information about occupants would be personal data covered by GDPR so I'm afraid I don't think I can be much help.'

Carla smiled. 'That's OK, I totally understand. I wonder if I could speak to your manager. It's just that we are desperately trying to locate the relatives of a woman in a murder investigation.'

'Murder?' The woman's voice was low and sounded as if she were holding the phone close to her mouth.

'Yes. I was just hoping there was a home address registered against the property. She was a student, so I assume you take another address in case you need to get money back after they have left? But I understand if you can't help.' Carla waited, in her experience, people found it hard to resist playing a bit part in a murder inquiry.

'Hold on, let me have a look. What dates are we looking at?'

Carla gave the date the car was registered in Liverpool and waited. Minutes later, the woman came back on the phone.

'Got it,' she said, 'sorry, it took longer than I thought, it's quite a long time ago. An alternative address was given as the main point of contact. It was stressed this was the main contact point.'

'Oh that's so helpful, thank you.' Carla picked up her pen and wrote down the address as the woman read it out. Carla opened up Google maps, typed in the address, and stared at it – a house in the Cotswolds? What were they, royalty? She clicked on 'images' resulting in a sprawling estate which didn't even fit in one window, then clicked on several other images: an outdoor pool, tennis courts, stables and a hunting lodge before she even got to the extensive woodland acres beyond.

'Why do you say this address was stressed as a main contact point?' she asked. 'Isn't that usual for students? A parental contact point?'

'Well usually, yes. But in this file the word "any" is underlined,' the woman said. 'Which is a bit odd.'

Carla didn't understand. 'Sorry, could you elaborate?'

'I don't know, it's just we don't usually make any particular comment on the files so it must have been important to someone for it to be underlined.'

'Someone?'

'Well yes, generally we like to ensure students are independent of their parents, but in this case the parents are listed as the main contact.'

'So, all communications about Rachel had to go through her parents?' Carla asked.

'Seems so,' the woman replied.

Hanging up, Carla wondered why the parents had to be in control of Rachel's communications, surely, as the woman had said, one of the points of going to university was to learn independence? At least, it had been for her. Still preoccupied with this thought she typed in the father's name, Malcolm DAVIDSON, convinced she wouldn't get any hits it came as a surprise to find pages of them.

Clicking open the first, she began to read the article, detailing a Christian project in America which had received a million-pound donation from Rachel's father, a multi-millionaire and apparently a major philanthropist; donation after donation to various causes, all with the proceeds of the money he had made in computing back in the 70s.

How the hell had she missed all this during her checks on Rachel? But then she'd been checking for Rachel Morris, not Rachel Davidson. Annoyed with herself, Carla checked the last entry on the page. 'Multi-millionaire backs church in centre of LGBT row.' Scanning the article, Carla read that Malcolm Davidson had no qualms about donating half a million pounds to a Liverpool-based church, which believed gay people could be cured of their homosexuality. Clicking on the church website, she scrolled through the pages, each one filled with more anti-homosexual rhetoric than the last.

'Anything good?' Bremer was by the door, two takeout coffees in hand. Carla barely noticed. She was opening and scanning page after page, increasingly disturbed by what she was seeing.

If I Fall

You shall not lie with a male as with a woman; it is an abomination. (Leviticus 18:22)

If a man lies with a male as with a woman, both of them have committed an abomination; they shall surely be put to death; their blood is upon them. (Leviticus 20:13)

Line after line of Bible quotes, streams of lectures all obsessed with homosexuality, each consigning gay people to a life of damnation in increasingly angry terms.

'Carla?' Bremer walked over and put a coffee on her desk. She jumped.

'God, sorry.' Then, noting the coffee, 'Thank you.'

'Two sugars, right?' He handed her two sachets. 'You OK?' He peered down at her and she pointed to the screen. 'Just a little freaked out by Rachel's parents. Turns out they're multi-millionaire bigots.'

'What?' Pulling over a chair he took hold of the mouse and opened a page. Ten seconds later, he sat back and looked at Carla.

'Thoughts?'

'How awful it is that people hold these views and, worse, make them so public?'

'Agreed, but relevance to the case?' Bremer looked back at the screen. 'I thought this was something that only happened in Amercia, no?' He looked back at Carla, who shrugged.

'I did too but all this' – she pointed to the screen 'suggests otherwise. And it gets worse' She flicked through to the last page on the website. 'Here they offer courses on how to cure people of their gayness. I mean, how insane is that? It's like a Liverpudlian version of the Westboro Baptist Church.'

Bremer pulled himself closer to the screen. 'I still don't see the relevance though.' He glanced at Carla, who hesitated, unsure if she wanted another overreaction to her theory.

'Problem?' he asked.

'No.' She gave a short smile. 'OK, hear me out. I think Rachel may be gay.' She told him about Laura's comments in the pub, the way Rachel reacted to Nell. 'And it links in with Alice. Maybe they met when Rachel visited Simon and had some sort of fling, or developed a crush, an obsession with Alice?'

Bremer considered her. 'But Nell doesn't get the same impression? About Rachel being gay, I mean.'

'She says not.'

He tipped his head slightly to one side. 'And you don't believe her?'

'I don't know.'

'What are the implications to the case if she were gay?' he asked. 'For argument's sake.'

'Well it's a motive for killing Simon. She's married to a man when she wants to be free to be with a woman.'

Bremer nodded. 'True. But then they've been together years, why now?'

'She'd just had enough of the lies?'

'Hmmm.' He looked back at the screen. 'Not sure it works like that. And why wouldn't she just divorce him?'

'Because of her parents.' She pointed to the screen. 'If they are highly religious then divorce would be a sin, so Rachel could have felt trapped and that her only option was to kill him.'

Bremer was scanning the screen.

'I'm pretty sure murder is more of a sin, no?' Carla conceded he had a point.

He glanced over at her. 'Can you do some digging on all this? See how involved the parents are, what, if any, connection it has to Simon. Hadn't they known each other since they were kids? So the parents must know each other; look into that and see if there is a relationship beyond that of in-laws.'

Carla nodded and turned back to the computer screen. Bremer put his hand on her arm just as she was about to click on a page.

'From what very little I know, this stuff isn't pleasant. If this starts to get too much, or you read anything that upsets you beyond the normal levels, you tell me, OK?'

'Sure.'

His hand stayed where it was.

'I promise, OK?' She smiled at him and moved his hand to the table. 'I'll let you know what I come up with.'

Bremer looked unsure.

'Go! How can I get any work done with you sitting there!'

'Point taken.' He picked up his coffee. 'Oh, and Alice's HR file will be on my desk by this afternoon, so soon we'll have all the details of the complaint against her.'

Carla laughed. 'Rank wins every time.'

'You know it, Brown,' he said.

When he'd gone, Carla turned back to the screen. Shutting

down the pages relating to Rachel's parents, she opened up a new Google tab. If she was going to research them, she wanted to go in prepared, know what to look for.

She began typing: 'Gay conversion therapy, UK,' then pressed send.

She assumed that whatever came back would surely be less messed-up than the USA fanatics peddling the same theories? That seemed to consist of camps in the middle of nowhere, with guards who policed your every move and punishments for any transgression – real or perceived. The UK at least didn't breed lunatic bigots to the same level, and had far more limited geography when it came to camps in the middle of nowhere.

She glanced at the Davidsons' house, hidden in an expanse of land. Maybe the UK disciples didn't need a desert or a forest. Maybe all they needed was a haven tucked away in a corner of the Cotswolds, next to one of the most famous cities in the world.

Thirty-five

I stand at the garden door of my family home, the drawing room behind me a collage of green, and let my eyes wander across the shrubs and bushes, now heavy with the weight of winter. The garden had been a retreat for me when I was a child, hiding in the dilapidated garage, and I'd had that with Ash, until he left me there alone.

My mum arrives behind me, cup and saucer in hand. 'Here you go, my darling.'

I take it and follow her to the narrow sofa; uncomfortable, so much so that I wonder if it was deliberately so – to make those coming for guidance and respite sit up and pay attention, to reiterate that the words of my parents were to be listened to with seriousness and suffering. There had been so many people through the old house across the years, I wouldn't have been able to count even if I'd been allowed to meet them. Instead, I'd hide on the stairs, peering through the dark oak banisters, trying to hear the words being chanted – until finally it became my turn to hear them first-hand.

My mum smiles, hands neatly folded on her lap. 'I've taken Laura upstairs and given her the spare room down the hall from us.' She's studying my face for signs of disappointment that Laura won't be closer to me but, as I don't care, I just smile.

'Lovely, thank you. I'm sure it's just a precaution and she won't be here long.'

My dad appears at the door, Bible in hand. 'Rachel.' He opens his arms to me and I oblige by standing and walking to him. 'So relieved to have you back.'

We sit back down and my dad smiles. 'Do you remember Reverend John?'

The cup starts to shake on the saucer. I put it down on the glass coffee table, trying not to remember the smell of the Liverpool church; the feel of that man's hands on my body, or hear the chanting as I was held down on the stone-flagged floor.

'Yes.' It's all I can manage as my stomach churns and my mouth goes dry.

'We can send you back to Reverend John if it would help.'

I look to my mum but her eyes are closed, lips moving quickly, with the words she was praying.

I feel myself start to panic, the loss of control coming back to me quicker than a train, the memories of fear, guilt, and self-hate, collapsing on me with a force that almost pushes me backwards. I tell myself, everything is OK, you are going to be fine, over and over, until my heart starts to slow and my head starts to still. Focus, Rachel, focus on why you are here.

'I don't think I need to see Reverend John again.' I smile at my dad, who nods, and opens his Bible.

'Do you remember God's words in Romans, Rachel?'

'Yes,' I say quietly.

'Then tell me them now.'

I look to the floor, stone flagged like the church in Liverpool, equally hard, equally cold, and I begin. 'They exchanged the truth about God for a lie, and worshipped and served created things rather than the Creator – who is forever praised. Amen. Because of this, God gave them over to shameful lusts. Even their women exchanged natural sexual relations for unnatural ones. In the same way the men also abandoned natural relations with women and were inflamed with lust for one another. Men committed shameful acts with other men and received in themselves the due penalty for their error. Furthermore, just as they did not think it worthwhile to retain the knowledge of God, so God gave them over to a depraved mind, so that they do what ought not to be done. They have become filled with every kind of wickedness, evil, greed and depravity. They are full of envy, murder, strife, deceit and malice.'

My dad smiles. 'Very good. And those words stay with you every day?'

'They do,' I reply obediently.

'Now that Simon is gone, those words should remain the first thought of your day and the last of your night.' He leans forward and takes my hands in his. 'No more lies now, my love. If you are to stay in our house, we can't have the police back at our door over misunderstandings, can we?'

I shake my head.

'It almost killed your mother.' He shook his head. 'When I think of the things you told them about us, the things you said we'd done.' His hands tighten around mine. 'You cannot blame us for your behaviour, nor for how we chose to offer our help. The Bible says, "The person who sins is the one who will die. The child will not be punished for the parent's sins, and the parent will not be punished for the child's sins. Righteous people will be rewarded for their own righteous behaviour, and wicked people will be punished for their own wickedness." So remember, Rachel, as parents we will not be punished for your sins, but we will still be alone in heaven without you, knowing you were in the blazing furnace, shackled in chains of darkness, awaiting judgement.'

I try to ignore the words, ones I've heard so many times before, let them wash over me. I need to get to their study, I need to know if they paid Hannah, I need to know if they harmed Alice. I close my eyes. Everything is OK. You're going to be fine.

'Rachel?' Laura is standing by the door, a mixture of concern and bemusement on her face. 'Can we just discuss security for a moment?'

I look to my dad and he nods permission, although I can tell her presence irritates him. But I don't care because the minute I'm in the cold dark hall, I feel bathed in relief.

'What do you want to know about security?' I ask, and Laura grins.

'Nothing, it just looked like you might want to escape.'

I almost laugh; at her bravery, at how little she comprehends what my father is capable of, at how kind it was of her to want to rescue me. 'Let's go outside,' I say. 'I fancy some fresh air.'

We walk around the garden, me pointing out flowers I planted, where I'd hurt my knee, almost broken my arm.

'It sounds like you had a happy childhood.' She smiles.

'I did,' and it's not exactly a lie. We stop by the old garage. 'I used to play hide and seek in there with myself. It's so full of random bits and bobs I would spend hours just rummaging around.'

Laura laughs. 'How can you play hide and seek with yourself?'

I look at her, before bursting out laughing. 'I have no idea, I can't remember.'

I glance back at the house. My parents are standing at a window, watching us, and all I want to do is run from that cold dark house as fast as I can. Because one thing I knew: when I left – when I'd done what I came here to do – I was never going back.

Thirty-six

The more Carla read about gay conversion therapy, the angrier she became. It was all so extreme and she had no idea it was practised in the UK. But it turned out whether it was families doing it by themselves, or a more organised version such as at the church in Liverpool, it was very much alive.

Bremer sat down next to her. 'How's it going?'

Carla grimaced. 'It's not easy reading. I've been going through survivor stories, mostly from the US, I admit, and it's so damaging. In the US they use therapy to "cure" you and that can be sexual "healing", where they make you have sex with someone of the opposite sex, or talking therapy. So I assume they use the same techniques here.'

Bremer stared at her. 'Are you kidding me about the sex thing?'

'No. And they make you watch pornographic films over and

over and then make you talk through how you felt watching it. I mean, some of these are kids of sixteen or younger.'

'Jesus, but this is all illegal, right? At least here?'

'Nope. Government chickened out of banning it in 2018. They did strongly condemn it, as has the Church of England, but from what I can tell, and I've only done a really quick whiz through Google, it just goes unreported now. Religious institutions know it's frowned on here so it's all been swept under the table. If you think about it, I bet you know someone who thinks being gay is a choice.' She looked at him, his profile, and slightly furrowed brow as he thought.

'I don't know really. I suppose so.'

Something in his tone made her ask, 'Do you think it's a choice?'

'Shit, Carla, I don't know. I'm not gay – how do I know if it's a choice or not?'

It was the first time Carla had seen him even the slightest bit ruffled. 'Did you choose to be heterosexual?'

'No.'

A one-word answer, sensible. 'So what you're really saying is heterosexuality is the norm, so you didn't need to make a choice, but homosexuality is not the norm so they needed to make a choice to not be straight?'

'That's a bit of a jump.'

She looked out of the window. Maybe it was a jump, but she was also right; why the hell could people not spend the slightest time examining why they felt the way they did?

'Putting the fact that you're cross with me aside,' Bremer said, 'are you any clearer on how this impacts the case?'

'Well, I've been thinking about that. One of the things about survivors of this is that they are consumed by self-doubt, guilt, much like other abuse survivors, often unable to leave their abuser or, if they do, there are mental health consequences such as depression, self-harm and even suicide. If Rachal had been forced to undergo this, maybe even forced to marry Simon, it could have taken years for her to get to the point where she finally snapped and killed him.'

'But she could have divorced him,' Bremer pointed out.

'Yes, but if her parents exposed her to years of abuse, where she was made to feel as if she was wrong to feel the way she did, and controlled by them in what decisions she could and couldn't make, her fear of them may have made killing him preferable over facing them with a divorce.'

'That would have to be some fear.'

Carla felt a flash of anger. 'A third of people undergoing gay conversion therapy attempted suicide. That's here in the UK, not America, where God only knows what the stats are. Choosing death rather than face society as a gay person is also some fear, wouldn't you say?'

Bremer held up his hands. 'True, very true. Sorry.'

Carla didn't reply, anger prevented her, so when it was clear she wasn't going to, Bremer said, 'Fancy a little trip to the Cotswolds?'

Carla turned to him. 'To meet the parents?'

Bremer nodded. 'I'd like to get an idea of them in person.'

And despite Carla usually protesting at their impromptu visits out of the office, in this instance, she very much wanted to join him.

The Davidsons' house was situated just outside Great Tew – a small village with a scattering of thatched cottages, seated alongside a landed estate of the same name – with narrow roads, unreachable by any satnav.

The driveway to the Davidsons' was long and winding, lined with large oaks, which obscured the view of the main house. When it came into view, Carla almost let out a shout, so impressive was it; she'd only ever seen its like in films.

'That's one big house,' Bremer said, turning the engine off and peering up at the turrets at either end of the building. Carla spotted two little outhouses to the right of the main building, like two mini holiday houses, although she doubted they would be used for that.

The man who opened the door to Bremer's knock stared frostily down at them, which turned to outright hostility once Bremer had introduced them.

'What now?'

Carla was taken aback. That was the sort of greeting she'd expect if they'd knocked on the door of a career criminal, not a philanthropist millionaire. Bremer tucked his warrant card into his back pocket. 'Do police visit you often, sir?'

Carla could hear the faint amusement in his voice and hoped the man didn't pick up on it. And if he did get visited a lot, there'd been no trace of it on any of the intel databases.

The man put his hands in his pockets. 'What do you want, Inspector?'

'I'd like to have a chat with you about your daughter, if that's possible. And with your wife if she's home?' He craned his neck to look past Mr Davidson, who moved to block his view.

'What about Rachel?' His tone was suspicious, but Carla thought she detected a hint of concern. 'You can't speak with her, she's gone to the shops with that policewoman of yours.'

'It's not Rachel we'd like to speak to.' Bremer smiled. 'It's about her.' When Mr Davidson didn't move, Bremer took a step forward. 'Sir, I do think it would be best if we came inside. We just want to confirm a few things about your daughter, specifically about her time at university and a group of friends she hung out with.'

Mr Davidson's face coloured. 'I'm not having you coming in here and stirring all that up again. My wife went through hell because of Rachel's actions. I will not stand for it again.'

Carla didn't have a clue what he meant – was he talking about Rachel being gay? It was a possibility, but for some reason she sensed Mr Davidson was being more specific, so what had Rachel done which could make him so angry? She glanced at Bremer who, despite being as in the dark as she was, didn't miss a beat. Instead he said, 'I'm sure it was a very difficult time, sir, and I have no wish to upset your wife, but it really would help us in what is a complex inquiry.'

'Inquiry? You're doing an inquiry because of her lies? This really is too much; it was years ago and there is absolutely no evidence whatsoever. It's her word against ours and frankly I would have thought you had better things to do than investigate age-old allegations made by a disturbed teenager.' His voice was now raised and Carla saw a woman appear on the stairs.

She stood, one hand on the banister, one clutched to a necklace hanging from her neck. 'Malcolm? What is it?'

Mr Davidson didn't move his eyes from Bremer. 'Nothing, Hilary, nothing at all, just go back upstairs.'

'Is it the police?' she called, taking a step down. 'Is it Rachel? Is she OK? She's only just left. Has she been hurt?'

Finally, a parent asking the obvious question. Carla called over Mr Davidson's shoulder, 'She's OK, Mrs Davidson, we just need to speak with you about a few things if that's all right.' She ignored the murderous look that Mr Davidson gave her and flashed a smile at his wife who by now was approaching the door.

'Darling?' She looked to her husband. 'What's going on?'

Mr Davidson gave a sigh which Carla sensed was one of both frustration and resignation.

'She's started on the allegations again.'

Hilary paled. She looked from Carla to Bremer then back to Carla. 'But we were told there was no further action to be taken. There would be no record of it at all. Why would she make it all up again? And why wouldn't she tell us? She's been here all morning.' She looked to her husband. 'Why would she lie to us?'

Carla wanted to tell her she was right, there was no record relating to either parent, but no record of what?

Hilary looked at her husband. 'We didn't harm her, did we,

Malcolm? We just tried to help her and her friend.' She turned back to Carla. 'That's all it was, help they both needed so we offered it.'

'Help with what?' Bremer asked.

Hilary looked confused. 'Well, with the homosexuality issue, of course. Rachel says we abused her' She clutched at her neck 'Reported it to the police and came out with the most dreadful lies; how we beat her and mentally abused her. Thankfully, of course, her friend made it clear she wasn't telling the truth, or goodness knows what would have happened.'

Rachel accused her parents of abuse? Why hadn't Carla been able to find a record of it? Surely someone would have documented it, even if it was later found to be untrue? She sensed Bremer was about to speak, probably to clear up the confusion over why they were there, and she knew it would mean they'd clam up about the abuse and she'd get nothing more from them if all records had gone.

'Friend?' she asked, ignoring Bremer's look of surprise. 'Which friend?'

'The lovely one, oh, what was his name dear?'

'Asheem, I believe, Asheem Desai. Good friend of Simon's,' Mr Davidson replied.

Ash. Why had he been involved in a report to the police made by Rachel against her parents? And why had he told the police Rachel was a liar? Did he believe it, or was he siding with her parents for some other reason? Carla thought of the survivor testimonies she'd read, their inability to escape from abusers because of the coercive nature of the abuse, and wondered if Ash had been, at some point, a victim like Rachel? In which case, how would Rachel feel towards him betraying her like that, because there was only one thing Carla could think of – Rachel wanted her revenge on Ash.

Thirty-seven

Paul drew to a stop outside Ash's home address, but the house looked to be in darkness.

'What is it with this guy?' Nell said, as Paul unclicked his seatbelt. 'Is he ever home?'

Paul stared up at the darkened windows. 'What time did uniform go over yesterday? When Ash left after getting the phone call. Maybe he works odd hours?'

'He's an academic at the university, the proper one,' she added. 'So I think it would be pretty standard hours and I doubt he'd have left this early.'

Paul was grinning at her.

'What?'

'Don't let Oxford Brookes hear you call Oxford the proper university.'

'Well, if they are as good, why didn't he choose to be an academic there then?' She wasn't in the mood for Paul to argue, last night's conversation with Carla and Laura was still irritating her, and for the life of her she couldn't work out why.

'What's wrong with you?' Paul asked as he approached the door, which Nell knew would go unanswered.

'Tired, that's all.' She knocked, ignoring the look he gave her telling her he didn't believe her, and waited. Nothing. Predictable. This whole case was beginning to consist of knocking on numerous unanswered doors.

'Come on,' she said, turning back to the car. 'I'm sick of not getting anywhere. Let's go and find Luci, buy her a coffee and some cigs, see if she can move us forward.'

It took them a while to find her, tucked down an alley next to the New Theatre on Oxford's George Street, clutching a large cider bottle, her dog Billy growling at their approach.

'Luci?' Nell held out her warrant card and nodded at Guy, who had stepped forward protectively when Nell had reached into her pocket.

'Yeah? What of it?' Luci's eyes were slightly glazed but Nell still thought she could get some sense out of her.

'I've come to chat about Alice.' Nell knelt down to Luci's level and made her hold her eye. 'We really need to find out more about her; how she came to be on the roof, why she was invited to the reunion. Can you try to help me with that? For Alice's sake?'

Luci glanced at Guy who shook his head.

'Please, Luci, just a few questions, I'll buy you a coffee down the road if you'd like.'

'Wine would be better.'

'Yeah well, it's only coffee on offer, I'm afraid. Might be able to stretch to a sandwich.' Nell gave what she hoped was an encouraging smile before standing. Pulling out a packet of cigarettes, she offered one to Guy who shook his head. Tough crowd, she thought, taking one out of the packet and lighting it before handing it to Luci. Billy growled, hackles raised. Nell looked to Guy, who just shrugged. Great, two attack dogs for the price of one.

Luci pushed herself off the floor. 'It's OK, Billy.' She stroked his head and the dog fell silent, eyes still fixed on Nell. Luci picked up his lead. 'All right. Coffee and a sandwich.'

Nell looked at Guy. 'You want to come?'

Guy looked to Luci then down at Billy. 'Nah, I'll hang out here with the dog.' He reached to take the lead and then sat down in Luci's space on the pavement.

'Right,' Nell said, 'best leave that here mind.' She took the bottle from Luci's hand and tried not to think what it had been in contact with as she guided Luci up the street towards The Old Fire Station café.

They sat by the patio doors, which in the summer opened out onto the narrow pavement – stumpy palm trees trying vainly to distract from buses and tourists – but were now just a reflection of the café's brightly lit interior.

Luci stirred three sugars into her black coffee and looked across at Nell. 'Go on then, what do you want to know?' Her tone was borderline aggressive, expression defensive, and Nell hoped the alcohol would wear off before it prevented her from getting any sense out of Luci.

'I was wondering about the days before her death. What was she like? Sad, happy, unsettled?'

Luci's face seemed to soften as she thought back to her time with Alice, and Nell felt a pang of hope.

'She was OK,' Luci said. 'She'd been a bit tense which meant she'd had trouble sleeping.'

'Do you know what about?'

'No. She wouldn't tell me so we argued.' She took a sip of coffee and sniffed as she placed the cup back on the table. 'But she'd been like it for a few weeks, all snappy and distant.'

'Can you remember exactly when she started to be like that?'

Luci added another sugar to her coffee. 'No, but it was around the time this woman turned up. Kept popping up, she did, and her and Alice would scurry off for a little chat and then she'd come back all pissed about something.'

'But she didn't tell you what had annoyed her about the chat?'

Luci shook her head. Nell considered her for a moment. Maybe Alice had been getting involved with drugs? But then why hide that from Luci, who clearly wasn't averse to the odd narcotic or two.

'So she'd been off about something and you think it was down to this woman?' Nell asked.

'Yes. I think it was something from her past.'

'Why did you think that?'

'Because how else would she know her? I met her the day she landed on the streets and we'd been together ever since. So where would she have met her that I wouldn't have known about? And Guy didn't know her either, and after me, she knew Guy the best, so the only way it makes sense was if she was from Alice's past.'

Nell had to admit it did make sense. But if it was from her past, why hide it from Luci? What could the woman coming back have meant to Alice that made her afraid of sharing it with the two people closest to her?

'That woman turned up the day Alice died,' Luci went on. 'She just turned up like she always did, without any warning, and dragged Alice off.' Luci leant forward, pointed her finger at Nell. 'But this time I followed her. I was sick of it, all the lies and the hiding away. I mean, I had a right to know if she was shagging her, didn't I?'

It hadn't occurred to Nell that had been an option, but she supposed it was a credible assumption to make. 'And were they?'

'If they were it wasn't going well. When I followed them, they were arguing about something, going at it like Billy goes for a cop.'

Nell ignored the dig. 'Did you hear what they were arguing about?'

'No. I couldn't get close enough without them seeing me, so I just left them to it. When Alice got back she wouldn't tell me what was wrong, but she was in a hell of a mood.'

'And this all happened the day she died?'

Luci took a drink of coffee. 'Yep.'

'Do you think the argument contributed to her taking her life?'

Luci flashed Nell a warning look. 'She didn't take her own life. She wouldn't do that. She wouldn't have left me here, she promised to never leave me, and I believed her.'

Nell gave her a moment to settle before she replied. 'Sometimes things happen to make people break their promises.'

'I know that. I'm homeless, not stupid. But she told me she'd never leave me because someone had done that to her. That's why she'd ended up on the street, so she'd never be able to do that to anyone, especially me.'

Nell decided to go with it. 'Was it the woman who came back? Was she the one who hurt her?'

Luci looked close to tears but she brushed at her face. 'Don't know. Maybe. It would explain why she was so cross, I suppose.' She looked at Nell, suddenly alert. 'Maybe the woman came back to get her and Alice said no. See.' She held her coffee up as if holding up a medal. 'I told you she didn't kill herself, she wanted to stay with me, that proves it.'

Nell rather thought it didn't, but she let Luci have it. She was far more interested in who this woman was and why she'd upset Alice.

'Could you describe the woman for me, Luci?'

Luci looked out of the window, thinking. 'Brown hair but I don't know the length as it was up in a ponytail.'

Not short then.

'And she was pale, about my height.'

White, 5 foot 7.

'And she spoke with a normal voice.'

'Normal?'

'You know, just a normal one, like not Scottish or anything.'

'No accent, you mean?'

'Yeah, like I said, normal.'

The description wasn't much help and it pretty much fitted the description of both Hannah and Rachel, but if Nell had to put a tenner on it, she'd pin it on being Rachel. Maybe Carla was right about Rachel and Alice. That would fit with it being her who came back after ditching Alice during her university days. But why come back? And why now?

'Was Alice still angry when she left to go to The Varsity Club?' Nell asked.

Luci shook her head. 'She'd gone all quiet by then, didn't really speak, and when she did she seemed confused. It upset her, I think, that she was having trouble thinking straight. That's what arguments do – they make you so tangled up you can't get your thoughts out. I told her not to go, to stay with me, but she was having none of it.'

'Did she say why it was so important for her to go?'

Luci took a mouthful of coffee and thought. 'Just something about how she'd find the answer. Like I said, she wasn't making too much sense, so couldn't explain what she meant when I asked.'

So, Alice had gone to the club, confused and upset, hoping to find an answer. But to what? Nell watched Luci start the sandwich.

'If I came back with a photo,' she asked, 'do you think you would recognise the woman?'

'Maybe. I could give it a go.'

'And Alice never told you what she'd come back for; nothing the woman said she wanted from Alice? Something she had, maybe?'

Luci laughed. 'Like what? The pot of gold we kept in the sleeping bag?'

Nell didn't know, but she'd turned up in Alice's life for a reason and Nell was damn sure it had something to do with the case. But what?

Rain started to hammer the window. Nell saw Guy standing across the road, watching them, Billy at his side – both already drenched.

She turned back to Luci. 'Get yourself in the shelter tonight, OK? It's going to be cold.'

Luci shrugged again and carried on eating, finishing the last mouthful with a swig of coffee. 'Costs money to get in the shelter,' she said pointedly.

Nell pulled out her wallet and handed over a ten-pound note. 'You'll check out a photo if I bring one back?' Nell asked, wishing she'd got one of Rachel so they could pin Luci down there and then. God knows where the woman could be tomorrow.

'Sure, I'll help all I can. Guy might have a look too, but he's a bit, you know.'

Nell did. Guy was police-shy, otherwise known as having spent too long in their company, and not in a good way.

'But he loved Alice too,' Luci said, frowning at the expression on Nell's face. 'So, he'll help if he can. She didn't do it, you know; she didn't kill herself.'

Nell wanted to let her believe it, she really did, but facts were facts and sometimes it was better to accept that, move on. 'There were lots of witnesses, Luci, they all say she jumped and no one was near enough to have pushed her.'

'Oh, I know that.' Luci waved to Guy to say she was coming. 'I mean someone made her want to die. That's still murder, right?'

And while Nell wasn't sure that would hold up in a court of law, she thought Luci probably had a point. Following Luci to the door and holding it open, she said, 'One last question. We've found a mobile for Alice, do you know the passcode?'

Luci had her back to her but the rise of the shoulders, the refusal to turn around to answer the question made Nell think the reply was going to be a lie.

'No,' Luci said, as she started off into the rain.

Thirty-eight

Ash was walking home when he heard a car pull up behind him and what sounded like the opening of a car door, then the boot. He pulled out his phone to message Eric and say he was on his way, partly because Eric always fussed if he was late, but also because he'd had a sudden sense of unease – a feeling of being watched, as if the cloak of anonymity he normally donned when walking down the road had been pulled away.

As he pulled Eric's number to the screen, he heard footsteps – quick, purposeful – and he was about to turn around when he felt himself being propelled forward, stumbling to stay on his feet, a sharp pain in his neck as if a wasp had just struck. And then, the pavement too close, heart pumping too quickly, a streetlight too far away, before, nothing.

*

At first, Ash thought he was paralysed. The room, such as it was, came into view – a mass of dust and broken bits of furniture in the middle of which he seemed to be seated – but his arms and legs wouldn't move despite desperate attempts to make them.

He made himself stop trying, take time to focus, look at his surroundings; fighting the desire to wrestle his arms and legs free, he took long deep breaths and tried to concentrate.

The room had a low ceiling, the floor a patchwork of barely laid concrete, while a thin wooden staircase sat to the left of him. A basement. But where? Ash tried to listen for sounds of traffic, people speaking, anything to give him an idea of where he might be, but it was total silence. He didn't even know if he was still in Oxford, as he had no idea how long he'd been unconscious, and with that thought he remembered the wasp-like sting and moved his neck – a dull throb confirming all this was real.

He heard a noise from upstairs and strained to hear it more clearly. Footsteps, he was sure of it, but coming towards the basement or away from it? He listened to each creak of floor-board, the soft tap of someone walking. It occurred to him he should scream, yell for them to hear him, because who was to say it was the person who put him here? But then Eric always said, 'People die in horror films because they do dumb things.' He didn't want to die. He wanted to be at home, with the fire on, a book on his lap and glasses falling down the bridge of his nose.

The footsteps stopped. Ash waited. He couldn't make sense of where they were now, how close to the basement door, to him – until the door handle at the top of the stairs turned and someone began to walk down.

Ash froze. He could see a gloved hand on the staircase rail, a heavy pair of walking boots, then, click, a flash of light in the greyness and the person was gone.

Thirty-nine

Mr Davidson finally relented and allowed Bremer and Carla to enter their home, guiding them into a large, ornate room, vases depicting colourful scenes scattered on sideboards, all in various autumnal shades, dark reds complementing the oak wooden floors and garish – but undoubtedly expensive – wallpaper.

Rachel's parents sat at either end of a large sofa. Carla watched the pair's body language, the way they mirrored each other, anticipated any new move like a tilt of the head or crossing of a leg, which suggested they were a close couple; but there was something cold about them, a lack of eye contact, perhaps, or the way Hilary's legs were turned away from her husband's, which suggested their display of unity might not be an entirely true reflection of their marriage.

'Can you tell me a bit more about these allegations that Rachel made against you and how they relate to Ash Desai?' Bremer asked.

'Why? How is that relevant to our son-in-law's death?' Mr Davidson snapped.

'I don't know, which is why I'd like more information, if that's OK.' It wasn't a question and Mr Davidson knew it. Carla saw his cheek twitch, the slight squint of the left eye. He took his time in replying, but when he did his voice was steady.

'Growing up, Rachel was a very normal child. She did everything other kids did and we had no concerns about her at all.'

'Not even with homework,' Mrs Davidson interrupted. 'She always did it on time without being chided.'

Her husband nodded his agreement. 'But then things started to change, around the time she was seventeen, and we grew concerned. Just little things, the music she liked, the friends she chose. We became worried she was starting to stray from the word of God, something which is very important to our family, and so we decided to conduct an intervention.'

Carla watched as Mrs Davidson began to rub the cross around her neck.

'We asked a couple we know who lived in the village,' Mr Davidson went on. 'And they agreed to encourage Rachel to spend more time with their son, Simon, who is, was,' he corrected, 'a lovely reliable and stable person.'

Bremer remained silent, so Mr Davidson continued, 'We set them up and Rachel seemed resistant. She refused to see him or leave the house if he was waiting for her.'

'He waited for her?' Bremer interrupted. 'Even when she'd said she didn't want to see him?'

'Well yes, I mean it wasn't going to be easy, was it, so we asked him to be patient. Gave him the odd quid here and there – his parents had very little, you see; they lived in one of the affordable homes provided by the council – and he agreed to stay outside the house to try to catch her when she left.'

Carla tried to imagine how she would have felt at seventeen, stuck up in her bedroom, being stalked by a boy being paid by her parents – claustrophobic, fearful, frustrated, angry, she imagined.

Mr Davidson continued. 'When she still refused to leave her room, we told her she couldn't have dinner unless she came downstairs. When she still refused, we included lunch too. It was all done to help her. All she had to do was comply, like the good girl she'd always been before.'

Carla glanced at Bremer. What the hell kind of parents starved their child in order to make her go out with a boy?

'Did you ever assault Rachel physically,' Bremer asked, 'to make her "comply"?'

Mr Davidson crossed his legs. 'I reprimanded her according to the behaviour she presented to us and that afforded to us by the scriptures. "Withhold not correction from the child: for if thou beatest him with the rod, he shall not die. Thou shalt beat him with the rod, and shalt deliver his soul from hell."'

'So, yes,' Bremer said.

Mr Davidson didn't answer.

'And it was at this point that Rachel went to the police?'

Carla wondered how she could have done that, being locked in a room and probably too weak to walk, but Mr Davidson replied, 'No, that was later. I was trying to help you understand the character of my daughter and how duplicitous she could be.'

Carla saw Bremer frown. 'So this wasn't what prompted Alice to go to the police?'

Carla could hear the incredulity in Bremer's voice.

Mr Davidson nodded. 'The time concerned was while she was at university. She'd brought her friend, Ash, home with her, the summer of her third year, and asked for our help in curing him of his homosexuality. His family were close to disowning him and he wanted to be saved. We did what we could and Rachel was happy to support him by going through the process with him. It helped her to have a reminder of the path of God.' Mr Davidson leant forward. 'You see the Bible tells us we all have sinned and fall short of the glory of God, but it is very clear that those who persist in sin will be judged the harshest.' Mr Davidson spoke to Bremer as if delivering a sermon. 'Hebrews 10:26, 27. "For if we practise sin wilfully after having received the accurate knowledge of the truth, there is no longer any sacrifice for sins left, but there is a certain fearful expectation of judgement and a burning indignation that is going to consume those in opposition."'

'But after agreeing to help Ash, Rachel decided to end the . . .' Bremer paused. 'The "process"? Why did she just not tell you she wanted to stop?'

Mr Davidson let out a sharp laugh. 'Well, if it ended when one wanted it to rather than when God intended it to, the process wouldn't be successful, now would it?'

'OK.' Bremer's tone was level, thoughtful almost. 'So, Rachel escapes, makes the allegations and then you get called to the police station?'

Mr Davidson nodded.

'But there is no record of that. Do you know why that might be?'

'It was a small village with a small village police station. The inspector knew us and knew how absurd her claims were. We brought Rachel's friend in, Ash, to support our case. He'd come to us a few months previously asking for help. He was from a very religious family, you see, and they recognised homosexuality as the sin it is, so he wanted us to help him.

'So we helped him and he came to the police station to offer us his support by way of thanks. The officer made sure Rachel came home with us and assured us nothing further would be said about it. Life would just return to normal. And it did.'

Not for Rachel, Carla thought. Life didn't look as if it went on the way she'd intended it to at all.

'Let's go back a bit,' Bremer said. 'You'd worn Rachel down to such an extent she agreed to date Simon, which ended up with her marrying him.'

Carla watched Mrs Davidson nod. She didn't even want to think about the ways in which they might have worn Rachel down.

'Rachel goes to visit Simon at university and becomes friends with his friends. Do you remember who they were?'

'Yes, Hannah – lovely girl, she was always very nice to Rachel.'

'Did you pay her to do that?'

Mr Davidson looked cross. 'No, of course not.'

'And who else was she friends with?'

'That boy, Ash, and Simon, obviously.'

'Small group,' Bremer noted. Mr Davidson nodded.

'Any friends at her own university?'

'No. She was quite content to be with Simon.'

'Did you prevent her from making friends? Were you worried, for instance, she might revert back to her previous behaviour if she was left alone?'

'No. She had come to her senses by then, but we ensured Simon was there to support her. And of course, the church in Liverpool was very supportive of her.'

Carla thought the half a million donation might have helped with that. God, the poor woman, they'd got every base covered.

'Did you pay Simon to date Rachel?' Bremer asked.

Mr Davidson sighed. 'He was living in an expensive city, which he wouldn't have been able to do if we hadn't helped him. We were supporting our potential son-in-law, which is what any parent would do. We weren't bribing him to marry our daughter, if that's what you are implying.'

That's exactly what he's implying, Carla thought, and that's because you did. She suddenly felt overwhelmingly sorry for Rachel. She bet they carried on paying him too; she made a mental note to check his finances when they got back to the office.

'Let's go back to Ash, shall we?

Mrs Davidson leant forward, cheeks flushed. 'Oh, he was marvellous. He came to us about his problem, about the thoughts he was having that he knew were wrong. He loved his parents so much, you see, and he knew how devastated they would be if they ever found out he wasn't normal.' She seemed to say this both to express pride in his devotion to his parents as much as to highlight Rachel's lack of it.

'We told him how we'd helped Rachel and said if he could commit to staying with us for one week, we would be able to convert him. He agreed and, with no problem at all, he left seven days later, a full man.' She said this with such joy, Carla almost leant over and slapped her. She didn't even want to imagine what they'd done to him in that week.

'And the best part was we could always show Rachel the proof that what we had done not only worked, but made a difference to another person's life. I mean, what a glorious thing.'

Carla wondered how Rachel felt about Ash for being that beacon of her parents, an ever-present reminder to prove she could never escape them. Carla started to get a sense of unease. If Rachel was the one behind the reunion, and she'd killed Simon, would she now go after Ash? They needed to get back to the office, start putting all the pieces together until they could see the full picture. She looked to Bremer, who clearly thought the same, and gave her a brief nod.

'OK, well, thank you both for your time, you've been very helpful.' He stood. 'One last thing. Did Rachel ever find out about the payments you made to Simon? Or was that your little secret?'

Mr Davidson stood and Hilary joined him, her hands clasped in front of her.

'No, we never felt the need to tell her; it was for her own good and Simon didn't want us to. He loved her, you see, so he thought it might make her doubt him.'

Doubt him or want to murder him. Probably both. It was pretty clear Rachel had the motive and probably the means to kill him. Now all they needed to do was work out why she wanted Alice dead too. It was the only flaw in Carla's theory, because if Rachel loved Alice – and Carla was increasingly of the opinion she did – what made her want to kill her? Unless she hadn't. In which case her whole theory was going to be wrong.

Forty

Nell and Paul were halfway down George Street before Nell realised. 'Shit, we have got a picture of Rachel and Hannah.' She pulled out her mobile phone and clicked on Facebook. 'See?' She held it up to Paul, The Reunion Facebook page glowing on the screen. 'There's a picture of them right there.'

Paul looked back towards the Old Fire Station. 'If we run, we might catch her, otherwise there's no telling where she'll be.'

Nell was staring at the screen. She zoomed in on the picture which had been newly uploaded. 'Oh my God, Paul, look.' She gave him the phone and watched his face as the realisation of what he was looking at dawned.

'What the hell?' He looked over at her as she took back the phone and dialled Bremer.

'God only knows, he looks alive, yes?' she asked him as

Bremer's phone went to answerphone. She hung up and dialled again.

'Yeah, looks like it, but hard to be sure.'

'I'm going to work on the assumption he is, shit.' Nell hung up, cutting off the recorded message, and stared down at the picture of Ash tied to a chair, a look of fear in his eyes as he sat, staring across at whoever was holding the camera.

It took Nell longer than she would have liked to get to the station, a combination of rush-hour traffic and what seemed like fifty temporary traffic lights, ensuring their journey was painfully slow. All the while she was ringing Bremer, but each call just went to voicemail.

'What the hell is he doing?' Nell said as she unclicked her seatbelt before Paul had even stopped the car in the back yard. 'If he's out somewhere with Carla again I really think I'm going to lose my shit.'

Paul kept quiet as they climbed the stairs to the office.

'I mean, seriously,' she said as she pushed open the door, 'we are midway through a murder inquiry and the DCI is nowhere to be found. How can that be right?'

Nell threw her bag on the desk, flicked on her computer, before realising Laura was sitting in the corner by the wipe board. 'What are you doing here? I thought you were with Rachel?'

Laura walked over to her desk. 'She wanted me to pop back to her house and grab a couple of things, so I dropped her off at her parents and came here to get a spare radio battery.' She obviously clocked Nell's look of concern because she added, 'Quite frankly, Nell, from what I've seen of the Davidsons, Rachel is safer there than in a police cell. They're a pair of pit-bulls.'

Nell had to hope Laura was correct, because right now they had more important things to worry about. 'You know anything about Facebook?'

'In what way?'

Nell showed Laura the photo of Ash, tied to a chair. 'How to find where he is, that IP stuff, know anything about that?'

'Well, I do actually. Although you're not going to like what I'm going to tell you.'

'Why?'

Laura handed the phone back. 'We had a stalking case in my first couple of weeks. No one was interested because, you know, a woman getting terrorised by an ex-boyfriend was boring, right? So I took it on myself to try to locate him. He'd gone to ground, you see, hiding so he could continue to taunt her, which he mainly did via social media, Facebook to be exact. Anyway, I took the account to a tech guy I knew, not in the job but a friend, and asked him to trace where he was posting the pictures from. I hoped if I could prove he was a credible threat, everyone would have to act to help her.'

'But you couldn't.'

'Nope. Facebook pictures have all metadata removed.' She obviously clocked the blank expression on Nell's face because she explained: 'Photos have data attached to them. Information such as when it was taken, by what phone, where it was at the time, that sort of thing. It's called metadata.'

'But Facebook take that off?'

'Yep. They strip it all away.'

'OK, so what about the IP stuff?' Nell asked.

Laura gave a short laugh. 'Well, Facebook will have that, but good luck trying to prise it out of them. And anyway, IP addresses are overrated. I mean I could go into a coffee shop, use their Wi-Fi to post something, walk down the street and connect to a hotspot to post something, and then post again when I'm using my home Wi-Fi. It's difficult to pin someone down using it and it's certainly not the golden goose everyone thinks it is.'

Nell sat on the chair next to Laura and looked at the picture of Ash. He looked terrified. She zoomed in on his eyes and stared at them, unable to let go. 'Well how the hell do we find him then?' She said it more to herself than to Laura or Paul, so barely noticed when neither replied. What sort of messed-up shit was going on with this reunion? First a woman kills herself, next a man is murdered, and now another one of them was tied to a chair. She looked at Paul.

'OK. The only person left on the reunion list is Hannah, isn't it?'

Paul nodded. 'Yeah, if we don't include Rachel.'

'She wasn't on the list so she doesn't count. Let's bring Hannah in. Either for safety or as a suspect, I don't care.' She gave Bremer's phone one last try.

'Bremer, Nell. When you get this, ring me urgently.' Then, shoving it back in her bag, she threw the car keys to Paul.

Merilyn Davies

Catching them he said, 'Maybe when she sees Ash she'll think a bit harder about who might want to be doing this to them all.'

'I wouldn't bet on it. She's seen a woman she knows kill herself in front of her and a man she knows murdered. Whatever secret she's keeping is obviously a big one.' As they reached the door she turned to Laura. 'Go back to the Davidsons' and speak with Rachel—'

'But they don't want me there. I can't make them let me in,' Laura interrupted.

'I don't care. Find a way. Ask her about Ash. How well she knew him, would she consider him a friend, when she last saw him. That kind of thing, and let me know what she says.'

Laura looked less than hopeful. 'Will do.'

'But don't tell her about the picture, not yet.' Nell grabbed a pen and dragged a piece of paper from the printer tray. She scribbled 'research known addresses for Ash' and put it on the table. 'And stick this to Carla's computer,' she said, pointing to the page. 'Hopefully between Hannah and Carla we can get some idea of where Ash is likely to be.'

Forty-one

Carla listened to Nell's message to Bremer as soon as she got in the car. Hanging up, she googled 'The Reunion Facebook page' and stared at the picture of Ash that appeared on the screen.

'Let me see,' Bremer glanced over as she held it out to him. 'Jesus.' He looked back at the narrow village road. 'Ring Nell, tell her to bring Hannah in, mostly for her own protection, and make sure Laura is with Rachel so we know where she is. I want the chance to see what Hannah has to say before we bring Rachel in.' He was gripping the steering wheel, jaw clenched. 'But if Laura has any indication Rachel's a flight risk, I want her arrested.'

As Bremer put the car in reverse, Carla rang Nell. 'We've got your message.'

'Jesus, where are you, have you seen the picture?' Nell sounded out of breath.

'We've been with the Davidsons and yes, we've just seen it. Bremer wants you to bring Hannah in.'

'Already on it, we're almost at her address now.'

Carla relayed this to Bremer. 'And make Laura stick to Rachel like glue.'

'What?' Nell sounded concerned. 'Laura told me she'd dropped her off at the Davidsons' an hour ago? Isn't she there?'

Shit. Carla put her hand on Bremer's arm. 'No, she wasn't at the Davidsons'. So we don't know where Rachel is now?'

Bremer stopped the car and took Carla's phone. 'Nell, get Laura to Rachel's home address and if she's not there, get her to call me.' Hanging up, he put the car into reverse and spun it back into the Davidsons' drive.

The Davidsons responded to Bremer's banging on the door in much the same way they had the first time, but Bremer was having none of it. 'Rachel, where is she?'

Mr Davidson frowned. 'She's with one of your policewomen.'

'No, she isn't. I want to see her room.'

Mr Davidson stood aside as Mrs Davidson pointed to the stairs. 'It the one at the far end on the left.' She glanced at Carla. 'What's happening? Where is our daughter?'

Carla thought Bremer taking the stairs two at a time suggested no one knew the answer to that. 'It's fine, we just need to locate her.' She put a reassuring hand on the woman's arm before going after Bremer.

Rachel's room was small, containing only a single bed, a night-stand and a short stubby wardrobe which, Carla saw, was empty.

Bremer stood next to it, back to her. 'There's nothing. She's taken all her clothes.' He turned round to face her. 'How the hell did she get in and out again without us noticing?'

Carla looked around the sparse room. 'Probably the same way she got out all those years ago.'

Bremer walked over to the bed. 'Did you find any addresses for Ash when you originally researched him?'

'Only his home address.'

'And Rachel?'

'Just this one and her house on Woodstock Road.'

'If she's got him somewhere, it won't be at home, not with the possibility of Laura being there.' He looked at her. 'I need you to find me another address.'

Carla nodded. 'Get me to the office and I will.'

Back at her desk, Carla searched for any known addresses linked to either Ash or Rachel but drew a blank. Picking up the phone she dialled the Financial Unit.

'Hi, Carla here. I need an urgent check on a Hannah Barclay.' She gave her date of birth and home address. 'She's about to be interviewed, so can an urgent check be sent please?' If Hannah had been paid by Rachel's parents and denied it during the interview, those bank details were going to be crucial. But it still didn't get her an address for where Ash might be.

Nell popped her head around the door. 'I'm about to interview Hannah. Will you sit in the video suite, I want you to listen in, see if she says anything which could give you a lead.'

'Sure,' she said, grabbing her notebook.

Squeezing in beside Bremer, Carla looked at the screen.

Hannah was sitting, arms folded, plastic cup of coffee untouched in front of her. Nell seated across from her, Paul to her left.

'Hannah, we've shown you the pictures of Ash from a Facebook account set up by a person or persons unknown, used for the sole purpose of targeting you and three of your friends,' Nell was saying.

'Two,' Hannah corrected.

'Sorry?'

'Alice wasn't our friend. She had no involvement in our group.'

Carla saw Nell's knee start to jog. This wasn't going to end well if Hannah didn't start playing ball.

'You mentioned the word "group". And yet you assert you don't know who set up this group on Facebook or who invited you to the reunion?'

'No, why would I?'

Nell studied her for a second before folding her arms. 'Well, you yourself said it was a small friendship group, so I would have thought you might have an idea which of you set up the reunion?'

Hannah smiled. 'We are as much in the dark as you, detective.'

Nell returned the smile. 'Except "you" aren't, are "you"? Simon is dead, Alice is dead, and now Ash is missing and probably likely to end up dead. So that just leaves you as our main suspect, or, as our next victim.'

Carla expected Hannah to show – what? – panic, fear, a

realisation that what she was hiding wasn't worth it. But all she saw was Hannah's unwavering gaze at Nell.

They were at a stand-off. Hannah refusing to back down, Nell refusing to give her the space to. Carla was about to turn to Bremer, to get him to intervene, when Hannah said, 'I think she wanted to kill Simon and set this whole thing up as some elaborate framing exercise.'

Nell took her time. 'Who has framed who?'

'Well, as I'm the only one currently not dead or kidnapped, I'd say that was obvious, wouldn't you?' Hannah snapped.

Carla saw Nell tense. Paul must have seen it too, because he stepped in.

'Are you suggesting Rachel killed Simon and is trying to frame you?'

'I am, yes.'

'OK . . .' The doubt in Paul's voice was clear. 'And why would she do this?'

'Because she hates me, hated Simon for working with her parents to force her to marry him and for refusing to give her a divorce when she wanted one.'

'How do you know she asked him for a divorce?'

Hannah looked at him with utter contempt. 'Because he told me.'

Nell nodded, clearly giving Hannah time to settle, before she said, 'Was Simon being paid to stay with her?' The shock on Hannah's face was immediate.

'What?'

'Did Simon stay with Rachel because he was being paid?'

Hannah looked shocked, then angry. 'That's absurd.'

'Did you help Simon put a complaint to Oxford Brookes University, about Alice, because you were being paid by Rachel's parents?'

Hannah didn't reply.

'Well, your bank account details will tell us that.' Nell shrugged.

'My bank details?'

'Yes. And Simon's.'

Hannah opened her mouth to speak but Nell held up her hand.

'You see, we think Simon wasn't the only one being paid to ensure Rachel stayed in a straight relationship.'

Hannah visibly paled, her folded arms tightening across her chest.

'Do you know anything about the conversion therapy Rachel underwent at the behest of her parents?'

Hannah's jaw clenched tight shut.

'Strikes me that their willingness to take such extreme measures means they are pretty committed to ensuring Rachel isn't a lesbian, and so it also strikes me they would want to secure the results of their actions into the future. And what better way than to pay someone to help keep an eye on her. Monitor her movements, make sure she didn't' – Nell paused – 'waver from the path they'd forced her down. Now, a husband can only watch his wife so far, so it's probable they needed an extra set of eyes. Were they yours?'

Hannah had been watching Nell intently as she spoke, her face a mixture of doubt, shock and fear. But Carla couldn't tell if the latter was because Nell's words weren't true or because the realisation was dawning she was in a shed-load more trouble than she'd thought.

'I have not been paid to spy on Rachel. If Simon had, that's a matter for you to prove. And maybe that's why this is all happening.' She became suddenly animated. 'Rachel found out he was being paid and killed him in anger, then staged the whole reunion to cover her tracks.'

'The reunion invites were sent weeks before Simon's death,' Nell pointed out.

'OK then, maybe not in anger; maybe she planned it all meticulously.' She was gesturing now, leaning close to the table, eyes flitting between them all.

'She gets everyone together to witness Alice's death, then kills Simon, so confusing you all into thinking his death was linked to our time at Oxford Brookes when it wasn't at all, it was just her way to kill him because she found out about her parents.'

Nell sat back. 'But how would she have convinced Alice to kill herself when her girlfriend is pretty adamant they were happy together?'

Hannah snorted her disdain. 'What, Luci? I'd be surprised if she stayed sober long enough to remember Alice's name.'

Carla leant forward, looked between Nell and Paul on the screen, but neither seemed to have noticed the significance of what Hannah had just said – no one had mentioned the name Luci.

'And where does Ash fit into all this?' Nell asked.

'What?'

'Well, if Rachel killed Simon, and somehow persuaded Alice to kill herself' – Nell's tone told them what she thought of that idea – 'why has Rachel now taken Ash? For what purpose? There is no ransom demand, no threatening message associated with the image, so why has she done it?'

Hannah threw her hands in the air. 'How should I know? If it's part of a plan then how can I guess what she's going to do next?'

'Did you know Ash also underwent the same conversion therapy as Rachel?'

Hannah laughed. 'Really? This is England, not America. Do you believe everything you're told? And if Ash underwent this conversion therapy, why did he get married to a man called Eric?'

Carla looked at Nell, who reacted to the information with indifference, and, instead, pointed at Hannah's coffee.

'That looks cold. I'll get you a new one. I'm sure we could all use a little break.'

In the viewing room, Carla stood, 'I need to speak to Nell,' she explained to Bremer, 'back in a minute.'

She found Nell standing, back to the wall, staring at the ceiling. On seeing Carla she said, 'Man, I've never wanted to punch anyone more.'

'Wasn't at all obvious, honestly.'

Nell rolled her head round to Carla, then went back to staring at the ceiling. 'Poker face has never been my strong point.'

'You know when you mentioned Alice's girlfriend and she said Luci would be too out of it to remember her name?'

Nell turned her head towards her. 'Yeah?'

'Well, how did she know her name? We haven't told her, right? So if we didn't tell her, how does Hannah know who Alice's girlfriend is?'

Nell stared at her for what felt like a full minute before pushing herself off the wall. 'You're right. How does Hannah know Alice's girlfriend is called Luci, unless she knew of her prior to Alice's murder, in which case it means she'd had contact with Alice prior to her death!'

'Or,' Carla said, 'it means Hannah had contact with Luci that didn't go through Alice.'

Nell looked uncertain. 'You're saying we need to look into Hannah knowing Luci?'

Carla held up her hands. 'I'm not saying anything, other than we've never mentioned Luci's name to Hannah before.'

Nell looked towards the interview room. 'How long will it take you to research a link between Hannah and Luci?'

'An hour, tops.'

Nell looked back at her. 'One hour.'

Carla nodded. Nell looked back down the corridor. 'OK, do it.'

Forty-two

It took a moment for Ash's eyes to become accustomed to the dark and another for him to realise his hands were tied tightly behind his back. He was in a room, the low ceiling above chipped brick walls made him think it was a cellar. It was empty save for the chair he sat on, piles of rubble dotted the edges of the floor; windowless, a dark wooden door to his left was pulled tight shut. He began to panic. Tape was across his mouth, his nose began to sting, but the harder he tried the harder it felt to find air. All he could think about was the lack of breath, of needing to fill his lungs. Desperately he began to pull at the ties around his wrists, sharp pains shooting to his shoulders, air seeming to be further away, the darkness of the room, the smell of damp and dust, until the blackness overwhelmed him completely.

*

Coming round, he felt a hand on his arm. Jerking back he saw a woman crouched by the edge of his chair, holding out a glass of water. He tried to focus on her but, without his glasses, all he could see was a blurred outline of a slim woman with dark hair. The tape from his mouth had gone and he sucked in air, the relief of it filling his lungs, momentarily dulling his fear. It was only when she spoke that he realised who it was.

'You need to drink,' she said, tipping the glass to his mouth until water ran down his chin. Only when she'd stopped could he speak.

'Rachel?'

The figure reached forward and Ash flinched, before his glasses were placed on the bridge of his nose, and Rachel came into view.

'Hello, Ash.' She was dressed in a white shirt and oversized trousers, boots he'd seen earlier still on her feet, hair piled high on her head. It took a moment for him to filter through all the words he wanted to say.

'Rachel, what the hell is going on?'

Rachel held up both hands. 'I know this will all seem extreme, but I need your help.'

Ash stared at her. 'My help?' He scanned her face for signs she was having some sort of mental health episode, anything to give him an indication of the seriousness of his position, how reasonable she was going to be; but all he saw was the Rachel he knew, staring back at him, the faintest smile on her lips.

Rachel rocked back off her haunches and sat cross-legged in

front of him. Picking up a narrow piece of wood, she began to trace shapes out of dust from the concrete floor. 'Do you remember that night, when I managed to get out of the house, and made it to the police?'

Ash was studying her face for signs of anger, anything to pre-warn him of what she might do next. 'Yes.'

She nodded, studying the floor. 'Do you remember how we spent hours every night, lying there on the floorboards, hungry and scared, planning how one of us was going to make it out and bring the police back for the other one?'

He looked at her, arms aching, feet numb. 'Yes. You were sup-posed to bring them to the house and we would go together to the station and tell them what they were doing to us.'

Rachel nodded. 'Because we knew it had to be both of us or we would never be believed.' She looked up at him. 'And what did you do, Ash?'

He tried to swallow but his mouth was too dry. 'Your parents were right next to me, Rachel, staring at me, that copper inspector of theirs next to them. I just couldn't say the words.' He knew it was pointless trying to explain. He'd helped her escape, then betrayed her at the last moment, her one hope of finally getting her parents revealed as the danger they were gone.

Rachel leant towards him. 'Ash. I can't go back to that house, you know that. With Simon dead, that's what's going to happen, unless you help me.'

Ash stared at her. 'Why not just ask, why all this?' He nodded to the room. 'You know I'll always help you.'

'Well, that's the thing isn't it, Ash? I don't know you'll always help me because when I needed you to most, you failed.' She gestured around the room. 'I just needed to remind you of why you had to help me, of what you took from me that day you refused to tell the police what you knew. I wanted to scare you, to make you feel just one bit of what I felt the day you turned your back on me, so that I could make sure this time you'd help me.' She paused for a moment before continuing. 'My whole life, Ash, to be spent with a man who didn't love me, who I hated; all because you were too scared to speak up.' Rachel stood. 'I thought that was my one chance, my only chance to have the life I wanted, but I was wrong. This is my chance, right now, to get a life I want, and you're going to make sure this time I get it.'

Forty-three

Nell caught up with Laura in the stairwell. 'What you doing here? You're supposed to be at Rachel's.'

'She's not there and she's been declining my calls, so I came back to see what you wanted me to do now.'

Nell stared at her. 'And you didn't think to ring me? To tell me you hadn't made contact with her. She could be anywhere.'

Laura shuffled uncomfortably on the stairs. 'Well, I thought you'd been in with Hannah and didn't want to bother you.'

Christ, served her right for trusting in a probationer. 'Get back there now and tell me if she's still not there. Immediately, OK?'

'In my defence, you didn't say she was a suspect. Has that changed? I was under the impression I was just babysitting.' Laura sounded annoyed but Nell didn't have time to reassure her, she was getting a headache, desperately needed nicotine, and puppy-sitting a new recruit was the last thing she needed.

'As of now, consider her a person of interest. We've got a man missing, potentially kidnapped, and no idea where he is. From now on I want to know where she is and what she's doing, got it?'

Laura nodded. 'Got it.'

Nell got back to the office. 'Rachel is still AWOL and Laura didn't bother to tell me. Christ, she could have been with Ash for all we know. Forget about Hannah and Luci, is there any way you can see if Rachel's made any calls which might give us an idea of where she is? Have you got up-to-date call data you could check?'

'No, I've got it up until this morning but nothing since. I'll put in an urgent request now.' She hesitated.

Nell walked over to her desk. 'What?'

'Well, you know Rachel was staying with her parents the night of the reunion?'

Nell pulled a chair over and sat next to Carla. 'Yes.'

'OK. I got a fresh phone bill in, I was scanning them to check for a link between Hannah and Luci, but I found this.' She pointed to the screen. 'Turns out Rachel called her parents about three hours after Simon's suspected time of death. And they spoke for ten minutes and forty-five seconds.'

Nell didn't get it. 'Why would she ring them if she was there at the house?'

Carla's inbox pinged. 'Exactly. Hold on, it's the financial data.'

Nell waited while Carla trawled row upon row of data – highlighting the odd row here and there – until she turned around, face serious.

'The data here' – she pointed to the screen – 'shows financial transactions made and received by Hannah.' She pointed to a row midway down the page. 'And here, Hannah received the sum of £35,000, from a Mr and Mrs Davidson. Two weeks before the death of Alice and Simon.'

Nell leant back on the chair. 'My God.'

Carla looked back at the screen. 'I'd say we now have proof Rachel's parents were paying Hannah a significant sum and that she accepted it.'

'And is it just one-off, or are there more over a period of time?'

'A one-off for now, but I haven't checked past data. For now, all I can say for sure is that Rachel's parents have potentially lied to us about two things: one, Rachel's whereabouts on the night Alice died, and two, payments made to Hannah.'

Nell leant forward, rested her hands on her thighs. 'What about Ash? Have we got anything to link her parents to him, either payments or phone calls?'

Carla looked up at her. 'You think they've got something to do with his disappearance?'

'Don't you?'

It was plain from her face she hadn't considered it. 'But that would mean they have access to the Facebook page, wouldn't it?' she said. 'In order to post the photo.' Carla frowned. 'Do you think Rachel and her parents are working together? I mean, it could make sense. If Rachel is so brainwashed by them, she would do anything they told her, wouldn't she?'

Nell nodded. 'She would. But what are they telling her to do, and why kill Simon now, if at all? The way they saw it, he was their insurance policy against Rachel going to hell.' Nell pointed to the screen. 'I need you to find me some form of contact between Ash and Mr and Mrs Davidson so we can seize their laptop. There's got to be something on it, but we're going to need as much as we can if a magistrate is going to sign it off.' Nell turned to Paul and threw him her wallet. 'Can you get some coffee from Budgens down the road? I can't face any more canteen crap.'

He pulled his jacket from the back of the chair, retrieving the wallet from the desk. 'Sure, Carla, want anything?'

Carla, staring at the screen, held up her hand. 'Might want to grab that on the way to Mr and Mrs Davidson's.'

She wheeled the chair round and pointed to a highlighted row on the call data spreadsheet. 'A call from Ash's mobile to Rachel's parents' landline, time 17:08, date' – she looked at Nell – 'yesterday.'

Nell leant over the screen. 'How long was the call?'

'Just under thirty seconds.'

You couldn't discuss much in thirty seconds, but that didn't matter, this gave them cause to search the computer and any other records they might have at the house. 'Good job,' she said to Carla, pulling on her jacket and grabbing the car keys from the desk.

'I'll get hold of Bremer,' Carla was saying as Nell headed to the door. 'But I don't think we'll get an out-of-hours court sign-off within the hour.'

Nell paused. She was right; they'd be at the house with no way of entering, and that would give the Davidsons plenty of time to destroy any evidence.

'We could arrest them, seize the computer that way?' Paul said.

Nell shook her head. 'No, we'd be showing our hand too early.' And potentially shutting down an avenue that had only just opened up. No, she needed access to the house, the laptop, hard evidence, before they brought the Davidsons in. She turned to Paul. 'Let's go to the house. If the warrant doesn't arrive in time, we'll get creative.' The ends would justify the means. She just had to hope Bremer would agree.

Forty-four

I outline my plan to Ash. When I'm finished he just stares at me. He's free of the ropes now and we are sitting upstairs in the little cottage owned by my parents, a rental property that's been empty for months.

'I don't understand,' he says finally. 'You think Hannah organised the reunion and you know because Luci told you?'

'Yes.' I take a chip from the takeout box.

'But you said Luci hit you, that she chased you away when you went to find Alice.'

I lick salt from my fingers. 'I lied.'

'What?'

I look at him. 'I lied to you. She did hit me but that's because I told her to. I need there to be no link between me and Luci if the rest of the plan is to work, so I needed to make sure people saw her refuse to speak to me.'

Ash hasn't eaten a thing, he's in shock. I get it, but I don't have the time to go gentle on him. 'Ash, Hannah killed Alice, I know it, and now I'm going to prove it, and I'm going to prove it was my parents who paid her to do it.' I lean forward, arms on my thighs. 'Don't you see? If I can prove the link, they'll go to jail, and that's the only way I'm going to be free.'

'But what's Luci got to do with that?'

I smile. 'The less you know, the better. Let's just say she's helped me out and will be adequately rewarded. And I don't mean with a place in heaven,' I add.

He's looking at me as if I'm mad, and maybe I am a little. The world certainly feels more vibrant, more real, more possible now. And if that's what mad is, I'll take it. I stand. 'I'll be back in a couple of hours. Make sure you eat.'

Luci is sitting by the McDonald's next to Carfax Tower, seemingly asleep. I crouch down next to her and put my hand on her arm. 'Luci?'

She looks up at me and it takes her a second to remember who I am. 'Hey.'

'Are you OK?'

Luci doesn't seem drunk, more tired. The kind of tiredness that countless hours of sleep wouldn't solve. She pushes herself to sit upright, yanking the duvet from her legs. 'It's all done. Guy and me did it earlier.'

'And no one saw you?' My heart is pounding.

'No, thought they were going to catch us for a second but it was OK.' Luci eyes me cautiously. 'That Ash bloke went for it then?'

'Let's just say he owes me.' I look behind me, then down the street a little, before turning to Luci. 'Come on, let's get something in McDonald's. Last time we met, you punched me, remember? I don't want people seeing us talking as if nothing happened.'

Luci pushes herself off the pavement. 'Yeah, sorry about your face. Did it hurt?' she asks, gathering her belongings into a neat pile before following me into McDonald's.

'Yes, but worth every penny, Luci.'

Minutes later, and with our coffee, burger and chips, we go upstairs and take a seat by the window.

'So we can keep an eye out for Guy,' Luci explains.

I watch as she adds three sugars and get a flutter of nerves at what she'd said. 'I thought he was on board? We can't have him backing out now, Luci.'

She takes a bite of her burger and chews. 'Don't you think we both know that?' she says, mouth still full. I pull out my mobile.

'Luci, this all hinges on me being right about who killed Alice. If I show you a picture of her, will you see if you recognise her, honestly, and whether you'd seen her hanging around in the days leading up to Alice's death? If it's not her, I want you to tell me, OK?'

Luci nods, so I push my mobile phone across the table, a picture of Hannah from her Facebook account filling the screen.

'That's her,' Luci says.

'And you agree you think she had something to do with Alice's death?' I have to know how invested she is in this, if it means as much to Luci as it did to me. Luci puts her burger down.

'We taped her.'

I stare at her. 'What?'

'I knew that Hannah woman was saying shit to Alice. Every time she came back from seeing her, Alice would be all . . .' Luci searches for the right word. 'I don't know, vacant but also agitated, angry, distant.' She falls silent. 'Just, very emotional, and she wouldn't let me in.' She looks at me and the pain she'd felt at the sense of rejection and confusion was still there in her eyes.

'So anyway,' she continues, 'I made her promise to record their next meeting on her phone so I could work out what was going on. So I could prove to Alice the woman was messing with her head and that she needed to refuse to see her again.'

Clever, I thought, very clever. 'What did it say?' I ask. Luci stops chewing.

'I don't know. She met Hannah the evening they were going to that reunion at The Varsity Club, and I didn't see her again.'

'Hannah met Alice the night of the reunion?'

Luci nods. 'I assumed she'd recorded the meeting, so that's why Guy went to get Alice's stuff,' Luci went on, 'so we could get the recording and prove Hannah had been messing with Alice's head, but they wouldn't let him have it because the police needed it and I never got to hear what had been recorded.'

'The police have Alice's phone?' Maybe there was still the possibility Luci's recording plan could help them.

If I Fall

Luci picks up a chip and dips it in ketchup. 'Well, I assumed so, but when they came to speak to me they asked me if she had one, which means the mobile wasn't with her belongings or on her when she died.'

'So where is it?' They needed that phone; it was the final bit of proof that Hannah killed Alice.

It was a good question. A dead person's belongings would be the first thing the police would check. So if they didn't have Alice's phone, then where was it?

Luci holds the paper coffee mug between her hands, warming them. 'I'd never met anyone like Alice, you know?' She smiles. 'She just had this life inside her that shone out of her.' Luci gestured to the pavement outside. 'She just took it all in her stride, always tried to help people, and even though I knew she had this really deep sadness in her, she didn't let it win.' She takes a deep breath and exhales loudly. 'That's why I'll help you with Hannah. I don't need the money; I'll do it anyway.'

I think of the cash under my bed, what I could do with the part I've earmarked for Luci, but dismiss the thought. I need Luci to help me get Hannah, but I also need her to be silent, and taking that money makes her as complicit as I am in what's to come.

Forty-five

With Bremer briefed and on his way to meet the out-of-hours magistrate, Carla got to work on finding a link between Hannah and Luci.

Starting with Facebook, she searched both accounts for signs they were in contact but drew a blank, as did their phone bills and financial transactions. Frustrated, she took a sip of cold coffee. Maybe she'd got it wrong. Maybe they had mentioned Luci's name and that's why Hannah knew it? But even with all evidence to the contrary, she knew she wasn't wrong.

Her mobile rung. Baz. Her heart sank, braced for a fight about something else she'd done wrong, which was only a pretence for what she actually had done wrong; they both knew it, both pretended they didn't, both waiting for the other to be the brave one and end it.

She pressed answer. 'Hey.'

'Hey.'

A brief, awkward silence, something they'd become used to, before:

'So, when are you home?'

Carla looked at the clock. Shit. Seven thirty already. 'Not sure. Just got a few more checks to do. About nine?'

'No worries,' he said lightly, 'see you then.'

Blindsided, she hung up, staring at her phone until it went dark. She had a sudden stab of panic at the thought of him ending it, the idea of going back to an empty flat night after night, the solo trips to Sainsburys and lonely nights in Was that why people stayed together? The fear of being alone? Of having to unpick years of habits and redo them again into something new and unknown; always the fear it would be worse than the life you'd left behind.

Feeling despondent, Carla opened Google. Maybe if Facebook failed her, Twitter would come good; but five minutes later, sifting through username after username, she drew a blank. About to close it down, she saw a tweet from an account with a cute picture of a Staffie street dog looking like it was grinning up at the camera. There was something about it which made her click on it – memories of Luci's dog, Billy, maybe, with his brand-new harness and coat – and she started to scroll through picture after picture of homeless people's street dogs, taken by a charity in London, who, every week, visited homeless people and their dogs, providing them with veterinary support and essentials such as dog coats and food.

Carla tapped her pen on the table. Hannah was a vet in a relatively poor part of town; what if she'd connected with the charity and volunteered for them when they came to Oxford? And then she remembered Billy the dog growling around her feet, his brand-new dog coat bearing the name of the charity.

As she scrolled, she came across a post from a few months back, the cross of Bonn Square, in the centre of Oxford, visible in the distance. Carla clicked on it and read the thread. The team had begun outreach in Oxford a year ago, no doubt aware a rising homeless population here meant a similar rise in dogs, and they posted regular call-outs to local vets to volunteer a few hours of their time each month.

Carla leant back in her chair. What if Hannah had been one of the vets? Could that be how she'd come across Alice? If Hannah had volunteered, it made sense she would have come across Luci and Billy, and Alice would inevitably have been there too. It had to be the link. She needed more than that though, a definite link between Hannah and Luci, some proof to her growing theory that Hannah was the woman who'd come back into Alice's life and left her so upset.

Clicking on the charity's website, Carla retrieved her mobile from her bag and dialled the number on the screen. 'Hello? Yes, my name's Carla Brown and I'm calling from Thames Valley Police. I was wondering if I could ask you about a possible volunteer vet you work with?'

'We don't give out details of our volunteers,' the man's tone pretty much adding, 'and certainly not to the police,' at the end.

'I understand, but we're working on a murder investigation, so it would really help if you could just confirm a name for me? Obviously, I could always get a court order to requisition your files, but time is really of the essence as I'm sure you'll understand.' She waited as the man considered how difficult he wanted to be.

Bremer appeared at the door. She waved him over. Joining her at the desk, he held up the court order to seize the Davidsons' computer, then looked questioningly at the screen. Carla put her hand over the phone. 'Trying to get a link between Hannah and Luci, I think these guys might be it.'

The man on the phone cleared his throat. Decision obviously made. 'OK. I'll confirm the vet's name if I can, but that's it. I'm not confirming when they worked or where without some form of official request.'

'Great, thank you, I appreciate that.' They would need the times Hannah worked to be sure, but for now, just confirming she had been a volunteer was enough.

'The name is Hannah Barclay. And she would have worked on one of your Oxford runs.'

'Hold on.'

Carla heard the man call to someone across the office, pulling her notepad aside as Bremer went to sit on the edge of her desk.

'Hello? Yes, I can confirm Hannah Barclay has been a volunteer vet with us.'

'For the London runs as well or just Oxford?' She was pushing her luck but the man answered, 'I told you I wouldn't confirm times and places and, anyway, you said you only wanted information on the Oxford runs. I'd have to check if she worked the London runs too and for that I'll need an official request.'

Carla smiled. 'That's OK, thank you, the Oxford run is enough for now.' Hanging up, she pushed her chair round to face Bremer and explained about the connection. 'The man helpfully confirmed not only that she worked for them but also it was in Oxford. Luci has a street dog, Billy, and I saw him wearing one of their dog coats.'

Bremer looked sceptical.

'I know it's not enough yet, but it's a start. I'm going to check through Luci and Guy's Facebook. They obsessively post about the dog, so if they did take Billy they'll have put a picture up. And then I'm going to search all pictures from the charity to see if we can put Hannah in Oxford at the same time. I'm sure that's how she found Alice.'

'And where's Hannah now?'

'In an interview room. She's not being held, though, so I doubt she'll be there for long unless you charge her. But we now know she lied about taking money from Rachel's parents and we know she withheld information from us about knowing Luci, so—'

'That's not enough for an arrest,' Bremer interrupted. 'If Hannah's connection to Simon's case is only Alice, we've got nothing on her. Alice's death is still being treated as a suicide, and until we hear otherwise from the coroner my hands are tied. What we need to work out is how this' – he pointed to the screen – 'Hannah and the dog charity, connects Alice's death to Simon's.'

'Or to Ash,' Carla added. 'It's all one and the same, all links back to the reunion, and can it be a coincidence Hannah is the only one so far not affected by that? I mean, she's sitting alive and well over there' – she gestured behind her to the door – 'while Simon and Alice are dead, and Ash is missing.'

Bremer studied the screen. 'But it's still not enough to hold her. We need more, something concrete.' He looked down at her. 'Nothing on Ash's phone, no trace?'

'Nothing. It's either off or run out of battery, and last time it pinged a phone mast was in central Oxford, Turl Street, and that was hours before the picture was put up on line. It's like looking for a needle in a haystack, and unless I get something from the Davidsons' computer, I don't see where else I can go with it.' She nodded to the piece of paper resting on his knee. 'Speaking of which, don't you need to get that to Nell?'

'I took a photo and texted it to her, said if they didn't let her in I'd drive it over, but I'm pretty sure just seeing the words "magistrate's" and "warrant" will be enough.' He looked distracted. 'Our main focus for both Ash's disappearance and Simon's murder are Hannah, Rachel and potentially the Davidsons. Laura is with Rachel, right?'

'Yeah, Nell said she'd gone over to her home address.'

'And Hannah is in the interview room, and Nell is over at the Davidsons', so who's left?'

Carla didn't understand what he meant. Seeing her expression, he clarified, 'There is no one left, or certainly no one we are aware of, which means wherever Ash is, he's alone. But at some point, whoever is holding him is going to have to go and check on him, take him food.'

Carla got where he was going. 'And we can follow them when they do?'

'Precisely.' Bremer stood and walked over to the wall where pictures of their suspects hung. Hands behind his back, he contemplated them. 'It takes eight cars to mount a surveillance team. With four suspects that's thirty-two cars and that's impossible. Not enough manpower and certainly not enough money to mount that level of operation.'

Carla joined him at the wall. 'We need to narrow it down, focus on one of them, use the surveillance team for our best option.'

Bremer looked between the photos. 'Agreed. That has to be our next step. We can't have Ash out there much longer and I don't see we have many more options left open to us.'

Carla agreed. He turned to her. 'We wait to see what Nell gets from the Davidsons, you dig a bit more on Hannah, although' – he looked at the clock – 'I don't want you here for longer than an hour. It's been a long day and I want you fresh for tomorrow.' He turned back to the wall. 'And then we'll wait to see if Laura gets anything from Rachel, and make our decision which subject to get behind in the morning.'

Forty-six

Mr Davidson opened the door to Paul and Nell dressed in his nightwear and with a look of shocked incomprehension on his face. Nell held out the picture of the warrant on her mobile phone.

'You're too late. They've already been,' he snapped, without looking at it. Nell glanced at Paul, frowning.

'Sorry, who has been?' she asked.

'Your lot. We heard a noise in the back garden and called 999.'

Nell nodded to Paul to check round the back.

'They didn't find anything,' Mr Davidson shouted after him.

'DC Hare will go and take a look anyway, just in case.' It was probably a fox. Even if it was a burglar, Paul's size tens knocking round the garden would soon see them off if uniforms hadn't already.

Mrs Davidson appeared behind her husband, dressing gown

clutched to her chest. Nell held up her mobile phone. 'Mr and Mrs Davidson, we have obtained a warrant from the magistrates which allows us to retrieve electronic communications from your house in relation to the murder of Simon Morris.'

The couple didn't move.

'I don't understand,' Mr Davidson said, after a moment. 'Are you suggesting we are involved in Simon's death?'

'We just need to check your laptops or computers. It's purely routine, nothing for you to worry about.' Nell wondered if anyone ever bought that line. It was clear the Davidsons didn't. 'If you could take us to these devices, that would be a great help, sir.'

Mr Davidson looked at his wife. 'Go to the kitchen. Pour us a whisky each and I'll be in when this lot have gone. And make sure you lock the back door,' he called after her.

Nell followed him up the stairs, across a wide but darkened landing, to an office at the rear of the house.

'You'll find everything in there,' he said, his tone now not even bothering to hide his disdain. Nell threw him the brightest smile she could and began to unplug two laptops and a standalone computer.

'Thank you, we'll be out of here in no time. Oh,' she said, as he was about to leave, 'can we get your Facebook log-in details, passwords to files, any other social media you might use?'

Mr Davidson looked disgusted. 'We don't use Facebook. It perpetuates sin.'

Nell smiled. 'Oh right, yes, sorry, that had slipped my mind. Must be with all the homosexual sin I'm struggling with.' She shouldn't have said it, but the man had it coming. How dare he be so arrogant as to judge who she was, what sexual orientation she'd been born with? And why were men like him so obsessed with sex anyway? It was just plain creepy.

He stared at her as she went back to bagging the equipment, standing by the door, watching her, so it was a relief to be by the front door ten minutes later.

Paul came jogging back from the garden.

'Anything?' she asked.

He shook his head. 'I only had my phone torch but I'm pretty sure it's clear.'

'I'm telling you, there was someone there,' Mr Davidson snapped, pointing through the house to the back door. 'It was a few hours ago, just after your DCI left.'

'Did you see anyone?' Nell asked, handing Paul a laptop and bag.

'No but we heard them, didn't we, Hilary?'

Hilary was hovering in the background by the kitchen, clutching two half-filled whisky glasses. She nodded.

'Well, make sure you have all the windows and doors locked, OK? And call 999 again if you hear anything,' she added. Mr Davidson looked at her as if she was stupid. She smiled again and nodded to the laptop in her arms. 'We'll have this back to you when our investigations are complete.'

'I don't know what you're hoping to find on there. We use it for accounting, emails and that's it.'

'Well, a quick check of the search history will prove that,' Nell replied. Mr Davidson's expression didn't alter and, after giving her a quick look up and down, he slammed the door in their faces.

Paul nodded over his shoulder as they walked to the car. 'You've got a right fan there.'

'A pair who like to get their own way,' she said.

'Yeah. Sometimes it feels good to make them see who's really in charge, and that certainly felt good.' Paul grinned.

He was right, it didn't hurt to remind people that the police had the power. A warning shot. Not that she thought they'd heed it.

With the equipment booked in, Nell left Paul chatting to a young blonde DC, whose smile up at him suggested to Nell it wasn't the first time they'd met, and headed out to the car. Her mobile buzzed in her pocket.

'DS Jackson speaking.'

'Nell, it's Laura. I'm with Rachel now and she's asking to see you.'

Nell beeped open the car door. 'Did she say why?'

'No, she looks pretty upset though.'

'Did she say where she'd been?' Nell asked, slamming the car door and turning on the engine.

'No, she says she'll only speak to you.'

Great. That was all she needed. 'I'll be right over.' And though she knew she shouldn't, Nell couldn't help but feel pleased at the idea of seeing Rachel again.

*

Laura opened the front door and pointed to the front room. 'She's in her usual place.'

Nell nodded. 'Why don't you get off, I'll take it from here.'

Laura looked uncertain. 'You sure?'

'Yeah, it's been a long day. Go and relax and I'll text you where to be in the morning.'

Seeing Laura off, Nell walked to the front room. The fire was out and the room was lit by a single lamp on the table next to Rachel. A bottle of wine under it, two glasses by its side. Nell glanced at them. She was not going to have wine. The woman was a suspect in the murder of her husband, for God's sake, so even if she did find her attractive, which she didn't, you just didn't go around sharing wine with suspects. She'd be pleasant, maybe have a cup of tea and then leave. Job done. Easy.

Rachel smiled. 'Thanks for coming.' She unfolded herself from the chair and picked up a glass, pouring wine until it was half full. She held it out to Nell. 'Please join me.'

Nell shook her head to explain she couldn't as Rachel shoved it into her hand.

'I won't tell anyone, I promise, just one glass to make me feel better,' she said before turning back to the sofa, silk dressing gown billowing behind her, the briefest glimpse of her bare leg.

Nell sat on the other end of the sofa and sipped at the wine. God it was good. Definitely not a five-pound bottle from the Co-op like she was used to. She took two more mouthfuls and enjoyed the brief hit from the alcohol, slight dizziness, day's events falling away if only for a few seconds.

'Any developments on the case?' Rachel asked, dark brown, almost black eyes, gazing at Nell, her lips edged red from wine.

None that she was going to tell her about, Nell thought. 'A few leads but nothing concrete yet.' Nell kept her eyes low, tried to ignore the curve of Rachel's shoulder, the smooth line of her collar bone.

'What about Ash? Laura implied something had happened to him.'

Nell was going to kill Laura in the morning. She hadn't wanted Rachel to know about Ash until she was clearer on how it fitted into Simon's murder investigation, until she could determine if Rachel was involved somehow or not. And after all, Rachel may be a person of interest, but she was still Simon's wife, and they owed her a duty of care because of it. 'In the absence of evidence to locate him, all we can do is keep trying. We're doing all we can, I assure you.' Nell took a swig of wine and hoped the computer would give them something before he turned up dead on the Facebook page. She didn't like the idea of not working through the night to find him, but they'd be more use after at least a bit of sleep. Another good reason not to be drinking wine.

'Did you know Ash well?' she asked.

Rachel shook her head. She tucked her legs under her, gown falling apart slightly, to show the beginning of her thigh. Nell quickly looked away, aware she risked her eyes wandering further up Rachel's leg if she didn't.

'He was more Simon's friend than mine,' Rachel said. 'I

hadn't seen him in years, not really since university. Oh, and of course, our wedding,' she added, glancing at the picture on the mantelpiece where the invitation to the reunion had once sat, but was now bagged up in some forensic lab to be tested for DNA.

'He was a nice man,' she continued, smiling across at Nell, head slightly lowered.

'Is,' Nell corrected.

Rachel blushed. 'God, yes, of course. I didn't mean I thought he was dead.' Her hand rose to her hair, patting it nervously. Interesting slip-up, although Nell hoped it didn't mean he was. Maybe it just indicated how little contact they'd had since Simon and Rachel's wedding. Carla hadn't found any contact between Rachel and Ash, so it was a fair presumption to make. Nell took a sip of wine. Maybe they'd been wrong to think Rachel was involved. Her parents could be acting on their own, but then where had Rachel been these last couple of hours?

'He was married a few years ago, I think. To a man.' She looked at Nell, face serious. 'After all those years pretending not to be gay, he just one day popped up with an invite to a wedding to someone called Eric, and that was that. No apology for lying to us for all those years, no explanation for how he could have got away with pretending, or for how he made us feel when we thought he'd been gay during university but then told us he wasn't.' She seemed increasingly angry and then, as if realising it, she smoothed down her dressing gown and reached over to top up her wine. 'Sorry. It just felt like a betrayal. I'm not sure why.'

Nell knew why – it had been a betrayal, of sorts. 'How did it make you feel,' she asked, 'when you thought he was gay, but then wasn't?'

Rachel considered the question for a moment. 'I felt alone. Trapped. But mostly, I felt invisible again.'

'And Ash being gay had made you feel visible?'

'Yes, like I was seen for once, like I had someone on my side.'

Nell nodded. 'Did Alice make you feel like that?'

Rachel looked so sad at the mention of Alice, it made Nell's heart actually ache. She couldn't imagine hiding her sexuality all her life, how it would feel to be told you were evil, to have people trying to beat or pray or starve it out of you. How does someone come out the other side of that? Maybe they never do.

'Yes, she did. I used to watch her across the cafeteria, laughing at what someone had said, walking across the quad with a pile of books in her arms, or reading on a bench.' Rachel laughed. 'She had this frown she made when she was totally immersed in a book.'

Nell smiled. But there was something odd about the way Nell spoke about Alice. She couldn't put her finger on it, but it unsettled her. She needed to get out of there, note down all Rachel's comments, and clear her head.

'Would you like some more?' Rachel had risen, standing over Nell, wine bottle in hand.

'Oh no, thanks, I have to get going, early start.' Nell stood. Catching Rachel's eye, she leant to put her wine glass down. And then before Nell could stop her, Rachel had leant over and kissed her.

Forty-seven

Carla opened the front door with the same sense of dread she'd had for weeks; memories of Baz's bags packed by the entrance, the sniping and undermining that had gone on since his return, sitting like a dead weight where the love had been.

She heard music – soft, light – coming from the front room. Slinging her bag by the hall table, keys on top, she walked to the door and stared around the room. Every bookshelf, coffee table, windowsill had a candle dousing the room with a warm orange glow. The table next to the window was covered in flowers, and three dishes sat in the middle, filling the room with the smell of curry.

'Baz?'

He popped his head out of their small kitchen, apron around

his waist, grin on his face. 'Thought we'd do curry night with a difference.'

He walked over and she took the wine he offered, leaning into his kiss, but only briefly.

'Wow,' she said, stepping back a little. 'This is a surprise.'

His brow furrowed. 'A good one?'

Her heart flipped with guilt at not being more effusive. She stepped forward to give him a kiss, lingering this time, just like they used to. 'It's lovely. Thank you.'

Relief on his face, he guided her towards the table, pulling out a chair. She laughed. 'Since when have you ever done that?!'

Baz knelt down beside her, holding her eyes in his, 'Since I want to make things better, OK?'

She scanned his face: earnest, hopeful, pleading. 'OK,' she said, and tried to feel something, anything, which would make that statement true.

The meal was as good as it smelt; they laughed about the jobs Baz had come back from which had ended up worthy of a scene from *Only Fools and Horses*, Carla giving a brief outline of the job she was working on; it was like the old times. When they'd finished, they sat on the sofa, Carla's legs curled round him, his hands on her thigh, and poured more wine.

'See,' he said, handing her a glass. 'It can be good.'

She felt tears and took a swig of the wine. Oh, the times she'd heard that after a brief spell of being happy. Because there were good spells – hours, days, but never weeks – but they always ended in the slow descent back to how things were – fewer kisses, heavier silences, nights spent later at work even when you didn't have to. Saying it reminded her this would only be the start of another time when hope gave way to resignation, then to sadness and pain – the briefest of respites until it all began again.

'What's the matter?' He brushed at her cheek, as if seeing the tears falling before they did. She didn't reply. He leant in, kissed her neck, her hand, her lips. 'Let's go to bed.'

And she wanted to scream; scream he shouldn't have to suggest it, it should just happen, that by asking he was acknowledging it never did any more, and therefore the reasons why. It was as good as a cup of cold water being thrown over them, why couldn't he see that?

Her phone rang. Relief flooded her with such force it took her aback.

'Don't,' he said as she reached for her mobile, but Nell's name was flashing. She pointed to it.

'I have to.'

'Seriously?' He pulled away and stared at her, furious, disbelieving.

'I'm sorry.'

But he turned his back on her, picked up his wine, and stood. Fighting the feeling of obligation she felt to call him back, she pressed accept. 'Nell?'

'Carla? Shit, man, I need you to come over, can you?' She sounded drunk, words blurring over each other, but the panic was evident.

'What's happened?'

'I can't tell you over the phone, just come over, please?'

Carla glanced at the kitchen, Baz's back to her. Shit. 'OK, I'll call a taxi, won't be long.' Hanging up, she held the phone in her lap. Baz's back was still to her, shoulders tense; he downed his glass of wine and reached for another bottle.

'I'm sorry,' she said.

Baz turned to face her. 'You know most men wouldn't have come back, after what you did. Month after month pretending you were as disappointed about not being pregnant as I was. I'm trying, Carla, I'm really trying here, but it's like you won't even help me make an effort, like you don't even want me to try to make things right when really it's you who should be trying, not me.' He finished speaking and poured another glass of wine, taking a deep swig. Carla watched him, a feeling of familiarity so vivid she could almost touch it, the pain of it was what kept her there – unable to let him go, unable to want him to stay.

She stood. 'It was a lovely meal, and I'm so sorry, but Nell needs me.'

Baz glared at her, anger, humiliation on his face. 'I bloody need you.'

What could she say? Choosing the coward's way out she took her phone, picked up her bag and went outside to call a taxi.

By the time Carla got to the three-storey town house in Jericho, Nell was chain-smoking and drunk.

'What the hell happened?' Carla asked, following a barely upright Nell downstairs to the kitchen which spanned the length of the house. The garden doors were open onto a small courtyard garden; despite the chill, Carla was glad that some shred of air was fighting the ceiling of cigarette smoke.

Nell sat down on a battered velvet sofa and put her glass of wine on the dark grey rug by her feet, spilling a little which was absorbed before Carla could move for a towel. Kneeling down in front of her, she repeated the question.

'What happened, Nell?'

Nell shook her head and reached for the packet of cigarettes next to her. 'I've been a total dick, that's what. I told myself to not have the wine and now if we get anything on her she'll bring it up in court and the case will be thrown out.'

'I don't understand. What wine? And which "she"?'

Nell looked at her and shivered. 'I'm cold.'

Carla looked at the back doors but couldn't bear to shut out the air. Instead, she turned and began building a fire in the log burner opposite them. Crouched on the rug, methodically piling logs upon kindling, she tried to work out what Nell meant. She'd been with the Davidsons, hadn't she? Had they given her and Paul wine? But there was no way they'd have accepted that, so who the hell did she mean?

With the fire lit she turned back to Nell, who was now smoking while cupping the glass of wine in her hands. Carla fetched a glass and filled it with red wine from one of two bottles open by the sink. Sitting back down on the rug, she took one of Nell's cigarettes and lit it. 'Come on, you're not making any sense. Explain.'

The fire began to spit and hum. She watched the light of the flames flicker over Nell's face as it began to warm her back. Then she listened as Nell explained.

'Shit. She kissed you?' Carla said, when she'd finished. 'What the hell did you do?'

'What do you think I did? I got the hell out of there.'

'Did she say anything?'

'She followed me to the door, apologising again and again.'

'Did she threaten to tell Bremer? Or report you?'

Nell shook her head and took a mouthful of wine. 'But now she's been on her own all night and Hannah's in a cell when I should have gone back to interview her and I've just royally fucked up, Carla.'

Hannah was fine, Rachel was probably panicking about kissing Nell, so all Carla wanted to know right then was how much of a mess this kiss could become.

'Did she say anything about the case before she kissed you?'

Nell frowned, clearly trying to focus. 'Like what?'

'I don't know. Where she thought Ash might be? Who she thought was behind it?'

Nell didn't reply.

'Nell? What?'

'She was really angry about Ash coming out as gay. I think she's got Ash somewhere and she's doing it to punish him for betraying her and allowing her parents to think their conversion crap works. I think she murdered Simon and somehow messed with Alice's mind enough to make her kill herself and I think

I've just buggered up any chance we've had of convicting her for all that.' She gave a hiccup which could have been a sob and lit another cigarette.

As drunken theories went, Carla had to admit that was a good one. But if Bremer could get the funding for surveillance, that theory might form the basis of who they chose to follow. She just had to hope Rachel wouldn't do anything to Ash in the meantime.

Carla stood and sat down next to Nell. She pulled the rug from the back of the sofa and pulled it over them, then stared at the fire, watching the way it danced and fought with itself, letting herself enjoy the feel of heat on her cheeks.

Truth was, she didn't have a clue if what Nell had done would ruin the case, because she wasn't a police officer. She didn't really get involved in liaising with the CPS about charging and trials, she just provided her evidence to them when they did. So Nell might be right, or she might be hanging drunk and exaggerating. One thing was certain, they wouldn't achieve anything by obsessing over it all night. Nell needed to stop drinking and get to bed. They could sort it in the morning.

After a brief skirmish, Carla managed to get Nell as far up as the sofa in the second-floor living room, before depositing her there for the night; glass of water and a bowl on the floor, two blankets tucked over her in the hope she wouldn't fall off. Then Carla walked back down to the fire, sat cross-legged in front of it and took out her phone. She opened up The Reunion Facebook page and stared at the picture of Ash. No updates. No comments or notes added. Just the same scared man looking out at her. What was he doing now? Was he warm, cold, scared, hungry?

As she leant her head back on the sofa, sleepy, Carla thought about Nell's conviction that Rachel was the one behind it all. Carla wasn't so sure. It was the parents she was interested in, although she certainly didn't rule Rachel out. Anyone who had the balls to try to get a police officer drunk and kiss her – midway through an investigation into your own husband's murder – was someone worth being on a suspect list.

She started to feel her head go heavy with impending sleep. It was the parents, Hannah or Rachel; Carla was just going to have to make sure she got something from the Davidsons' computer in the morning to prove which theory was right.

Forty-eight

I put on jeans and a large black jumper, before grabbing my coat and car keys. As I drive to Ash, I think of Nell's kiss, the way she'd smelt of cigarettes, tasted of wine. She was the first woman I have ever kissed, and it felt like I'd always imagined kissing Alice would be – like coming home, a return to where I should be, should always have been. As I park the car in the small alley, I feel a surge of something – power, hope – and I know everything is going to be OK, I am going to be fine.

Ash is lying on the sofa curled up under his coat. The room is freezing, not helped by the light snow which has begun to fall outside. I pull a pair of threadbare curtains across the window, a pointless attempt to shut out the cold, and consider the fireplace. Could we risk a fire? God only knows how Ash had managed to keep going in this temperature.

I sit down next to him, laying the back of my hand against his cheek, feeling guilt when I note the icy cold of it. 'Ash?'

He wakes with a start, trying to push himself upright but, seeing it's me, relaxes back down. 'Where have you been?'

I explain about seeing Luci, having to placate Laura. I omit to mention Nell. 'Have you been OK?'

'No, Rachel, I've been freezing, and why the hell did you lock me in?'

I want to say, 'For the very reason you knew it was locked, because I knew you'd try to get out,' but instead I say, 'You hungry?'

Ten minutes later we are eating chips from paper bags on our laps. It had been a risk, but the taste of salt and vinegar on my lips made it worth it. I pick up two more chips, suddenly hungry.

'What now?' Ash asks. 'Eric is going to go to the police if I don't get back soon. If he hasn't already, that is.'

I lean back against the tiny sofa, springs digging into my thighs. 'You can go when you've finished your chips.'

Ash looks up, surprised. 'And how will I get there? You want me to go to the Witney police station, yes? But we're in Chipping Norton, and that's fifteen miles away.'

I lick the salt from my fingers. 'I'll drop you a little way away from the police station. You'll say you hitchhiked there but can't remember the make of car and didn't get a name from the driver.'

Ash looks suddenly worried. 'Do you think they're going to believe me? What if they start asking me loads of questions?'

'Like what? You've just been kidnapped and tied to a chair for hours, they have proof – the picture.' I haven't told him about the injury he'll have to sustain to make that part realistic. 'We'll go down and make the room look like you escaped, just in case they do find this place, and you just need to play the distressed victim.'

He is staring at me in panic. 'I thought you said they wouldn't find this place?'

He is beginning annoy me. 'They won't, but better to cover all bases.'

Ash bundles the chip paper into a ball. 'I'll put this in the bin outside and then we can get going. The sooner this is over, the better.'

I watch him pull the door open and duck outside before pulling the kitchen knife from my bag. I'll have to make sure I don't hit a vein or it could all go very wrong.

I wait for Ash to come back and think of Nell. Maybe, when this is all over, we could go on a date. I'd never been on one of those and, now Simon was dead, I could do anything I wanted; I could date as many women as I wanted as soon as I got my parents out of the way. I try to imagine sitting in a restaurant, holding hands across the table, a kiss in the doorway as we go to leave. That would be nice.

Ash pushes the door open, blowing in his hands. 'Cold out there,' he stops, and looks at me, then at the knife. 'What's that for?'

I stand. 'We need to make it realistic, Ash, just a little injury to make it look like you struggled to escape.'

He doesn't move. 'That wasn't part of the plan.'

I smile. 'It is now.'

Forty-nine

It took Nell a moment to work out where she was and then about two more to remember why. She rolled over, picked up the glass of water and downed it in one before regretting it as her stomach churned.

'Coffee?' Carla was leaning against the door, cup in hand, looking annoyingly fresh.

Nell sat up, holding the arm of the sofa as the room spun. 'Ugh.' She took the coffee and moved the blankets for Carla to sit.

'How you feeling?'

Nell hoped her look told her what she thought of that question.

'I meant about Rachel.'

Images of Rachel leaning over to kiss her, her gown falling

open, the silky smell of her perfume. 'Oh God, I'm going to throw up.'

Carla held the bowl, and Nell's hair, as Nell retched into it. When she'd finished, Nell leant back against the cushions and tried to breathe without gagging. 'What am I going to tell Bremer?'

'Nothing.'

Nell stared at her. Was she mad? She'd kissed a subject in a murder case, for God's sake. 'How can I not?'

'There's no point. Our focus needs to be finding Ash and Simon's murderer. So what if she kissed you? It's going to look bad on her, trying to bribe an officer with sexual favours.' She gave a supportive smile.

Nell considered Carla. It actually made sense. This did look worse for Rachel than her. She took a sip of the coffee, then another after her stomach accepted the first, until she'd finished the cup. 'OK, so what now?'

Carla stood. 'You need a shower and then we are going to check out the computer and find Ash.'

Nell nodded, then clutched her head.

'And I'll make you a takeout coffee for the ride in,' Carla added.

Lugging the computer up the stairs, Nell kicked open the office door, deposited it on Carla's desk and threw her notebook down next to it. 'Passwords are in there.'

Carla plugged it in and flipped open the notebook. 'Deliverance?' She looked at Nell.

'Seems about right to me. Religion seems to be the theme of Simon's murder, after all. Mutilation, religious messages.' Nell shivered, her hangover oscillating between raging heat and cold sweats.

Carla was looking at her in thoughtful amusement. 'Did they seem that way, though? When I met them they seemed, well, normal.'

'What's normal, Carla?' She took out a cigarette but, finding she couldn't face it, rolled it round in her fingers instead. 'I would have thought nine years here would've told you whatever people look like on the surface can hide a multitude of sins. To use a religious analogy.'

Carla went back to the computer, starting it up to reveal a picture of Simon and Rachel on their wedding day. She raised her eyes at Nell before going back to the screen. 'Give me five, OK?'

Nell went to her desk and scrolled through the messages on her phone. Two from her sister and four from Rachel, each one increasingly hysterical at Nell's exit last night. She shoved the mobile in her desk drawer and shut her eyes. What a fuck-up.

'Nell.' The tone in Carla's voice made her eyes snap open.

'What?'

'He's here, Ash. The picture is on their hard drive.' Carla looked like she could barely believe it and Nell didn't blame her. She'd thought it was a long shot, putting the parents in the frame; seemed like they might have been right after all.

'Can you trace it?'

Carla shook her head. 'I don't know, I've not done much work on this kind of thing.'

'I can,' Laura said, from the door. Carla and Nell turned to look at her as she walked over to the desk and took a seat next to the screen. 'As long as you don't mind,' she added to Carla, who shook her head.

'Not at all.'

Laura took the mouse. 'Remember that stalking case I mentioned, the one where we couldn't trace the photos he was posting on Facebook because of the metadata? Well, we got hold of his laptop and traced the evidence from there. See' – she pointed to the screen – 'each picture has a property, like a little stamp saying when it was taken, by what device and, crucially to this case, where it was taken.'

Nell stared at the screen as Laura opened up the picture properties box and there it was: Apple iPhone, date, the day Ash disappeared. 'But the location is blank?' she said.

Laura grinned. 'That's where Apple comes into its own. Look . . .' She clicked on a places album in the picture folder. Ash appeared, superimposed over a map of England.

Nell couldn't believe it. 'So can we scroll in and find a more specific location?'

'No need.' Laura double-clicked on Ash's picture. It popped up in an album of its own titled 'Chipping Norton'. Laura pointed to it. 'That's your location, Chippy.'

Nell peered closer. 'But nothing more? Nothing exact.'

Carla took the mouse from Laura. 'No, but that's narrowed it down enough.' Nell watched as Carla brought up the parents' phone bills. Entering the dialling code for Chipping Norton, she pressed search. One result showed up on the screen and it wasn't their own, which meant there was another address in Chipping Norton connected to them. Nell grabbed a pen and scribbled it down then picked up the phone. 'DS Jackson here, Thames Valley Police. I need the address registered to a landline.' She read out the number, tapping the pen on her thigh, before taking down the address as it was read to her.

'And the bill payer?'

Andrew Johns. The name wasn't familiar, but she handed the piece of paper to Carla. 'Check it for cars, people associated with it, risk-assess the hell out of it and check out who this Andrew is. I'm going to ring Bremer.'

Leaving Carla to do the research, she went into Bremer's office, took three paracetamol and rang him. 'We've got a possible location for Ash. Carla's bottoming it out but I want Paul and me down there ASAP, with backup if possible.'

'Hold on, let's not get ahead of ourselves.' From the sound of it he was on his hands-free. 'I'm three minutes away, give Carla time to get us as fully armed as possible, then we can decide on resources.'

Nell tapped the pen on her thigh, faster now. She could also hear him thinking, 'we don't want a repeat of what happened last time', and she got it: the last time they'd done a house entry, Nell had ended up in hospital for two weeks – and while the stab wounds had healed, panic attacks remained, like scar tissue on her brain.

'Wait till I get there, Nell,' he said, his voice making it clear it was a warning.

With Bremer and Paul in, they all gathered round Carla's desk as she told them what she'd found on the property and the Andrew Johns who owned it. Which was basically nothing. 'I can't find anything on Andrew at all, other than being registered as the account holder for the phone and the listing to the address in Chipping Norton: no vehicle, no council tax, nothing.'

Nell wound a cigarette through her fingers. 'A made-up name then? Parents are using it to hide their tracks, for tax maybe, and are now using it to hold Ash?'

'Maybe,' Carla replied, 'or maybe he was a previous last tenant who didn't cancel the account. I can check that out, but for our purposes all we need to know is the house is listed as for rent through a local letting agency, and when I checked with the council tax for current occupiers, it's listed as empty. There is no Andrew living there, no cars registered to it, and no one has registered an account with utility companies.'

'Perfect place to take someone then.' Bremer looked to Nell. 'I'll get you a uniform unit as backup.' Then, looking back to Carla, 'Anything to suggest a threat to officer safety?'

Carla shook her head. 'Nothing on the intel database, no. And I double-checked,' she added. Nell grabbed her car keys. Obviously everyone was jittery, they'd missed a firearm last time and they all knew how that had turned out, but while she was glad Carla was being cautious, it was also in the forefront of her mind that caution wasn't going to find Ash.

Bremer put his hand on her arm. 'Make sure you wear your vest, and take a taser with you; use it if you need to.'

She started to move away but he stopped her. 'Nell?'

'Got it,' she snapped. 'I'll book one out now.' He didn't need to tell her to be careful, it'd taken eight months after leaving hospital for the panic attacks to ease, but it didn't help being reminded of them now. She got their concern, she appreciated it, but she didn't want to think of the bone-crushing fear she'd felt when the air left her lungs, when all she could think of was how she was going to die but desperately didn't want to, just before they were about to do a forced entry.

She felt her chest constrict at the memory, aware of Bremer studying her, heart pelting stones at her ribs.

'If you can't do it, Paul will, OK?'

'I can do it,' she said, with the last bit of air in her lungs. She put her hand on the desk and took deep breaths, anger at herself only lessened by her concentration on getting back control.

Bremer put his hand on her back. 'Nell, I don't think you're ready for this. I have a duty of care to you and I'm—'

'I'm ready,' she interrupted, standing upright and pulling her jacket from the back of her chair. 'I'll let you know as soon as we are in the address.' And ignoring the fact Bremer was about to speak, she nodded to Paul, picked up her stab vest and left.

Fifty

Carla could tell Bremer was unsettled, rolling up his sleeves, he was staring at the floor with a distracted intensity.

'She'll be fine. She hasn't had a panic attack for weeks now.'

Bremer glanced over at her. 'Yes, but she hasn't had to do a forced entry for weeks either, has she?' He took the chair next to her. 'You really think she'll be OK?'

Carla nodded. 'I do.' It wasn't a lie; she knew Nell could fight any fears that came her way and, besides, the hangover would be a distraction. 'She said she'd let us know when they're there, so we need to be ready to bring the parents in when they do.'

Bremer seemed to relax, back on sure ground, focusing on where the investigation needed to go now. 'The picture isn't enough,' he said. 'I want to prove the Davidsons are behind this whole thing: the reunion invites, Alice's suicide, Simon's murder, and we'll need more than a picture on their computer for the CPS to take it on. I'm not sure Ash being at an address owned by them would swing it, because any defence could throw doubt on that – someone broke in as they knew it was empty, that kind of thing – so I want to hear Hannah's explanation for why she lied about taking money from the parents and what that money was for. The more things we can get leading back to the Davidsons, the more chance we stand.'

'You think Hannah's working with them?' Carla asked.

'With them or for them. It's not like she doesn't have form for happily stabbing her friend in the back at their request, so it wouldn't be that much of a jump for her to go that extra mile and help set this whole thing up.'

Carla wasn't so sure. 'But murdering Simon? That took force, and to be able to just walk away and speak with the police as if it never happened? I mean, that takes some doing.'

'It does, but we haven't put that to her yet, have we? The minute we do she may fall apart.' He stood. 'And in the absence of a murder weapon, we're going to need a confession. Get me as much as you can from there' – he pointed to the screen – 'linking Hannah to the parents and both to the reunion and we'll bring the Davidsons in.'

After he'd closed his office door, Carla opened up the Facebook account on the computer; it was already logged onto The Reunion page. She smiled; the CPS were going to love her. A picture might not be enough, but it proved their involvement without a doubt.

She checked to make sure they had administrative rights on The Reunion page and was about to call Bremer to tell him they had, when she noticed another administrator was listed; alongside Mr Davidson was Hannah. My God, Bremer was right. The woman wasn't just being paid by Rachel's parents, she was actively supporting them. But why? Surely it couldn't just be for money. Hannah was a vet, for God's sake.

Carla clicked back to the spreadsheet of Hannah's finances. She'd been so preoccupied with finding a deposit linked to Rachel's parents, she'd missed the most glaring thing of the whole data – Hannah was drowning in debt to the tune of £36,700 and that was after the parents' payment and before Carla had checked for loans, credit cards or Hannah's business account. Certainly it went a long way to explain why she was willing to throw years of professional training down the drain.

Making notes on her iPad as she went along, Carla went back to the Davidsons' computer and began to search their files. The usual ones appeared: Passwords, Car, Utilities, Insurance, but two stood out – 'Payments' and 'Will'.

Opening the first, 'Payments', she scanned the Excel spreadsheet and found row upon row of payments to Simon and Hannah. Each one was dated and spanned the last two years. But while the amount paid to Simon was the same each month, the payments to Hannah changed: some months there was none, but during some months £1,000 was paid into her account, and during another they deposited between £500 and £600. Why the variations? she wondered.

She checked back through the dates but the file ended midway through 2018. She pressed print. Bremer would want to be able to refer to it when he questioned Hannah about each payment and Carla hoped she'd be there to hear the explanation.

As the printer kicked in, Carla closed down the file and opened up the folder titled 'Will'. There were only two benefi-ciaries, Rachel and Simon, but it was the stipulations which made her call for Bremer.

'What you got?' He pulled Nell's chair over and sat down.

'The Davidsons have put some pretty wild conditions in their will, but the most surprising thing is they don't leave the bulk of their substantial fortune to their daughter, but rather to Simon, their son-in-law.'

'How much are we talking?'

'Well over two hundred million.'

'Two hundred million? Jesus. No wonder he stayed with her. I presume the thirty-five a year was just pocket money then.' He leant closer to the screen. 'What if Rachel divorces him, surely she gets the money?'

'Nope. Simon does. Well, it's written in legal speak, but from what I can make out, he gets it if she files for divorce but not if he does.'

'So if he files for divorce, she gets the money?'

'Yes, same if Simon dies. But, she has to never marry or be in a relationship with another woman and they've appointed a kind of board of trustees to check that she doesn't. In the event she doesn't remain straight, the money goes to the church in Liverpool.'

Bremer leant back. 'That's pretty messed up. I mean, who is so obsessed with what kind of sex their child is having that they even write it into their will? And appoint a body to police it?'

Carla had thought about that while she read it and could only offer one conclusion. 'Because they love her so much.'

Bremer looked incredulous. 'Seriously?'

'Yes. Look, these people, rightly or wrongly, believe homosexuality to be the ultimate sin, right? And the only reason a sin matters is because it stops you getting into heaven for all eternity. They want her with them in heaven. Simple as that.'

Bremer looked doubtful. 'I'm not seeing heaven as their first port of call somehow, are you?'

'You know what I mean. If her parents get to heaven, they will have to spend all of eternity while their beloved child is down in hell because of who she chose to sleep with. What greater torture could there be than that? So they try to guarantee her place alongside them by paying all the money they have to ensure she remains pure and free of sin.'

Bremer didn't speak. She couldn't tell if he was digesting her words or trying to think of where to start contradicting her.

'I think we've got enough to bring them in, regardless of what Nell finds in Chippy. Print that off for me.' He pointed to the will as his mobile rang. He reached into his pocket. 'And print off all the research you did on the crackpot church. I want to be fully armed when I speak to them.' He pressed the mobile's screen. 'Bremer speaking.'

Carla opened up Google but turned back when he said, 'To

clarify, Ash Desai has just presented himself to your police station?' He nodded at the reply. 'Get him checked out by the doctor and then, if he's fit enough, put him in an interview room, I'll be right there.' Hanging up, he looked at Carla. 'Ash is at Witney police station.'

'What? How?'

'I don't know. He presented there half an hour ago and asked to speak to me.'

'He asked to speak specifically to you?'

'Looks like it. They said he seems shocked but unhurt. Come on.' He disappeared into his office before appearing again, coat in hand. 'Let's go and get him. And ring Nell, let her know she doesn't have to do the forced entry. Tell her to stand down immediately.'

Fifty-one

The address in Chipping Norton was down a narrow alley. Nell manoeuvred the car into a spot so tight she wasn't sure she'd get out again, as two police cars made the wiser choice, parking at the top by the main street. A light dusting of snow covered the road and pavement, the odd flake still falling as Nell strapped on her protective vest.

'You OK?' Paul asked as he did the same.

'Sure.' She double-checked the fastenings then checked again, ignoring her heart underneath, trying to break out. *You're being ridiculous*, she told herself, *it's just another house entry like you've done dozens of times before. There is no one inside with a gun ready to shoot you, no man brandishing a knife, Carla has checked.* But then analysts had been wrong before; she'd got the scars to prove it. She noticed her hands were shaking as the officers joined them – all five wearing officer safety equipment, one carrying a battering ram. She saw Paul looking at her hands and shoved them in her jacket pockets.

'You gain entry, we'll follow, secure each room. We're looking for this man.' She held up a picture of Ash, taken from his driver's licence. 'He may be disorientated, so go slow, don't panic him.' She saw the officers share a look – don't tell a grandma how to suck eggs – but she didn't care. It was her job, she was in charge, and if anything went wrong it was on her head not theirs, so she'd make damn sure the operation was as tight as it could be.

She gave the officer holding the battering ram a nod. 'Go ahead.' Standing back she looked over the house, which was in complete darkness, and tried to convince herself that was a good sign, that it meant Ash was in there alone.

It took three attempts to gain entry but, once they had, Nell's hope they'd find Ash diminished with each empty room. They secured each area then regrouped by the front door.

'Where's Paul?'

'Securing the basement.'

His silence gave her no hope Ash was down there. Shit. Was it the wrong address or had Ash been moved? She looked at the exposed beams, the worn wooden floor, stone walls, the general state of disrepair and lack of furniture. She didn't think forensics would thank her for calling them out to find something amongst that mess. But then the picture had been taken here, so there must be something left behind, something to link it to Ash?

Thanking the officers, she closed the door behind them and

went to find Paul. Treading carefully on the well-worn steps down to the basement, she found him crouched by a chair standing in the middle of a long, low-ceilinged room which spanned the length of the house.

'Got anything?'

Paul didn't look up. His phone's torch directed to the chair's legs. 'Not sure. But look, seems like fibres of rope, tiny bits of material anyway, maybe used to tie him with? I've checked the picture on Facebook and the chair seems to match, as does the background.'

Nell crouched next to him, examining the tiny brown worms of material. 'You think he was cut free?'

'Maybe.'

'Looks like they used rope Not very sophisticated . . .'

He looked over to her. 'But effective and easy to come by.'

Nell pictured the Davidsons' outhouse and garage. They'd need to secure that, go over it, see if they could match this rope to theirs.

'I'll ring forensics and Bremer.' She stood, head suddenly spinning as her hangover kicked back in.

'Don't envy them getting fingerprints from this.' He waved round the room. 'They couldn't have chosen a better spot.'

Walking up the lane in order to get a phone signal, Nell dialled Bremer. He was right. But then everyone knew about crime scenes these days; didn't take a genius to know a basement as dirty as a building site would be hard to examine.

Bremer's phone went to answerphone. She dialled Carla.

'Nell, we've been trying to ring you. Ash has presented himself at Witney station. We're on the way there now.'

Nell could hear the beep of her phone as each answerphone message they'd left started to load. 'What? What the hell is he doing there? Did they find him?'

'Not 100 per cent certain yet. It appears he just turned up.'

'Has he said where he's been, who had him?'

'Not that I'm aware of. Hold on, I'm putting you on speaker . . .'

Nell waited as Carla fixed her phone to the hands-free set before Bremer came on the line. 'Did you force entry?'

'Yes, all secure.'

'Anything?'

'Not sure. I'm calling out forensics and I'd like to search the Davidsons' place for rope.'

'Rope?'

'Yeah, some potential evidence here which may prove a link.' She knew she didn't sound hopeful and that was because she wasn't. They were in an empty house, looking for a hostage who had turned up miles away, and every suspect looking no more convincing than the last. But it was more than that; she had this increasing sense she was being played – like she was being left crumbs of evidence to find.

'What if this is all a game?' she said. 'And we're part of this whole reunion thing, with them making us jump through hoops, while directing the case all along so it's just out of our reach?' It was possible, after all. One of the only things they knew about the case was it was linked to Alice and Simon's time at Oxford

Brookes. Whether it was payback from the complaint he'd made against her or not was still up for grabs, but it was payback for something, so what had the police done back then to warrant revenge?

Bremer's voice sounded distant. 'That would take some doing, Nell, to plan a suicide and a murder as well as using it as a way to beat the police. Let's wait to see what we get from Ash. Meet back at the station at four.' He hung up.

Nell shoved the phone into her pocket and took out her cigarettes.

'You don't really think this is all part of a game, do you?' Paul asked.

Did she? Bremer was right, it would take some doing, but she still couldn't shake the feeling she was being led in a certain direction when she should be going in another.

'Come on,' she said, 'I need a fag. And a coffee. Let's get out of here and leave it to forensics to see if they can make sense of it all,' because right now, hangover or not, Nell felt further away from finding Simon's killer than she had standing over his dead body two days ago, which irritated and frustrated her in equal measure. She didn't like being outfoxed and, if it was Rachel's parents behind all this, she was damned if she was going to be outfoxed by a couple of homophobes. 'Let's pop in on the Davidsons on the way back. Just a little peek in their garage, should they not object.'

Paul followed her up the basement steps. 'And if they do?'

'Then I'll probably end up arresting the pair of them,' she replied.

Fifty-two

Ash will be in the police station by now. The thought makes me restless. I go into Simon's office and sit in his chair. The room is dark, but central heating has warmed it, as well as the dust on the radiators which make it smelt musty – unused.

If the police put the pieces together, if they find the clues Luci left, by this evening I could be free: no Simon, no parents, and Hannah will be getting the punishment she deserves. I still don't know how she got Alice to jump off the wall, but I know she did and soon so will the police – all paid for by my mum and dad: emails, bank account details and phone calls to prove it. If the police are really clever, they'll have found where Ash was held, and it will be the icing on the cake of my parents' jail term.

I walk into the hall, my bags by the door, money in an envelope for Luci. I hope she goes far away and starts again, keeps hold of her life this time, rather than letting it be washed away in a bottle. Maybe I could have done things differently and Alice wouldn't be dead. But then Alice had never really been mine. All I'd been able to do was watch her from afar, following her to class, watching her walk around the lab, leaning over to help the students, and I'd picture the feel of her breath on my neck, the touch of her lips as they skimmed my cheek. But despite how much I'd tried to hide my love, to protect her from it, Simon had seen and I couldn't protect her from that.

I turn off the lights in the front room and do the same in the kitchen. I thought of the day Simon received his invitation to the reunion, the look on his face when he logged onto Facebook and saw the only others invited were Ash, Hannah, Alice and him: fear, disbelief, and a realisation this was all coming to an end. Hannah may have thought she'd devised a clever way to kill Alice, goading her into attending The Varsity Club, taunting her with memories of what the three of them did to Alice, but I was cleverer. I saw my chance to end things, and I took it; now she'll be in jail and I'll be free.

Fifty-three

Ash was in an interview room, wrapped in a blue blanket, clutching a cup of tea. His face looked drained of colour, heavy rings under his eyes suggesting lack of sleep. Bremer took a seat across from him, but it was Carla he looked at as she sat down. She smiled but he didn't return it. His eyes seemed blank, unseeing, the stubble on his jaw highlighting the hours he'd spent tied to a chair.

'Mr Desai, Ash, how are you feeling?' Bremer's tone was gentle, as if speaking to a child. Ash turned slowly to face him.

'Tired.'

Bremer nodded. 'We'll have you out of here and back to your bed as soon as we can, OK? I just need to ask you a few questions while events are still fresh in your mind if that's all right.'

As it wasn't a question, Ash didn't bother replying. Bremer took out his notepad.

'Can you tell us anything about the person who took you? Man, woman, height, accent, that sort of thing?'

Ash took a sip of his tea. 'He kept a mask on so I couldn't see his face but I'm sure it was a man.'

'How can you be sure?'

'He wore a T-shirt and there were no . . .' He paused, and shifted in his seat.

'Breasts?'

Ash nodded. 'No accent that I could hear. Height about the same as yours and a middle-aged sort of build.' Clocking the questioning look on Bremer's face he said, 'Saggy, bit wide around the middle.'

'What did the mask look like?'

'Just your ordinary black balaclava type. Wool, I'd say, two holes for the eyes and one for the mouth.'

'Thank you. Now, I'd like you to think back to when you were taken. Did you see anything suspicious just before? Anyone hanging around, any vehicles you wouldn't have expected to see?'

Ash stared off a little to the left, finger tapping the edge of his cup. He pulled the blanket over his shoulder where it had fallen off. 'I was on Broad Street and was just leaving Oxford College Library. It was about 11.30 at night as I'd been preparing for a class the next day and I can't recall seeing anyone at all. There was a car towards the end of the street by the entrance to Ship Street. I didn't notice anyone in it but I suppose there could have been.'

'Make and colour of car?'

Ash shook his head. 'I don't drive so I couldn't tell one car from the next and it was dark so it's hard to say what the colour was. I can say it was dark not light.'

Carla was amazed by Bremer's patience. How could anyone be so unaware of their surroundings? When Carla left work she logged every car, person and dog within her vision, and she worked in a police station, for God's sake.

'That's really helpful,' Bremer said. 'And then what happened?'

'I walked towards the car. I don't recall seeing anyone but, just as I passed it, I felt there was someone behind me. As the area was so quiet, I turned around.'

'Did you see anyone?'

'No, because that's when they put a hood over my head and shoved me into the car boot.'

'Did you struggle?'

Ash looked uncomfortable. 'Yes, but the surprise made me less able to react than normal, I suppose.'

It was said almost as an apology, and Carla wanted to tell him he didn't have to apologise, that fighting off your attacker or not, was no less or more an indication of the rights and wrongs of it.

'Do you know how long you were in the boot?'

'About twenty minutes, maybe half an hour?'

Carla judged that fitted with the distance between Oxford and Chipping Norton. They'd got the right address then, which was something at least.

'And when you arrived?'

'I was taken to what was, I assume, the basement, and tied to a chair.'

Bremer nodded. 'And how did you escape?'

Ash didn't reply straight away and Carla could see the muscles in his face working as he recalled it. He took a breath.

'I knew he'd gone out, I could always tell. Not so much because I stopped hearing him or heard the front door shut, but more because there was suddenly a sense of absence in the house. I knew I was alone. It had happened before but I'd been frozen, paralysed by fear that if I tried to escape he'd come back and find me before I could get out. I didn't know what he was intending to do to me . . .' He sounded as though he was pleading with them to understand his lack of action as he went on, 'I thought he would kill me, was going to kill me, and I wanted to stay alive for as long as possible. So I chose to comply. To stay tied.'

'So why did you change your mind?'

'Because of what he said.' He shifted a little, put his cup on the table, clasped his hands between his legs.

'He told me the reunion was punishment for Alice. For forcing her out of the university and onto the streets. That every one of us was responsible and every one of us would pay. He said . . .' He stopped, swallowed, jaw tight.

'He said Rachel was dead and so was Hannah and I was next. That he'd displayed their bodies on the Facebook page and was going to parade mine in the same way. So' – he breathed out – 'I decided I had nothing to lose. If he was going to kill me anyway, I may as well try to keep myself alive, so I chose to risk it. I chose not to fight in order to stay alive, then I chose to fight for the same reason.'

It made sense to Carla. Just because the choice wasn't an easy one either way, didn't make it any less of a choice.

'And how did you manage it, to escape?' Bremer asked.

'They had used rope to tie me. Rope frays. It was just a matter of freeing one hand then the rest would be simple.' He held up his wrist, hand wrapped in a bandage, swollen fingers protruding. 'Turns out it wasn't so simple after all.' He gave a tight smile. 'Took me hours, and at one point I thought I was going to saw through my wrist before I managed the rope.'

Carla tried not to wince. Would she have been able to do the same, facing that or death? She wasn't sure she could have intentionally inflicted that much pain on herself.

'And then I just ran,' he said, face lined with pain, eyes alive with it. Carla couldn't imagine having to sit here reliving it when all he must want was to go home and sink into a painkiller-induced sleep. Bremer clearly didn't feel the same.

'Why did you go to Witney police station?' he asked.

'Sorry?'

'Well, I'm struggling to understand why you'd travel all the way to Witney from Chipping Norton, a good half-hour away, with your wrist in that state.' He pointed to Ash's bandages. 'Or how people didn't stop you and ask if you needed help.'

Ash cradled one arm with the other. 'I just wanted to get away from there. The police station in Chipping Norton is closed, but I knew there was one here.'

Bremer nodded, made a note. 'And you travelled here by?'

'Car. I hitchhiked.' Ash looked to Carla, confused, then back to Bremer. 'Are you suggesting you don't believe me? That somehow I'm lying about someone kidnapping me and tying me to a chair? Because I feel like I'm being interrogated here.'

Bremer ignored the question and Carla felt the atmosphere in the room tighten.

'You chose to travel by car rather than dial 999?' Bremer asked.

'I didn't have a phone.'

Carla could sense the hostility and she didn't blame him. They had a photo of him tied up and his hand was clearly wrecked from escaping, so why was Bremer going in hard?

'You didn't think to ask the person driving the car to borrow theirs?'

Ash clenched his jaw. 'Unfortunately, I am not endowed with your white privilege. A bleeding Asian doesn't inspire concern, rather fear, so I just wanted to get here as quickly as I could so I could get help. Turns out it's not much different being here as a bleeding Asian as it is out there.' He tipped his head towards the door. 'But you live and learn.'

Bremer ignored the dig. 'Well, I'm sure CCTV will confirm your version of events. When you got here, the front desk say you asked to speak to me, why was that?'

Carla watched Ash's face which was, by now, set in a stony silence.

'Mr Desai, why did you ask specifically for me?'

'Because I remembered it was your team who were investigating Alice's death, from that night on the rooftop, I remembered it from there.'

Carla stared at him.

'OK, thank you very much,' Bremer said. 'I think we'll take a break now. I want to make sure you're well enough to continue.'

'Continue,' Ash almost shouted. 'Continue with what? I've told you everything I can remember.'

'It's just a few more questions and then we'll drive you home.' Bremer stood, conversation clearly closed. 'Shouldn't be more than an hour or so.' And before Ash could speak, he opened the door for Carla and guided her out.

Closing it behind them, she said, 'He's lying, isn't he?'

Bremer folded his arms. 'Yes.'

Carla pictured the wound on his wrist, the Facebook page with him staring out at them, scared and in distress. 'So who took that picture then? Of him sitting in the chair?'

Bremer smiled that irritating smile of his. 'I don't know, Carla. But if that man sawed his way out of a chair, got driven in a car for twenty-five minutes while bleeding profusely, and then remembered the name of an officer who wasn't even there? And who would really pick up a man in that state? He must have looked in distress, was bleeding, what person picks someone like that up and doesn't call 999? It doesn't add up. But' – he held up a finger – 'right now what we need to work out is whether he's lying because he's involved and has something to hide, or if he's been pressured to do so and is too scared to tell us.'

Fifty-four

Nell banged on the Davidsons' door, then again a few seconds later. Paul stood back and surveyed the windows.

'No lights, no car.' He pointed to the drive. 'Looks like they're out.'

'No shit, Sherlock.' Her head was pounding, mouth dry, so she didn't bother offering the apology she knew she should.

Walking down the steps and round to the side of the house, she pushed at the garden gate to reveal an extensive lawn surrounded by neatly tended flowers and shrubs, overlooked by ancient trees. A patio, grey and moss splattered, spanned the length of the house, a set of iron garden furniture sat upturned in its middle. Looking to the right she spotted a garage, shadowed in ivy; it appeared to merge into the surrounding foliage.

'Come on,' she called to Paul, 'I want to take a look over

there,' and, pulling her collar up against the drizzle, she crossed the lawn, boots leaving marks in the settling rain.

The door to the garage was partially open, patches of peeling cream paint revealing rotten wood underneath. Pushing it open she stared round the cluttered space. 'Christ.'

Paul appeared at her shoulder. 'How the hell are we going to find anything in here?'

Walking gingerly to what would once have a been a work surface, Nell started to pick through the dust-covered items. 'Well, the sooner we start, the sooner we can get out of here. Look for a rope, anything which could have been used for restraining Ash.'

Paul started at the other side, rummaging through boxes before pulling back with a yell. Nell spun round.

'What you got?'

'A massive bloody spider, that's what,' he said, brushing repeatedly at his trousers.

'Seriously?' Nell turned back to the worktop. 'I grew up in a Welsh farmhouse, where spiders were as big as cats, so we named them and kept them as pets.'

'Jesus, Nell.'

She laughed. 'Just kidding. They were big, mind.' She crouched down to examine under the bench and poked at a water-damaged box. 'Hey,' she called over her shoulder. 'Got any gloves?'

'Sure, you got something?' Paul pulled a pair of blue plastic gloves from the inside pocket of his jacket and walked over.

'Not sure yet,' she said, pulling them on, 'but could be a rope.' She tugged at the box, part of it falling away to reveal a rope, some scissors and a hammer, the newness of each a marked contrast to the decrepit state of the rest of the garage.

'I need an evidence bag, can you get one from the car?'

'Sure thing.' But as he stood, a cough came from the doorway. Startled, Nell looked over her shoulder, then slowly stood. Shit. Could there be worse timing? She walked to the door, hand extended. Mr Davidson did not take it.

'Mr Davidson, sorry to surprise you like this but you were out and we thought we'd have a little look around, just to check everything was OK. We were worried your garage seemed unsecured.'

Mr Davidson looked thunderously between them, before glancing over Nell's shoulder to the box on the floor.

'What are you doing searching my private property, Sergeant?'

'As I said, we were concerned over the security of your garage after the attempted break-in the other night and just wanted to check everything was in order.' They both knew it was bullshit, so the question was whether he was going to kick up a fuss, or back down. He chose the latter.

'Thank you for your concern but I'm afraid I'm going to have to ask you to leave.'

Mrs Davidson appeared behind him, hands fussing in her trademark manner, over a large wooden cross hanging round her neck. 'What's going on?' She looked at Nell and Paul before turning to her husband, 'Malcolm?'

'Nothing. The officers were just leaving.' He looked expectantly at Nell.

'I'm afraid that's not going to be possible.' She looked to Paul. 'Go and get the bag.'

'What bag?' Mrs Davidson asked as Paul walked past her. 'Why do you need a bag?'

Nell took a step forward and Mrs Davidson looked down at the box a few feet behind her.

'What's that?' she asked, pointing to it.

'I have reason to believe it may be evidence relating to the investigations into the disappearance of Ash Desai and the murder of Simon Morris.'

Mrs Davidson stared at her, mouth open, hands now clasping the cross against her chest. 'Simon's murder?'

Nell noted she didn't offer the same question for Ash. 'Yes. It contains some items of interest.'

'Like what?' She posed the question to her husband, but he just stared at Nell.

'Malcolm,' she snapped, 'do something. Why are you letting' – she threw her arm towards Nell – 'this woman have her own way?'

There was something about the way in which she said 'this woman' which made Nell tense. Nothing concrete but the undertones were there – she was one of 'them'.

Mr Davidson turned to his wife and put a hand around her shoulder. 'Let's just let them take away whatever it is they think they've found. We've nothing to hide, so the sooner they take it, the sooner that will be proved.'

Mrs Davidson shrugged off his arm. 'You're pathetic,' she hissed at him. 'A weak, pathetic man who can't defend his family against a woman like this.' She jerked a hand towards Nell and this time the implication was clear. Nell was starting to get seriously pissed off, but she didn't react. If she did that at every insult thrown her way, she'd never get her job done. But Mrs Davidson wasn't taking the hint of Nell's pointed silence and levelled stare.

'You know it doesn't matter what you think you've found,' she spat, pointing her finger close to Nell's face, 'because you are going to hell and you will burn in hell with the rest of your kind.'

Nell absorbed the hate in the woman's face, the way it contorted. OK. She'd bite. 'My kind?'

'The homosexuals.' Mrs Davidson's voice rose, her hand shaking now as she gripped the cross. 'Your rancid behaviour is a blight on the wonder of God's creation and you would do well to renounce it before you are punished with fire and eternal damnation.'

Nell raised her eyebrows. Both fire and eternal damnation, going in strong. She stood still, determined not to show the woman her words were anything other than that, but inside she was shaking, as if the attack had been a physically violent one.

Mrs Davidson raised the cross to Nell's face. 'The behaviour you indulge in is the depraved act of a sinner. You are a danger to children, to adults who are vulnerable to having their minds warped by your despicable beliefs, and to the whole of humanity.'

Nell had had enough. Her hangover was beyond words, she needed a cigarette and possibly a shot of hair of the dog. She also hated this woman more than she'd ever hated anyone before. 'Vulnerable like your daughter?' she asked. Mrs Davidson gaped at her, her face increasingly flushed, hands pulling at the cross around her neck.

'How dare you speak of my daughter,' she spat, spittle forming at the edges of her lips. 'Her marriage to Simon was proof of her renouncement of sin and her commitment to a godly life, and she will reside in heaven at God's right hand because of it. She is a proof your sins can be overcome.' She pointed a finger in Nell's face. 'But if you persist in your sins, with that knowledge in mind, you will be severely punished for it.'

The red mist came down. 'Like Ash was proof? Until he married a man? Is that why you took him, to bury the lie you had forced into your daughter's head?' Nell pointed a finger back at Mrs Davidson, focused only on taking this bigot down. 'The lie you tortured her with, paid people to persecute her for the rest of her life, to keep her pure?'

Paul appeared by the door. 'Nell?'

Mrs Davidson whirled round to face him, cross held up, inches from his face. He looked at it in surprise.

'You need to clean yourself from this woman's sin. Your contact with her puts you in danger of contaminating yourself with it.' She thrust the cross closer to his face. 'Repent therefore and be converted, that your sins may be blotted out, so that times of refreshing may come from the presence of the Lord.'

Nell took three steps forward, grabbed the wrist holding the cross and twisted it behind Mrs Davidson's back. Reaching for the handcuff in her back pocket she said, 'I am arresting you for the kidnap of Ash Desai. You do not have to say anything but it may harm your defence if you do not mention, when questioned, something that you later rely on in court. Anything you do say may be given in evidence.' She snapped on one cuff then dragged Mrs Davidson's right arm down and snapped the other on her wrist.

She nodded to Mr Davidson. 'Get him cuffed.' She'd had it with them both, let's see how far God's laws got them when put up in front of a judge, and let them just try and do her for wrongful arrest – if Nell had a hill to die on, this one was it, and no amount of police pension or overtime was going to stop her.

Fifty-five

It takes a while for me to find Luci, and in the end it is Billy who finds me. He comes up to me, still cautious, but tail wagging, and I find I feel a sort of pride that I've won him round.

Luci is chatting to a man I haven't seen before. Seeing me, she makes it clear he should leave, before standing and patting Billy on the head. 'I see you've made a friend. He doesn't like many people, you should be flattered.'

I smile down at the dog. 'He's a love. I'm glad you have him.' I look back at her. 'How's Guy?' then immediately regret it. Luci shrugs, her face closed, shuffling on the pavement as if it doesn't matter to her when it clearly does.

'He's had a few issues. I've found it hard to get him to talk to me, so he's sort of spiralled down – stupid fights, dealing in hard drugs, that kind of thing.'

If I Fall

I thought of Guy, Alice, Luci and Billy, this little makeshift family existing against all the odds but now with only Luci and Billy left. 'Will you get him to go with you when you leave?'

Luci shrugs. 'I'll try, but I can't make him.'

I hand her an envelope and scratch behind Billy's ear. 'Five thousand quid. Enough to get you started somewhere else.' I tuck inside a piece of paper with my phone number on it. 'You call if you need anything. I've taken out a SIM-only mobile and only you have the number. It's untraceable and safe, OK?'

Luci looks up the street, rain coming down in sheets, shoppers and Christmas work parties running for cover, laughing as they're drenched. 'It will be weird leaving Oxford. It was our home for over a year. It feels a bit like I'm leaving Alice behind too.' She looks back to me. 'Does that sound stupid?'

I shake my head. 'No.'

Luci pats Billy on the head. 'But I want to go. I want to give it our first shot.' She smiles and for the first time I see what Alice did – a soft intelligence which has never been allowed to poke above the soil, a smile which makes you feel welcomed home.

'Promise to ring if you need anything?' I say. Luci nods. I point at Billy. 'And you, my little fella, take care of her. Bite any-one who looks mean.'

I look back at Luci. 'Bye then.'

Luci is staring down at Billy. I reach out and touch her arm. 'Thank you.'

She looks at me, and for a moment I think she's going to hug me, but a second later she and Billy are gone, and with them, Alice.

Fifty-six

Carla watched Nell throw her keys on the desk and slump onto her chair. 'I'm not going to lie, Carla, I'm beat.' She looked pale, dark rings under her eyes, and Carla sensed it was more than just the hangover.

'I hear you've arrested Rachel's parents.' From what Paul had told her, Nell was lucky not to have been had up on an assault charge. 'Paul said you were a bit agitated. Everything OK?'

'Paul should keep his mouth shut.' She threw Carla an apologetic look. 'But yeah, I'm OK, just had enough of them shouting Bible verses in my face. God knows how Rachel put up with it all these years.'

Nell was watching her. 'You don't think I should have brought them in, do you?'

'It's not that. I'm sure you had good reason. It all just feels a little . . . easy, you know?'

Nell laughed, 'You're kidding, right? We've been chasing our tails since this started, I'd say it had been anything other than easy.'

'But that's my point. We've been floundering a little and it feels like someone has come along and joined up the dots for us. I'm just not sure it's the right picture.'

Nell stood and pulled off her jacket. 'Yeah, I know what you mean. I had a similar feeling – like I'm being played – but I found a rope and a hammer. The rope looks similar to the one found at the house where Ash was being held. You know what might have been used to kill Simon? A hammer. They're both at the lab now, so it's just a case of waiting to see if we're right.' Slumping back down, she said, 'Tell me about Ash.'

Nell listened as Carla told them about the interview, their conviction he was lying, but unsure as to why.

'Rachel's parents did that gay conversion stuff on him, didn't they?' Nell said when she'd finished. 'Stands to reason the bloke would be terrified of them. You haven't seen it when they go full-on God on you, Carla, it's bloody terrifying. They believe their words so much and the hate in their faces . . .' She exhaled, loudly. 'It's sick, that's what it is. And I know they are capable of violence, I'm 100 per cent sure of it. If Ash is lying, it's because he's scared, not because he's part of this.'

Carla thought she was probably right. Nell looked to Bremer's office. 'He in?'

Carla shook her head. 'When he heard you'd arrested the Davidsons, he went to find someone at the CPS, run it past them. He'll be back in half an hour – we're to debrief then.'

Nell didn't reply. Folding her arms, she closed her eyes. Hopefully after a thirty-minute recharge Nell would wake up in a better mood, but the frown on her forehead suggested to Carla she probably wouldn't.

Bremer strode across to the wipe board and gestured for them to join him.

'I've spoken to the CPS,' he said. 'They are happy to charge the Davidsons for Ash's abduction and for Simon's murder subject to forensics on the hammer and rope.'

'What if forensics comes back clean?' Carla asked. 'We'll still have the Facebook page, the pictures on the computer, and the fact Ash was abducted to a house the Davidsons own.'

'If the hammer comes back clean, then they won't run with it, so let's hope that doesn't happen,' Bremer replied. 'With regards to Hannah, they accept she received money from the Davidsons but they don't agree that's proof of any crime, especially as there are multiple witnesses to Alice's suicide.'

It didn't come as a surprise but Carla was disappointed nonetheless. 'How long for forensics on the hammer?'

'ASAP was all they could give me.'

'And what about Rachel,' Paul said, 'she's off the table now?'

Bremer looked at the board. 'We've got nothing on her. No

murder weapon to tie her to the murder, no motive, it's not exactly like she'd be doing it for the money—'

'What if she was?' Carla interrupted. 'The Davidsons' will says she gets nothing if Simon divorces her, he gets everything. We've seen Simon was asking for more money. What if he got sick of waiting and told Rachel he wanted a divorce?'

'But then why didn't he just divorce her years ago and take the money and run?' Paul asked.

'Well, two reasons.' Carla held up a finger. 'One, he'd have to wait until her parents were dead, but also, two, he'd have to know about the will. And going from what we know about the Davidsons, I'd say they weren't so stupid as to tell him, but were cruel enough to let Rachel in on their plan. As an added incentive to stay with him.'

Nell sat up. 'I agree with Carla. I fully admit I was all for Rachel being our number one suspect, but I think I was wrong.'

Bremer looked at her in surprise.

Nell folded her arms. 'I can admit when I'm wrong.'

Paul threw Carla a look and she tried not to smile. 'Who is going to tell Rachel we've arrested her parents for the murder of her husband?' Carla asked. 'Laura?'

Bremer shook his head. 'Nell, you take it. I want a ranked officer to tell her. This is undoubtedly going to kick off in the press – Thames Valley Police arrest philanthropist millionaire – so we need to make sure she's aware what's coming her way as well as, more importantly, make sure she's on our side.'

Carla looked at Nell, who steadfastly refused to look her way.

Fine, if she wanted to go back to Rachel's house after the woman had kissed her, Carla had to trust she knew what she was doing. But, going by Nell's current mood, Carla couldn't help feeling that it was a very bad idea.

Fifty-seven

Nell sat in the car and looked up at Rachel's house. How was she going to react when she heard about her parents being accused of the murder of her husband? Nell tried to think what she'd feel – relief, shame, anger, sadness? Probably all of them and more. She wondered what Rachel would do now, how she'd survive, with the two controlling factors in her life gone. Would she even know how to live a life on her own?

Nell unclicked her seatbelt, slammed the car door shut, and walked across the drive but, before she'd got a foot on the bottom step leading to the front door, Rachel opened it.

She stared down at Nell, expression unreadable, shrouded in shadows. 'Hello,' Rachel said finally.

Nell hesitated. Rachel's tone wasn't hostile but nor was it welcoming.

'Come in then,' Rachel said, moving back and holding the door open. 'It's freezing and I don't know about you, but I could do with a cup of tea.'

They walked to the kitchen, Nell explaining about her parents, as Rachel slowly placed teabags in a pot and laid out the cups. She said nothing, just listened, pouring boiling water into the teapot, giving the occasional nod, before putting everything on a tray and carrying it to the front room.

They sat for a while in silence, Nell letting the news settle while she poured them each a cup of tea and handed one to Rachel. Staring down at it, Rachel said, 'I'm sorry I put you in such an awkward position. I acted selfishly.'

'We know what your parents did to you.' Nell just came out with it, no sugar-coating, although she knew Rachel didn't need it. However weak Rachel thought she was, Nell knew she wasn't.

Rachel stayed silent. Nell wanted to tell her it was OK, there was nothing she could have done, that the nightmare was over. But it wasn't her place. Rachel would have to come to that realisation on her own. And she would, Nell was sure of it.

'The thing is,' Nell went on, 'it's likely there will be a lot of media interest surrounding their arrest and Simon's murder. You will have Laura with you at all times, but I wanted you to brace yourself for what may be a very intrusive time.'

Rachel looked up. 'Can I call you, if I have to?' she asked.

She should say no, tell her to contact Laura, but Nell nodded. 'Of course. Anytime.'

'I was thinking of going away for a little while,' Rachel said.

'Just for a break. This house' – she gestured around her – 'is filled with Simon's murder. Am I allowed to do that, to have a break?'

Nell smiled. 'Yes, that would be fine. Not abroad though, ideally. And we'd like details of where you're going, just in case we need to contact you.'

Rachel nodded, took a sip of her tea. 'I was thinking of Scotland. First-class train ride with nothing to do but look out the window, maybe read a book. I haven't sat down with a book in years.' She looked out of the back doors and Nell noticed a small suitcase tucked by the side of Rachel's chair.

'I've never been on holiday on my own,' Rachel went on. 'And while part of me is terrified, a bigger part of me wants to see what it's like.' She turned back to Nell and smiled. 'To just be able to go where you want, when you want, with no one watching you.' She laughed. 'I'm sure I sound quite pathetic!'

Nell shook her head. 'Not at all. Where will you stay?'

'A hotel in Edinburgh to start with, but then I was thinking of a cabin or apartment somewhere further out in the country. I think I could do with some time to plan what I'm going to do next. I mean, I haven't ever had a job.' She laughed again, light, free. Nell smiled.

'I'm not sure you're going to need one anytime soon.' She gestured to the room. 'And you'll get Simon's life insurance, so you should be all set for a while yet.'

Rachel looked suddenly serious. 'But I want one, I want to see what it's like, I want to meet people. I want to have friends! People who come around for a glass of wine.' Her words hung in the air and Nell felt herself grow hot.

'When's your train?'

Rachel checked her watch. 'I've booked a taxi to come in an hour.'

'Cancel the taxi,' Nell said.

Rachel looked confused. 'Sorry?'

'I'll take you,' Nell knew as she was saying it that she shouldn't, but what harm could come from dropping her at the train station? 'I don't have to be back at the office, we're just waiting for forensics,' she explained, when Rachel looked doubtful.

'Forensics?'

'Just checking on the rope used to tie Ash, as well as a potential murder weapon.'

'You found what they used to killed Simon?' Rachel had paled. Nell kicked herself for being so flippant.

'It's nothing to worry about. Just confirming your parents' involvement, that's all. We'll have all we need to charge them later this evening.'

When Rachel still looked concerned, Nell leant forward. 'We'll have them charged by this evening, Rachel,' she said. 'Don't worry. Just go and enjoy Scotland, you deserve it.'

Some colour had returned to Rachel's face. She smiled at Nell. 'Thank you,' she said. 'I'm so glad it's you who is working on the case.'

Nell returned the smile, but there was something in the way Rachel said it, with the lightest touch of arrogance, that made Nell suddenly doubt she meant it.

Fifty-eight

Mr Davidson was sitting, stony faced, in an interview room. Carla took her place in the video suite and watched Bremer repeat the caution, Paul to his right.

'Do you understand why you are here?' Bremer asked.

Mr Davidson glared at him. 'No.'

Bremer pulled out a file and flipped it open. Taking out a screenshot of The Reunion Facebook page, he slid it across the desk. 'Can you tell me if you've seen this before?'

Mr Davidson studied it. 'No, what is it?'

'It's a page on Facebook linked to the murder of Simon Morris and Alice Wilson. We found this on your computer. It lists you as an administrator of that page.'

Mr Davidson looked incredulous. 'That's absurd.'

Bremer pointed to Mr Davidson's name on the page, his

picture next to it. 'This rather suggests otherwise, wouldn't you say?'

'No, I wouldn't say. What it says is that someone is trying to frame my wife and me for the murder of my son-in-law.'

Bremer raised his eyebrows. 'Frame you?'

'Well obviously. How else would my name be on there?'

Bremer leant back, folded his arms. 'Does anyone other than you and your wife have access to this computer?'

Mr Davidson shook his head. 'No.'

'How about your daughter, Rachel?'

'I said no,' he snapped. Bremer pulled the page back.

'You can see our dilemma here, can't you, Mr Davidson? You say you're not the administrator on this page, and yet here it says you are, and you say you're being framed, yet no one else has access to your computer, so . . .' Bremer let his words hang for a moment and Carla watched as the seriousness of the situation began to dawn on the man opposite.

'We had a break-in, the night you came for the computer. It must have been them, they put this on our computer, and hid the items in the garage.' Mr Davidson was gesturing now. 'That has to be the explanation.'

Bremer pulled out a list of finances taken from the computer. He pushed it across to him. 'You will note the highlighted transaction midway down the page. A payment to Hannah Barclay for £35,000. What was that for?'

Mr Davidson folded his arms. 'I don't remember.'

Bremer nodded. He pushed over the screenshot again and

pointed to Hannah's name. 'You'll note the same Hannah Barclay is also listed as an administrator on The Reunion Facebook page.'

He remained silent.

'Can you explain that?'

Silence.

'Did you pay Hannah to ensure Alice Baxter's death? Did she help you to set up the Facebook page to entice Alice to The Varsity Club that night?'

'I told you, I didn't set up that page. Someone broke into my house and did it. I have no idea why Hannah's name is also there.'

Either the man was a damned good liar, or, Carla thought, he was telling the truth. And if someone had broken in to get access to his computer, it probably wasn't just to make sure the Facebook page would be open on their computer when the police found it, but also to make sure the picture of Ash was on it too.

Picking up her half-drunk coffee and notepad, she headed out of the suite and back to the office and dialled the local station. 'Hi, yes, Carla Brown here from HQ. I'm after a crime report or any intel associated with it.' She gave the date and time of the alleged break-in at the Davidsons' address. 'Can you email it across to me?'

Waiting, she sipped at her coffee. If Malcolm was telling the truth, and his theory about the break-in did stack up, and someone had put the picture of Ash on the Davidsons' computer for them to find, then who had done it? Rachel would have no need to break in, she'd have a key, and it seemed that the Davidsons were friendly enough with Hannah for her to go in through the front door. Unless there hadn't been a break-in, or it was entirely unrelated – but she didn't think for a second that was the case.

A few minutes later the file appeared in her inbox. Police had arrived at the Davidsons' house approximately fifteen minutes after they'd received the 999 call, but an initial sweep of the garden had found no evidence of an intruder. On speaking to the Davidsons, the officers were told the back door had been open at the time, after Mrs Davidson had visited the garden to fill the bird bath, fearing freezing temperatures overnight would leave the birds without fresh water. She had not shut the back door but had instead gone to the utility room to remove her shoes, which were muddy. She had then heard a sound from the kitchen, followed by one from the hall, and she 'sensed' it wasn't her husband, who she called out to. When he confirmed he had been in the front room all the while, they decided to call 999 rather than search the house themselves.

Carla took another sip of her coffee. It seemed legit, detailed enough to be believable, and the officer's report didn't indicate he found their account otherwise. She searched the staff directory and dialled the number for the officer in charge. 'PC Banner? Carla Brown here, HQ. I'm interested in an alleged break-in at an address in Great Tew. I wondered if you had a few moments to speak about it?' She could hear the sound of the police radio in the background, the hum of a car.

'Sure thing.' He sounded muffled, distracted. 'But if I get a call, I may have to cut you off.'

'Of course. I'm just interested in when you searched the address for signs of an intruder. Was there anything at all other than Mrs Davidson's account of hearing one?'

'Nah, nothing. We covered downstairs and upstairs and, other than the smallest speck of mud on the upstairs landing, everything was pristine. We spoke with the couple about the possibility the wind may have knocked the back door and frightened Mrs Davidson and advised them to ensure the door was closed when not in use.'

Carla scanned the report again for mention of mud – nothing. 'You say there was mud on the upstairs landing?'

'Yeah, but we put that down to the occupants. We'd given the garden a thorough examination and found no signs of footprints other than those matching the size of Mrs Davidson's.'

'But you said she took her shoes off in the utility room? How fresh was the mud?'

'I didn't check.' PC Banner sounded irritated now. 'There was obviously no one there, no items stolen, nothing even moved and no evidence of an intruder in the garden. I wasn't going to bag a piece of mud on the off-chance it wasn't theirs.'

Carla rather wished he had. 'OK, thank you for your time.'

Hanging up she wrote 'mud' on her notepad with a question mark next to it. Maybe there was a break-in. If someone had gone in there to put the reunion Facebook page and the picture of Ash on the Davidson's laptop, nothing would have appeared moved, would it? She dialled PC Banner back. 'Sorry, one last question.' She could hear sirens, the radio crackling updates.

'You'll have to hurry,' he shouted above the noise.

'When you went in the study, was the computer screen on or blank?'

'On,' but before she could thank him, he'd hung up.

Fifteen minutes from Mrs Davidson hearing a noise to the police attending. Was that time enough to tamper with the computer? You'd have to be pretty sure of what you were doing and confident you could get in and out in such a short period of time, which suggested a knowledge of the property. Still, it was possible, and anything that was possible had to be considered, especially if it meant they had the wrong man in the interview room.

Fifty-nine

Nell steered the car into Oxford's railway station, pulling over into the drop-off bay and turning off the engine. She was suddenly acutely aware of how close Rachel was, how their legs were almost touching. She moved her leg slightly away. 'How're you feeling?'

Rachel was staring straight ahead. 'Strange. Scared. Excited.' She gave Nell a brief smile. 'What's it like?' she asked. 'Being allowed to date other women, chat to them in a bar?'

Nell watched passengers hurry across the road, dodging buses and taxis, all crowded into a too-tight space. The question felt like a big deal, it being the first time Rachel had admitted her homosexuality – not just to her but possibly to anyone other than Alice – and she didn't know what to say. 'Well, picture how it felt with Alice, and it's like that, but better because it's not a secret.'

Rachel gave a strange smile, and again Nell felt as if there was something odd in the way she spoke of Alice – detached, removed almost, as if she couldn't remember what she had been like; or maybe they just hadn't been as close as Nell imagined. But then this whole thing had started with Alice, so what they had must have been real.

Rachel unclicked her seatbelt. 'Thanks for the lift.' She gave an unsure smile and paused. Nell leant across and pushed open the door.'

'It's going to be great, and you're going to be fine. I'll call when we have an update from forensics.'

Rachel pulled her suitcase from the back seat. 'Thank you.'

'Take care, Rachel, enjoy those bars in Scotland.' And as she watched Rachel get swallowed up into the crowd, Nell couldn't shake the nagging feeling that something wasn't quite right.

The office was full when Nell arrived back. Paul was on the phone gesturing, Laura by the back wall, writing on the board. Bremer's office door was closed. It felt tense. When Nell had left it had basically been job done, but now everyone was acting as they had in the first few hours again. What had happened?

'Where have you been?' Carla snapped before Nell had even put her bag down.

'What do you mean? I've been with Rachel and just dropped her off at the train station.'

Carla stared at her 'What the hell, Nell?'

Nell sat down. She really wasn't in the mood for this drama;

she felt oddly flat, and had the disconcerting thought it was to do with Rachel leaving – that things had been left unsaid, unexplored, but also she had the growing feeling she'd just been played and she couldn't work out how. She looked at Carla. 'What's wrong now?'

'She's part of a murder case. Why have you dropped her at the station?'

Nell was starting to regret telling Carla about the kiss; obviously she now thought Nell couldn't be trusted to do her job. 'She's a victim in a murder case and, correct me if I'm wrong, but there should be no problem about a victim going away for the weekend. And it's Scotland, so not technically abroad.' Nell sat down, hard, in her chair and glared at Carla. 'Bremer said to tell her about her parents being arrested, which I did. Turns out she was going away so I said I'd drive her, end of. We'll have the results back for the hammer later this evening and then it will be case closed.'

'We've had them back. The hammer didn't kill Simon.'

Nell stared at her. 'What?'

'Forensics came back and Alice had ketamine in her bloodstream. Ketamine is a drug used by vets, and they're testing it to see if it's from the same batch Hannah has at her surgery. Nell, Hannah's being arrested for murder right now.' Carla looked furious. 'And Simon wasn't killed with the hammer. They found traces of marble in his skull. Whatever he was hit with, it wasn't a metal object.'

The realisation of what Carla was saying started to sink in. Rachel had used her. She'd thrown Nell off the scent by manipulating her to feel things she shouldn't. 'But it's still the Davidsons for Simon's murder, no?' Marble, Nell was thinking hard, what was it reminding her of? Where had she seen marble before? 'Shit.' She looked up at Carla. 'The candlestick. The ones in Rachel's house. When I went to pick up the invitation, which was propped up against one, I noticed the other had a chip on it because it seemed out of place in an otherwise perfect room.' Nell looked to the window. 'Oh my God.'

Nell was off her chair and out the door before Carla had managed to pull on her coat. Running after her, she could barely see Nell, who was almost at the bottom of the stairs. 'Wait,' she called after her. 'For God's sake, Nell, wait.'

As she took the stairs two at a time, Paul appeared at the top. 'What the hell?'

'It's Rachel who killed Simon,' Carla shouted back up to him, 'it's been her all along, she's at the train station now.' She was on the ground floor by the time she'd finished speaking, the sound of Paul's steps pounding behind her.

Carla pushed open the back door to see Nell pull her car out of the back yard, swerving to miss a van as she sped towards the roundabout and disappeared. Paul ran past her, beeping open his car. 'Get Bremer,' he yelled to her, 'and get back-up.'

Carla turned back to HQ, bashing on the intercom, her pass sitting on her desk in the office. 'Officer assistance needed,' she shouted, 'hurry, please.' The gate buzzed and she dragged it open, desperate to get to Bremer before Nell did something stupid.

Sixty

Nell put the blue light on and sped down the Woodstock Road, cutting through Jericho, then down to Frideswide Square before pulling into the train station. It had taken no more than ten minutes from the office to there, but Nell still didn't know if she was going to be in time to stop Rachel from boarding the train.

Abandoning the car at the bus stop, she took the steps two at a time, vaulted the barrier – ignoring the shouts of the ticket collectors – and sprinted to the bridge, scanning the platform across from her for signs of Rachel. As she rounded the corner of the bridge she caught sight of the board – the train was running half an hour late. If Rachel hadn't been alerted to her coming, and Nell didn't see why she would have been, Nell was going to make it.

Just before the bottom of the stairs, she slowed, stepping out onto the platform while her eyes scanned the rows of people for signs of Rachel. Sliding in and out of the crowd, she made her way down the platform, hand on her baton. Where was she? Nell glanced behind her, making sure she hadn't missed her before turning back and making her way slowly forward. And then she saw her, no more than ten feet in front of her, suitcase by her feet.

Nell paused before starting to approach with caution, keen not to startle her. Walking with her hand in front of her, gesturing to people to move out of her way, she walked forward, baton extended, but held down by her thigh. As she neared Rachel, she paused, aware of someone behind her. Turning she saw Paul, baton out, and nodded towards where Rachel was standing, He nodded back, tipping his head to the adjacent platform. Nell glanced over. Bremer was slowly making his way down the platform, radio in hand, Carla a few feet behind him.

She turned back to Rachel as Paul moved to her side. 'Rachel?'

Rachel turned, surprised, eyes flitting between Nell and Paul. Passengers started to move away from her, crowding by the iron fence, watching, filming.

Rachel glanced to Nell's baton, then back to her face. 'What's going on?'

'It wasn't the hammer, Rachel. That didn't kill Simon, it was something made of marble.' Nell saw her flinch, only slightly, but it was there. Rachel put her hands in her pockets.

'Take your hands out of your pockets, Rachel, please, slowly.'

Rachel looked vaguely amused. 'Nell, you can't really think I'd kill my own husband? If I was going to do that, why wait and suffer eight long years with him? Why not just kill him in year one?'

'Rachel, take your hands out of your pockets.' Nell felt Paul move to the left of her, making sure he could cover any attempt Rachel might make to bolt.

'Now please, Rachel.'

Rachel slowly started removing her hands from her pockets, but Nell saw it, the glint of metal from the station lights. 'Paul,' she yelled, 'knife.'

Paul stopped, flicked his baton to extend it. 'Taser, Nell?'

Shit, it was in the office on her desk, her stab vest sitting next to it. Nell shook her head; eyes on Rachel, she started to walk forward. 'Rachel, put the knife down.'

Rachel began to back away towards the passengers by the fence. 'Or what?' she asked, before turning and holding the knife to the throat of a terrified man. She turned back to Nell, blade pushing at the man's skin. 'You know the point right here.' She dragged the knife over the man's neck, then stopped. 'If I push it in now, he'll be dead in under thirty seconds. You come near me with that baton, either of you' – she looked to Paul – 'and I will do it. It depends whose reflexes you think are faster, yours or mine.'

Nell stopped walking but raised her baton high up to the right. Paul did the same.

No one moved. Nell could hear movement behind her, officers clearing the platform, getting into position, but unless she could get Rachel to drop the knife at the man's throat, it wasn't going to do any good.

'Rachel. Everyone understands why you did it. We've documented the years of abuse you suffered, the payments to Simon, the same to Hannah. There is not a jury in this land that is going to give you a custodial sentence. Your defence will cite coercive control as mitigation, and they'll win on that. But if you do this,' Nell said, pointing to the man, 'you'll go down for life. Don't waste this opportunity to have the life you were denied. Think of the bars in Scotland.' She smiled but Rachel didn't return it. There was a faraway look in her eyes and Nell wasn't sure she'd even heard her.

'Rachel?' Bremer had approached from behind, stopping a foot behind Nell, a little to the left. 'Nell is right. We have all the evidence we need to charge your parents with abuse. They won't go unpunished.'

Rachel snapped her head round to face him. 'And what about Alice? Who pays for her death?'

He paused. Nell knew that answer wasn't going to be the one Rachel wanted. She glanced to Paul who nodded, aware she might make a run for it, or worse, use the knife.

'We have enough to charge Hannah with crimes relating to Alice's death,' Bremer said. 'But it's unlikely it will be for murder or even manslaughter. We know she gave Alice ketamine in the hope of influencing her to jump off the roof, and we know your parents paid her to, so she will be punished, Rachel, they all will. You have my word that Hannah will be made accountable for Alice's death. But you have to put the knife down.'

Rachel looked at Nell. 'Have you listened to the recording?'

Bremer glanced across at her, frowning, but Nell didn't know what she meant either. 'What recording?'

'Luci was concerned about what Hannah was saying to Alice, so she made Alice record the meeting they had, just before the reunion. It will be on Alice's phone.' Rachel looked to Bremer. 'If she is telling Alice to kill herself, after giving her ketamine to confuse her, would that be enough for a murder charge?'

A speck of blood appeared on the man's throat, and the colour drained from his face. Nell didn't care if that would be enough to get Hannah on a murder charge, she needed Bremer to tell Rachel it was and to tell her now.

'Yes,' he replied. 'It would.'

Rachel nodded. 'Thank you,' she said, as she thrust the knife into the man's neck.

Nell dived towards her as Bremer discharged his taser. Rachel lifted in the air then fell rigid on the ground. Nell crouched by Rachel, who was sucking in air, staring at the sky as her body starting to loosen. Behind her, Paul was shouting for an ambulance, hands on the man's throat, tying to stem the bleeding, Bremer calling for an air ambulance amidst screams from the passengers.

'Why?' Nell asked. 'Why, when you were so close to having everything you ever wanted, did you throw it away?'

Rachel's body went limp. She moved her eyes to Nell's. 'Do you think I would have been good in a bar?' When Nell didn't reply, Rachel said, 'I had to try and get them out of my life. They wanted me back in that house; if I'd gone back, I'd never have been able to leave. How is that any life to live?'

Nell got that, frame the parents, and who was she to say she wouldn't have done the same. 'But why stab this man?' She gestured to her side, paramedics working hard to keep him alive until the air ambulance could arrive.

'Because I couldn't be sure you'd convict me. It's not much evidence, is it? A marble candlestick, and who's to say that's even going to come back a match?'

Nell stared at her. Did she really try to kill a man as an insurance policy for going to jail?

'I've lived my life in a sort of cage,' Rachel went on. 'Even when I was on my own, I always knew I was being watched: by Simon; by my parents; by God. And the thing with God is, he's always watching, you can't escape Him, even in your sleep. Can you imagine that?' Rachel asked her. 'Can you imagine being watched every second of your life, just waiting to be caught out, not having so much as a second of freedom or rest from it? This way, I get to choose which type of cage I live in. If I can't be free outside, I'll be free inside. I don't care any more, just so long as my parents can never reach me.'

Nell watched the air ambulance appear over the station. She looked down at Rachel and pulled out her handcuffs. 'Rachel Morris, I'm arresting you for the murder of Simon Morris . . .' Reading out the rest of the caution, she gently rolled Rachel over, cuffed her, before pulling her to her feet. She handed her to Bremer. 'Can you book her in?'

He looked down at her, and for a moment Nell thought he was going to make her do it, but he just nodded, walking Rachel back down the now empty platform as the air paramedics rushed past them to save the man slowly bleeding to death by her feet.

Sixty-one

Carla sat by the office window, Paul behind her, having washed as much of the blood from him as possible. Nell was in the corner of the room, silent.

Bremer came to his door. 'I've got off the phone with the hospital. They think the man Rachel stabbed has a good chance of pulling through.' No one replied. He walked into the middle of the room. 'Look, I know it's been a shock, but we've got them all. The Davidsons for their part in Rachel's torture, Hannah for her involvement in Alice's death, and Rachel for murder and attempted murder. It might not have gone down quite as we'd have liked, but it's a result and a good one, nonetheless.

Carla saw Nell look up, her face grey. 'I just don't get why she did it. Why now, after all this time with Simon? What triggered it?'

Bremer sat on the edge of a desk. 'We found a lot of cash in her luggage, Nell, the sort it would have taken years to accrue. She'd been planning it, and maybe Alice's return was the trigger.'

'Do we know why Alice came back? Where she'd been before?' Paul asked.

'No,' replied Bremer, 'but we'll get Luci in over the next couple of days and try to piece together a clearer picture of Alice's life. I don't sense she came back for any other reason than she considered this her home. She'd been driven out and she wanted to come back, but Luci will be able to tell us more.'

'And when Hannah told Simon about seeing Alice, do we think that's when the idea formed to lure her to the rooftop by setting up the reunion?' Paul asked.

'I don't think it was until Hannah knew she could get money from the Davidsons,' Carla said. 'She was in over her head with debt and she knew the Davidsons paid out to protect their daughter. And the reunion was set up to mess with Alice's head, to remember how it felt to be their target; mix with the ketamine and Hannah just had to keep whispering in Alice's ear until she was ready to jump.'

Paul winced. 'That's really messed up. I prefer your bog-standard murders. Like Simon's, for example. I'm happy with that, but Alice's . . .'

'Well at least you're happy with Simon's murder, Paul.' Bremer smiled 'I'm glad we could give you one murder out of two to enjoy.'

'Do you think Rachel knew Hannah was going to harm Alice,

then?' Carla asked; because that didn't make sense, Rachel had no way of knowing what Hannah was planning.

'I don't think so, no' Bremer looked thoughtful. 'I think that was actually her undoing. She didn't just stop at killing Simon, she wanted to punish Hannah too. Without her setting up Ash's kidnap, planting the picture on her parents' laptop, we might never have found out she was our killer. She made it so complicated she was never going to be able to make it work.'

Carla thought of Rachel standing on the platform and thought she very nearly had. Nell walked over to her desk. 'Did you ever get access to Alice's phone?'

'Yes, it came through a few hours ago but I didn't have chance to go through it, and I suppose now I don't need to. Why?'

Nell pulled a chair over. 'Can I see?'

Carla pulled open a drawer and took out Alice's phone – passcode broken by tech support – and watched as Nell scrolled through the apps before stopping. She placed the phone on the desk and leant back as Hannah's voice filled the room.

'It's amazing you think Lui could love you. Have you seen yourself, Alice? You're just a washed-up old drunk, look at yourself, you can't even see straight. You're a failure, Alice, a waste of life, just something for people to step over on the street. Even Rachel doesn't love you any more. You know it was her, right? Watching you at Oxford Brookes, daydreaming about you, which is why Simon had to sort you out. Imagine that, your whole life reduced to sleeping on the street just because some little posh girl got a crush. I mean, the futility of it is enough to make you give up and die, really. So why don't you, Alice? Why don't you just give up and die?'

Nell pressed stop. The room remained silent, Carla staring at the phone, bile in her throat. She pictured Alice, standing on The Varsity Club rooftop, full of ketamine and the words Hannah had repeated to her over and over – because that was the last conversation they'd had, but Luci had said they'd met before, so God only knew how many times Hannah had told her to die before it got too much and she did.

Nell looked around the room. 'Anyone fancy a beer? I could really do with one after that.'

Bremer held up his phone. 'I'm going to be with the superintendent and CPS for half the night. Press is going to have a field day with this one, so have a beer and think of me.'

'And I need a shower.' Paul held up his hands, traces of blood on his fingertips.

Nell turned to Carla. 'Back to mine then?'

'You're on,' Carla replied.

It wasn't until she'd eaten half a pizza that Carla realised how hungry she was. Licking her fingers, she took a swig of beer, and the cigarette Nell was offering.

'How do you feel?' she asked.

Nell gave a light shrug. 'Like a complete grade-A idiot. I was totally sucked in and almost lost us the case. If Bremer ever found out, I'd be off the team like a shot, and maybe out of the force.'

'You weren't an idiot. You always had her pegged as a suspect. You weren't to know she'd been playing us.'

'I'm a cop, Carla, it's my job to know I'm being played.'

Carla leant back on the sofa and watched the fire huff and spit, beer and pizza making her feel dozy. 'I checked out the complaint file while I was waiting for the forensic results. Turns out Alice alleged Simon raped her but the police TFA'd it.'

Nell looked back at her, feet outstretched towards the fire. 'They No Further Actioned a rape allegation?'

'Looks like it. From what I could tell, Oxford Brookes wanted to press them to pursue it, but a "donation" was received and the matter was closed. Bet they're going to live to regret that when the CPS get hold of them.' Carla imagined there'd be lots of nervous people at Brookes right now. 'And maybe that's why Rachel made it more complicated than it had to be, why she singled me out, payback for failing Alice.' Carla had to hand it to the woman, she'd been nothing if not thorough.

Nell rested her head on the sofa and closed her eyes. 'What are you going to do about Baz?'

'Have his baby.'

Nell snapped her head up. 'What?'

Carla laughed. 'Kidding. And I don't know, is the honest truth. I think I quite like the idea of being single, but I know I'd miss him, and then there's the whole "where would I live" issue. Ugh.' She yawned. 'Why does life have to be so complicated?'

'I'm staying single for the rest of my life,' Nell said, closing her eyes.

Carla poked her with her beer bottle. 'You'll make someone a good wife, Jackson.'

'Bollocks would I, Brown, I'm a total nightmare.'

'Well, there is that.' And as she closed her eyes, she was glad to hear Nell laugh.

Epilogue

I lie on the bed, in a cell underneath the court, where minutes from now my guilt will be debated. I wish I had a paper and pen, to write my goodbye to Alice, to tell her she is missed and that Luci is OK.

I imagine myself, cross-legged, beginning to write.

Dear Alice,

I want you to know that Luci and Billy are OK. I've made sure of it. they're both in Manchester after Luci finally managed to persuade Guy to go with her, which makes me happy – I'd have hated her to be alone. She loved you very much and misses you every day, just like I do.

I want to tell you how much I loved you. You may never have known it but I thought you were bright and funny, and even when you found yourself homeless everyone said you were still kind and generous – you always thought of others first and no one is a failure in life when they do that.

And you were brave. My God, so brave. You endured what Simon did to you, and still managed to love another person – Luci – refusing to let his actions strip you of the right to love and be loved. What can be braver than that? To love is brave enough in itself, so your bravery was twofold.

I wished I'd been braver. I wished I could have told you how I felt and found out if you could love me back. But I tucked it away in a corner of my heart, where it grew, strong and bold. The fact that you were in the world gave me a feeling of calm, to know you were out there, and now you're gone things feel a little ragged and strange, like I've become untethered somehow and am not sure where to go. But I know I'll be OK.

I have to go now. Thank you for everything, Alice. Thank you for allowing me to see what love could be. I'm sorry I didn't do better. I hope you can forgive me.

All my love, Rachel

Acknowledgements

It's hard writing acknowledgements at the best of times, but during the pandemic it feels like it's taken me longer than it did to write the book. I started trying on a Monday then suddenly it was Friday, and before I knew it March was actually July, and it'll probably be November by Sunday. But I've made myself concentrate and I want to say a huge thank you to my editor, Emily, who I learn so much from with each edit. To Sonny, who is endlessly supportive, a great editor, and who came up with the title – a feat I can never manage. Thank you to everyone at Arrow, especially Helen Wynn-Smith in the production department, as well as the brilliant designer, Henry Petrides, for such a striking cover.

To Becky, my agent at A M Heath: thank you for always having my back and for talking me down from a few ledges. Your support is so appreciated and I'm glad you picked me to be one of your authors! We are a lucky bunch.

To A/DI Rob Hughes: thank you for taking me around Witney police station and for having the coolest cat in Freeland.

Thank you to Nell, Abe, Betty and Martin for putting up with me. None of you can decide if I'm harder to live with when I'm writing or when I'm not. Sorry about that.

And finally, to everyone in Hanborough and Freeland – these last few months (March to August, so far) should have seen me getting this book out into the world but instead I've spent them with you – getting the Blenheim van running deliveries, making sure people were OK during lockdown, and trying to keep us all upbeat despite the madness. I am so very lucky to be your District Councillor and, of all the people I could have spent the pandemic with, I'm really glad it was you.